The Quenching Fire

BOOK 2 IN THE SPRINGS OF ETERNAL LIFE SERIES

J. Suthern Hicks

To my One and only;
the only One worthy of praise.

Inquiries can be made by contacting the author at
HumbleEntertainment@yahoo.com

Cover Design and illustrations: Tatiana Minina
A Shophar So Good Book: www.shopharsogood.com

ISBN-13: 978-1966231028

"If you are on the wrong road, progress means doing an about-turn and walking back to the right road; and in that case, the man who turns back soonest is the most progressive." — C.S. Lewis

I believe a man is happier, and happy in a richer way, if he has "the freeborn mind." But I doubt whether he can have this without economic independence, which the new society is abolishing. For economic independence allows an education not controlled by the Government; and in adult life it is the man who needs, and asks, nothing of Government who can criticize its acts and snap his fingers at its ideology. —C.S. Lewis

The Quenching Fire

CONTENTS

Author's Note

CONTENTS

Author's Note

Welcome to *The Quenching Fire*, the second book in *The Springs of Eternal Life* prequel series.

For those familiar with my work, you'll notice a shift in structure. While the *Messengers and Thieves* trilogy was designed so each book could stand alone, this prequel series is a continuous, serialized narrative. Each installment builds directly upon the last to tell one grand, unfolding story. Because of this, you can expect the journey to continue seamlessly into the third and final book.

While you are welcome to start your journey anywhere, I believe the richest experience comes from reading the *Messengers and Thieves* trilogy first, followed by this prequel series. However you choose to travel through the Five Realms, I am honored to have you along for the ride!

Chapter 1

MARYBAH

(The Wedding)

Her face was covered with a large, dark scarf—just in case her daughter, the bride, happened to see her lurking amongst the invited guests. Although she had paid for the wedding, she had not been invited to attend.

Marybah thought it doubtful her daughter would have recognized her, even without the disguise. It had been many turnings since they had seen one another, and her physical transformation was profound. When no one was looking, Marybah reached into her bag for a treat. What she really craved was a hit from her pipe, but that would have drawn unwanted attention.

Time had not been kind to Marybah. Once, she had been

one of the loveliest citizens of Pixanese. Now, the lines on her face revealed a lifetime of anguish; she had few friends and lived a lonely, solitary life. Yet despite the rift between them, one thing remained: she still cared deeply for her daughter. After all, if not for Marybah, this grand wedding might never have taken place.

Her money had been well spent. Unbeknownst to Beely, her estranged mother had ensured the venue was affordable. Marybah had used the many secrets she kept against her enemies and friends alike to facilitate the grandest wedding the kingdom of Pixanese had ever seen—or would likely see for generations.

Beely—like Marybah's own mother—had always loved anything that grew from seed or spread from roots. For such a botanical enthusiast, there was no better place in all the Five Realms to hold the wedding of one's dreams than beneath the great falls of Pixanese.

Marybah walked as close to the majestic waterfall as she dared, careful not to let the cool mist ruin her hair or favorite scarf. She inhaled the sweet, fresh air as she gazed up at the tallest waterfall in all of the Five Realms as the water poured down from the heights of the High Forest.

Feeling the weight of the day's journey, she leaned against a tree fern, staying upwind of the roaring cascade. Partially hidden by a large frond, she could still see all the pre-wedding activity. She had originally planned to be long gone before the ceremony began; a veiled guest lurking behind a fern throughout the nuptials might draw unwanted attention.

She had scouted around the waterfall in the past, but never noticed just how beautiful the area truly was. On either side of the falls grew the famous carrier vines. They were ancient and thick, bearing flowers of deep red, dark purple, and bright yellow. She had once tried to get the vines to carry her to the top, but either it was a myth—or they felt her unworthy.

Marybah took another treat from her bag, lamenting that she had never witnessed the feat herself. The vines were very particular about whom they interacted with—and even more selective about whom, or what, they would carry.

She still had not seen Beely and suspected she would not see her anytime soon. She successfully fought the urge to have another treat as she watched the groom mingle with his guests. As it stood, she might never meet her son-in-law in person— but from afar, Maximilian was strikingly handsome.

The ceremonial wardrobe hugged his youthful, muscular frame commandingly. His shoulder-length, unbridled hair was free of any headdress. Marybah had not seen such a thick mane in many moons. Judging by the cluster of female guests around him, her daughter was clearly the envy of every eligible woman in Pixanese. There was no finer catch than Maximilian Wren.

Beauty and brawn, however, were not on any list Marybah might have had for suitable suitors. Mr. Wren came from one of—if not the—most respected families in all of Pixanese. Marybah suspected that, behind closed doors, they had protested their son's engagement. It had not been their plan for their only son to marry the daughter of a well-known Plotist— one who had divorced his wife, no less.

Beely's father had belonged to a small minority that most considered conspiracy theorists—unwelcome, especially in Pixanese. Marybah chuckled to herself, imagining how the groom's parents must have wondered how their son had ended up proposing to someone like Beely Rembree. The fact that Maximilian was his own man ranked high on her list of admirable qualities in a suitor.

The meeting between the Plotist's daughter and the son of Pixanese's most influential family had been no accident. Marybah would never have left such an encounter up to chance.

Marybah's mind drifted back to the day she met with Propo—her ex-husband's best friend and most loyal protégé. Propo had never been good at hiding the fact that he disliked his best friend's wife. He would never have agreed to meet her of his own accord—but even a genius like Propo needed work.

After Marybah's husband had died, Propo had found securing employment difficult. No one wanted to hire a rumored Plotist—someone who believed in "outlandish" theories and interpreted prophecy in ways unappreciated by the masses. Propo had become desperate, and Marybah knew it. The look on Propo's face when he walked in and saw Marybah behind a desk resembled someone coming face-to-face with a soiled diaper.

"Marybah?"

"Hi, Propo. It's been too long, hasn't it?"

"What are you doing here?"

Marybah rose and walked over to him. "What? No pleasantries before getting down to business?" Propo froze as she leaned in to kiss him on the cheek. His confused expression matched his disheveled appearance. He looked weathered beyond his actual age, with gray, thinning hair—an oddity in the Realms, where health and vitality were as common as air. He stroked his short beard with one hand and used the other to adjust the leather belt underneath his tunic.

"When has anything ever been pleasant with you, Marybah?"

"Touché, my friend, touché." She returned to the desk and sat. "Please, for the sake of old times—good or bad—sit and

4

hear what I have to say."

"And why should I do that?"

"Propo, my dear, have a curly and sit." She pushed the plate of curlies—one of her favorite treats—toward him. When it was obvious he was not receptive, she added, "Look, we may not like one another—"

"Like one another?" He shook his head and grunted. "There is only one person in the Realms I truly despise—and now I know she still lives both in sight and sound!"

"'Hatred is a root that never dies until it bores through the host, splitting it in two...' My mother told me that."

"Well, she knew you well, didn't she?"

"I understand our past," she said, brushing off the jab. "But I want to discuss the future—something I hear you're well-versed in."

"What could you possibly have to say that I would want to hear?"

"It concerns our Beely. I know you love her—possibly as much as I do."

At the mention of Beely, Propo softened. "What about Beely? Is she in trouble?"

"Not yet. But if we don't act, she could be in serious trouble—soon."

Slowly, and somewhat begrudgingly, he pulled back the only free chair and sat down. "I'm listening."

"I couldn't care less about prophecy or the Plotist agenda," she said flatly.

"Just get to the point—quickly," he demanded.

"The job you came to interview for is yours—if you want it."

He threw up a hand. "What does this have to do with Beely?"

"I knew the Realms would eventually face challenges. Change is inevitable, and things have been stagnant for centuries. For reasons that may differ from your own, I too believe even more difficult times are coming—perhaps even apocalyptic ones, if the Plotists are right."

He pressed her further. "And…?"

"Beely needs protection—something neither of us can give her. I can't, because she wants nothing to do with me. And you…because you have no means."

She noticed Propo becoming increasingly impatient with her assessment of his current state. As far as Marybah was concerned, she was simply expressing necessary facts. She paused, reconsidered, then got straight to the point. "Beely needs to marry into a family with influence."

"And you went to all this trouble just to get me here—why?" he asked.

"There is no other that Beely listens to and respects more than you—since her father passed, of course."

"I'm beginning to understand. Go on."

"There is a young man named Maximilian Wren."

"The Wren family, yes. I know none of them in a friendly way, and I'm the last person they would ever associate with."

"I don't need you to interact or influence them. I need you to make sure that when Beely meets their son, she does not let the opportunity pass her by."

Propo leaned over, examining the plate of treats, and picked a few of the finer offerings. He was not too proud to accept a handout in this precarious time of his life. "What opportunity?"

"An opportunity to marry up, to progress toward something greater in life, to be someone important."

One by one, Propo placed three curlies into his mouth and

chewed. He took his time before finally swallowing. "Beely needs no other person, man or otherwise, to advance her position in life. She is well liked in the community, even with her late father's much-maligned image. She is a woman of great character and talents, and most everyone in Pixanese knows this."

"All the more reason to make sure she secures her rightful place in Pixanese society."

Propo selected three more curlies and repeated his questionable consumption habit, further annoying Marybah in the process. He relished the look of disdain from his audience. "Marybah, what is all of this about?"

"Do you trust that I would put my daughter's best interests above even my own?"

"I would need to know to which interests you are referring."

"Must you be so hurtful?"

"Continue," he said dryly.

"In terms that you will understand—to make things as simple as possible—the Plotists' conjectures may not manifest as they predict, but the results will be the same," she said, finally gaining his full attention.

"Explain."

"Hell is coming to the Five Realms of Here, and if my daughter doesn't secure a position of authority, she will succumb to the whims of a dictator. She may not even survive. Most won't."

He sat back in his chair. "Interesting thoughts from someone who has fought the Plotists from the very beginning. You sound more like a believer than even Mikalo."

"My ex-husband was a dreamer. He was a philosopher. There wasn't a practical bone in his body. What I'm talking about is quite practical. There will be a power struggle, and Pixanese is the only realm equipped to bargain for its survival."

Propo took a small wooden pipe from his robe pocket. He watched Marybah's face as he lit the dry leaves and took his first drag. He knew she abhorred the smell of dead nettle leaf. He had given up smoking many moons ago and had only recently taken it up again. It was the only small luxury he could afford. It was even more luxurious to see the wealthy and pretentious Ms. Rembree squirm beneath the smell of dead nettle smoke floating all about her face.

"Tell me, is this about saving Pixanese or your daughter?"

She waved the smoke away. "Can't it be both?" After he rolled his eyes, she confessed. "My daughter, of course. Pixanese may just benefit because of her and our wise choices."

"You are as slick as an oarsman!" He thought for a moment before adding, "What would you have me do?"

"If she comes to you for advice—even if she doesn't—you need to encourage her about how great this man is. She trusts you. She loves you like a father or a brother; I've never been able to quite discern which. Be a father to her. Tell her the things that will save her life—that will help her flourish. If she marries Maximilian Wren, she will not only save her own life, but his, yours, and perhaps all of Pixanese as well."

"And you. Don't forget your life."

"Will you do it?" She was almost pleading.

"I will consider what you have proposed. If I agree, and I'm not saying I do, Beely must never find out about this conversation. If she ever finds out, you will not be happy with the result—I promise you that."

Propo took one more long drag from his pipe, exhaling in Marybah's direction, before he stood up to leave.

8

"The job is real, and it's yours if you want it," she said sincerely.

"No thanks. If you want to monitor me, you'll have to try much harder. How did you track me down, anyway?" he asked.

"If you want to stay hidden, *you'll* have to try much harder," she answered. Propo shrugged and left without looking back.

A harried wedding organizer placed a hand on Marybah's shoulder, startling her. "I'm sorry, we need to ask all guests to remain behind the pillars."

She pointed toward the large crowd. Marybah's reminiscing had caused her to lose all track of time. It was too late to leave the impending nuptials without being noticed.

Marybah lowered her head, further hiding her face. "I apologize." She walked briskly to her far right, avoiding as many guests as possible. She found a perfect spot inconspicuously located amidst several large ferns and a boulder. If she stood on the far side, no one would notice her interloping. She leaned her weary body against the large rock that was nearly twice her size.

All the guests she could see, without exposing herself, were beautifully adorned in their finest clothing and jewels. There were lots of red dresses and richly colored robes. Had there been enough light filtering through the trees, all the precious jewelry would have sparkled like stars. True to Marybah's prediction, there were too many guests to count. The union was a popular one in Pixanese. Everyone wanted to celebrate the adored young couple. Maximilian and Beely were practically royalty in a realm where such a concept had never before existed.

Marybah had to step away from the voluminous boulder to see the main attraction. Fortunately, everyone was looking in the other direction—toward the bride. She might have been imagining it, being so far away, but her daughter looked much like her maternal grandmother.

Beely was tall, graceful, and walked down to the front of the waterfall as if gliding on air. Her long, flowing hair was free of the usual braids. The little bit of light left from the day rebounded off the canyon wall, highlighting the bride's dark tresses like a halo.

Marybah hoped Max had learned that her daughter was more than just a pretty face. Ever since she was a small child, Beely had been strong, stubborn, and always breaking the rules. Beely would need a man who could match or even exceed her drive and ambition. Yet, on this special day, she was the perfect bride—calm, graceful, and exuding joy.

The early evening breeze blew away from Marybah. She could not hear all the words spoken, only the faint sound of water hitting rocks before heading downstream through the village.

She did not need to hear everything. She knew all too well the meaning of marriage in the Five Realms—if for no other reason than her own marriage, which had failed miserably and all too publicly. Ironically, the one line she heard the officiant clearly recite, as if he knew she were there, was, "The union of a man and a woman is a covenant before God, never to be broken." There were very few divorces in the Realms, but times were changing. Fortunately, thought Marybah, her daughter's marriage only needed to last long enough for her to become the magistrate of Pixanese. It was the nearest thing to a political leader that a society with no need for leaders would accept.

Now that the union was almost complete, Marybah just wanted to get home and smoke her pipe.

Then it happened.

The most incredible sight witnessed by the residents of Pixanese in a century. The carrier vines, adorned with the most extravagant and vibrant blooms, began to move. Right after the vows and a most passionate kiss, as if on cue, the thick, ancient vines gently wrapped around the bride and groom as a mother might caress her newborn child.

The woody fibers slowly lifted the newlyweds up until they disappeared behind the waterfall. The crowd gasped in unison. There was even a shriek. Marybah heard later that a woman fainted when the newlyweds vanished. It was a most spectacular sight, to be sure.

That's when she knew. Her daughter would be the first and only magistrate in all of the Five Realms of Here. Pixanese would survive what was coming. She, too, would survive.

Chapter 2

THE HUNT

The Scarlet Redback Hoofers were an ancient herd of four-legged beasts that had rarely been hunted. In fact, the very first of their kind had fallen by the sword less than eighty moons ago. Times had changed. Produce from wild plants and cultivated crops was the usual food sources, but when the Dry Death came, almost anything became fair game. The redbacks were attractive to hunters because they needed very little water to survive. Thus, they were a healthy and plentiful food source.

The prairie lands where they roamed were mostly within the

Realm of Okrad, but a small section crossed over into the Realm of Many. Their territory was only suitable for creatures that could survive for long periods without water. They numbered in the tens of thousands. Usually, their only mission in life was to search for food and, less often, water. Today was different. Their only mission was to survive.

To the fleeing redbacks, the huge brorayding was an alien in the sky. The massive herd kicked up so much dirt fleeing from the skyward threat that Propo could only see a cloud of dust. Propo was not skilled with weaponry and was even less adept at flying. Thus, he was given the simple task of scaring the herd toward the more experienced archers.

He tried to recall the signal to tell his ray—which broraydings were often called—to move upwards. If they kept on the current trajectory, he would be flying blind through a thick, smothering cloud. He tapped twice on the beast's left side, only to find it turning to the left in a steep decline. The fact that it was getting harder to breathe meant they were going in the right direction: chasing the herd toward the Salt Lands. Still, he needed his ray to ascend into the clear sky to ensure that the herd continued toward the awaiting pair of hunters.

Propo finally remembered the command to ascend. He rubbed two fingers in a circular motion just under the ray's horn. It immediately climbed up, and Propo took a deep breath of the clean air. He now had a better view of the landscape ahead. He commanded the beast to assume an aggressive attack position toward the herd below. The aerodynamic ray swooped up and down, banking sharply as it cut left and right through the currents. It worked. The herd continued their desperate, full-speed stampede toward the Salt Lands and the awaiting hunters.

The Salt Lands resided on the border of the Realm of Okrad, now known as the Realm of Mastad (by decree of its conquering ruler). Maximilian rode his ray, Searing, to one of the two spots where Propo would hopefully funnel the fleeing redbacks. He and Searing hovered high in the air, obscured by cloud cover.

The herd would not enter the Salt Lands. They knew that their scarlet coat would stand out against the ivory ground, making them easy prey for their pursuers. The salt would also burn their worn-down hooves, if they ventured too far or too long on the crystalline ground. Once the redbacks arrived near the border, they had two options: cut to the right toward Max or to the left toward Eudox. Eudox was an old man, but he knew how to wield a bow and command a ray. If the hunters were blessed, at least one, maybe two, harvested redbacks would be going to the hungry survivors in Pixanese.

Max stood upright on his massive ray. Searing was the largest female he had ever trained. She was the width of three grown men and even longer in length. Max had previously been bonded to an older, more experienced ray named Joshua, but in a very rare occurrence, Joshua relinquished his connection to Max and imprinted on Beely. He could not blame the beast. While Max was under the influence of the addictive Glouscenshire, he betrayed his wife, and the entirety of Pixanese as it turned out, by briefly and mistakenly conspiring with Mastad.

He deserved no one's loyalty, not even his wife nor his bonded ray. Max had a second chance with Searing. She imprinted on Max when he needed her most. Now, in defiance of Mastad and free from addiction, he held onto Searing's horn with one hand and held his bow with the other. As they quietly watched for any signs of the herd, he thought about a time when food was plentiful and hunting animals was unnecessary—the time before Mastad.

On the way to his strike point, Max looked down upon a small ghost town. The small thatched houses were in tatters and the canals were completely dry. He knew that most, if not all, of the villagers had died of starvation or dehydration, as most others in the Realms had. The exact number of deaths was impossible to calculate because a census had never been taken.

The survivors who remained, like those in Pixanese, mostly congregated together around the few springs still flowing, the largest one being deep in the canyon now known as the land of the Mara People. Max knew of one clan with a secret spring, the Mindalites, who so far had managed to remain hidden from Mastad. Pixanese, however, like most other villages, was not immune to the devastation of Mastad's rule.

Max felt intense guilt for his role in causing the natives of Pixanese to flee in search of food. The image of his friends and his own family wasting away from their addiction to the Glouscenshire haunted him. Those that chose to remain in Pixanese, less than a hundred at last count, needed sustenance, and Max was going to provide it, if it was the last thing he ever did. Pixanese was fortunate to have a small spring supplying water, but it was not enough to grow crops. There were few reserves remaining. Food was desperately needed; the hunt was a necessity. Killing was the new way of life in the Five Realms.

A huge dust cloud loomed in the distance, and Max immediately calculated the redback leader was just a few paces ahead. He and Searing waited patiently, careful not to scare them back the other way. Rays were excellent flyers, and Max was a proficient marksman, but if the herd ran back into the dust, he would be shooting blind.

This was his first real chance to begin making up for all the wrong he had done to those in Pixanese. Max looked down to a small pack on his hip and whispered, "Ask God for a victory, Thai. If it's God's will, the bounty will be ours." Thai was an empachic, a small, furry empathic creature that Max had saved from drug-addicted bullies before the village of Pixanese was all but abandoned. Near death, the tiny animal was being used as a kickball. Without Max's intervention, Thai would have died in a matter of hours. The two had been inseparable ever since. Max could feel Thai's reassuring vibration before his furry friend buried himself deep down in Max's rucksack.

The hunter refocused his attention on the mission. Once the herd knew they were being ambushed, they would retreat all the way into the dead woods where the canopy was too thick for a successful hunt. This was their best, if not only, chance to secure food. Max's heart rate increased. The excitement was real, and the consequences dire.

No sooner had he said a quick prayer than the herd turned toward him. He gave the command and Searing dropped out of the cloud and soared down so close to the ground that Max could smell the pungent odor of the redback's sweaty hides. He released his hold on Searing's antler, steadied his feet as if walking on a tightrope, and retrieved an arrow from his quiver.

He could see the whites of the frontrunner's eyes. The beast, surprised and panicked, feeling the draft and seeing the shadow from the ray's huge wings, lowered his rear and skidded several paces while twisting his body to the left. The herd behind him, in unison, did the same. It was a dance, choreographed and precise.

With his arrow strung and bow pulled tight, Max unleashed

seventy pounds of deadly draw weight. He struck the massive redback in its side. Blood darkened its scarlet hide as it trailed out of the wound. Still, the once proud leader, now in the rear of the herd, continued striking his strong legs against the hard ground.

The dust had not yet obscured Max's view as he released another arrow from his bow, striking the redback in its rump, directly above its left limb. The massive creature collapsed onto the hard ground, tumbling head over heels. As the majestic, but wounded beast, struggled to get back on its feet, Max sent a final lethal arrow through its side, puncturing a lung. All movement ceased as the beautiful Scarlet Redback Hoofer collapsed for the final time.

There was no chance for the predator to lament nor celebrate his fallen prey. By providence, there was another redback trailing behind the retreating herd. Dust had not yet overwhelmed them, and Max was able to fell a second animal; this time with one shot. It dropped not far from where its own leader lay.

Max, who abhorred killing, was surprised to feel a surge of euphoria. The blood rushed to his head, his skin tingled, and a sense of peace overwhelmed him. Standing victoriously tall on Searing, Maximilian lifted his fist and roared in victory. He then quietly recited a verse from the Word to thank the Lord. "The young lions roar after their prey and seek their food from God."

On the other side of the retreating herd, Eudox, sitting in a saddle, waited nervously. Unlike the younger and stronger Max, he did not trust his sense of balance flying through the air bareback with bow in hand. Noticing that one of the reins of his saddle had come loose, he instructed his ray to land.

They had only been on the ground for a few moments when

the herd came stampeding toward them. The thunder of a thousand galloping hooves shook the dirt beneath him. The ground vibrated in defiance of the otherwise peaceful day. With no time to find the hook and latch to secure the rein, Eudox quickly tied a knot with the loose strap.

If they did not become airborne in the next few seconds, they would surely be trampled to death. His limbs froze up and it felt as though he were moving in slow motion. He swallowed hard and tried to breathe normally. He looked up to see a wall of pure muscle charging toward him. The enraged beasts were only seconds away. He tugged on the poorly rigged rein, but it did not matter whether secure or not. He and Glider would need to get airborne immediately. He stepped up onto Glider, clicked the leather strap onto his belt and yelled, "Now!"

Glider lifted off the ground effortlessly—just in time. The draft from the stampede felt like a gust of wind underneath Glider's large body, giving him added lift. Although Glider could have taken flight at any time, he would have waited for his rider even at his own peril; there were not many creatures more loyal than the rays.

Once above the herd, Eudox wasted no time in positioning his bow. He quickly felled a full-grown redback with one well-placed arrow. He shouted as loud as his deep voice could, "The old man still has it, Glider!"

There was not much opportunity for a second attempt at another bag unless they could keep ahead of the herd. While rays were strong and agile, they were not as fast as a redback fleeing for its life. Still, they tried to get ahead of the herd and out of the oncoming dust headed their way. Glider made a swift turn that caused Eudox to lose the grip on his bow. He leaned forward to catch the falling weapon only to see the knot he had tied earlier slip.

As Glider slowed to turn, Eudox fell forward, unable to catch hold of the horn. He felt himself sliding off Glider's smooth leathery back. His stomach did a cartwheel and his mind went blank.

Miraculously, whether by luck or divine intervention, Eudox's foot had slipped under one of the remaining straps. As his body turned, his foot twisted in the strap. That's how Maximilian and Propo found him, hanging upside down from his ray, no bow, and a quiver emptied of arrows.

"My bet was on you," said Maximilian to Propo.

"What's that supposed to mean?" asked Propo.

"...to fall off your beast. You're not exactly the most experienced rider," said Max with a slight chuckle.

"I see. Very funny," Propo said flatly.

The two of them watched as Glider gently lowered Eudox to the ground. Glider held his wing up as Max attempted to free Eudox from the entanglement underneath. "How did you manage this?"

"Not very well, obviously." Once he was free of the reins, Eudox's lower half landed on the ground with a thud. "Is that any way to treat an old man?" asked Eudox while attempting to catch the breath that was just knocked out of him.

"Sorry, I lost hold of your foot," answered Max.

Eudox slid out from underneath the wing. He stood up, slightly embarrassed, and said to Propo, who was still mounted on his ray, "You should have seen me, hanging upside down with only one foot in the strap, yet I still managed to take the redback down with one shot." It was an exaggeration, but a necessary one, thought Eudox who felt compelled to assert his continued usefulness despite his age.

19

"Really? It took Max three arrows to land his first one."

"First one?" asked Eudox.

Max responded while he repositioned the saddle on Glider. "That's right. I bagged two." He smiled wryly and winked. "Of course, it was easier for me since I was on top of the ray."

They spent the rest of the day field dressing the three redbacks as Thai cautiously explored the area. Eudox taught Max and Propo where to cut and how to clean the redbacks the best they could in the field with few tools. Eudox was the only one of the three that had actually hunted and eaten big game.

He had been on the run for many seasons from those that would have preferred him as dead as the redbacks they were preparing to take back to Pixanese. Mastad's work to overtake every kingdom began much earlier than even Max or Beely knew. Mastad had been hunting potential rivals for many seasons before anyone even knew his name, any of his names.

Eudox was one of the few, along with Beely's father, who knew the prophecies, and they both suspected Mastad might be involved. If only they had acted sooner, perhaps the redbacks would still roam free—and so would the Realms.

Chapter 3

THE CELEBRATION

Something about the way he stood—tall and steady atop the great brorayding, soaring effortlessly—made Beely sigh with quiet delight. Maximilian was the strongest man she had ever known. He was also the most handsome. Thin, interwoven copper strands ran throughout his long, thick, raven-black hair, which flowed with the wind. Sharpened arrows and a beautifully carved wooden bow hung across his broad shoulders.

Seeing the bow strapped to his back reminded Beely of the horrific changes in the Five Realms. Never before had there been a need for protection. Never before had there been war, fighting, or murder. She thanked God every day that Maximilian was on her side. He was the protector of the Twelve, and he was her protector.

She knew he would lay down his life for her—though that had not always been the case. There was a time when he had doubted Beely and even conspired with the enemy. Like so many others, he had become a hollow shell—addicted and worthless—but that was many moons ago. It seemed a lifetime had passed since she first prayed for him to see the truth. She begged God to turn his mind and heart toward good. Those prayers had turned to celebration. So much was changing, but thankfully, not all of it was bad.

There were fewer than fifty inhabitants remaining in the village of Pixanese. The village center had been abandoned by all but a few grifters. Eighteen others now lived with the Wrens—alongside their empachics, Cogni-flora, and rays— some distance from the village. A few of them bunked in the outbuildings, some stayed in the main house, and Max had constructed temporary shelters for the rest.

Only one child remained in all of Pixanese, and his name was Johnny. He loved living "off the land," as he called it. The other families who survived "the dry" had moved to areas rumored to be more capable of supporting life. The location of the most productive water source—still permitted to flow by Mastad— was controlled by the Mara People: a ragtag mix of survivors from every realm that Mastad had exploited for experiments and slave labor.

Max and Beely's land had a small spring that had to sustain not only all the remaining people and animals in Pixanese, but also as much Cogni-flora as possible. Plants were considered sentient. Most could communicate in one form or another, and those that did not were still believed to possess the ability, even if not expressed in any recognizable way. The loss of life in Pixanese, whether rooted or not, was heart-wrenching.

Still, with so few resources, the Wren home—with its struggling gardens and crumbling structures—radiated with the love the survivors had for one another. It was as if the Wrens had planned for a time when hospitality would only be possible through imagination and hope. That was why the guests called the Wren house the "House of Hope."

Beely had been taught by her father, who eventually came to be considered one of the greatest and wisest philosophers to have ever lived. Even when most others doubted him, she had taken his writings and teachings to heart, which helped prepare her for the hard times he had predicted. She was wise like him—impartial, and gifted with unbridled common sense. Her title of "Magistrate" had originally come as mockery from the evil one, but those who knew her best used it with respect.

Maximilian's childhood had been far less chaotic than his wife's. He once called her a "child of the flowers"—someone who lived more by imagination and spontaneity than by rules and schedules. Even though he had only been teasing, she initially resented the connotation—until she eventually realized he was not entirely wrong. He hailed from a family that had been deeply respected as influential inhabitants of Pixanese for centuries. If nobility had existed in the Realms, the Wrens would have come from a long line of kings and queens. As it was, they were simply hard-working, God-fearing citizens of a land they deeply loved.

There were once no "rulers" in any of the kingdoms or villages, but that all changed not long after Maximilian and Beely were married. Okrad—now known as the Kingdom of

Mastad—introduced the very first ruler in the Realms. His name was Ankur, but he later became known as Prince Mastad. Many Nectarions—natives of Pixanese—felt they had no choice but to follow suit, bestowing a title upon their most noble citizen.

But before they could choose someone, Mastad himself had begun referring to Beely as the Magistrate of Pixanese. He needed someone to negotiate with—but of course, it was all a manipulation to keep Beely close. He needed her to fulfill a role foretold by the prophets. Unbeknownst to Beely, she was being used for Mastad's evil purposes. Even if Mastad had not chosen her, the people of Pixanese likely would have.

Beely fulfilled the role of Magistrate well by helping all those in Pixanese find temporary homes, securing their old homes in the hope they might return, settling disputes, and negotiating with an evil ruler set on conquering them all. As broken as the Kingdom of Pixanese appeared in its current state, most of the people survived the transition, with the help of their Magistrate.

Beely stood on a small, once-grassy knoll, watching as the Nectarions gathered to celebrate the successful redback hunt. She watched Max add coal to the fire as tables were set up for the first true feast in many turnings. The elderflowers provided many aromatic blooms for the beautiful centerpieces. There was wine, fermented from the fruit of the falls, and warm Ognatia tea.

The few fresh crops still available offered a variety of vegetables. Precious reserves were used to bake exquisite breads, both flat and raised. They were splurging in a time of scarcity—celebrating a successful hunt that brought hope for tomorrow and beyond.

Beely was jarred out of her grateful musings about the coming celebration by her dear—if not occasionally annoying—

friend, Duly. He was an orphaned braewicker. Braewickers typically lived underground in sand traps. Their faces were somewhat human—if a human had the face of a wrinkled hippopotamus. He had a wide, protruding mouth with huge jowls. His eyes were beady with prominent brow bones arching over them.

Braewickers had become expert thieves—of water and anything they deemed useful—and were given the derogatory label "sniblets" due to widespread disdain for their immoral habits. Duly had not been raised among other braewickers and now, fully grown, was the keeper of the Library of Truth—honest and forthright despite his heritage.

After Mastad's warriors and thieves raided the library, Duly was left without a job, and with too much time on his hands, he was constantly underfoot. He tapped Beely on the elbow, as he was too short to reach her shoulder. He then let out a horrendous sneeze, a sneeze so loud that the rays in the distant barn bucked in alarm.

He pulled a heavily soiled handkerchief from his satchel and, after wiping his short, snout-like nose, asked, "Do you think it wise to have all of us here together, out in the open like this?"

"I pray that your handkerchief is discolored from stains long since cleaned; if not, I sincerely request you go inside and retrieve as many handkerchiefs as you need. Max keeps a few in his bedside table. Help yourself," said Beely, staring down at the now snarly-mouthed braewicker.

His allergies were a bone of contention amongst several of the villagers. They were afraid he was contagious, but since most were already biased against braewickers, Beely chose to ignore their repeated requests to confine him to the barn with the rays.

Duly ignored her offer of a clean handkerchief and asked, "Did they all come?"

"All but two, but it's still early. I think we are all due a celebration of good food and companionship. What's the point in striving for better if we miss the little joys along the way? None of us is promised tomorrow, dear Duly."

"I'll never understand what you folks find so enjoyable about being near one another!"

"Perhaps if you weren't allergic to almost everyone and everything, you could take the time to find out."

"No thank you. The only benefit of the library being emptied by that evil monstrosity Mastad is the lack of dusty, grimy people clamoring over my books."

"Your books?"

"You know what I mean."

Beely smiled. "I do."

No one loved books more than Duly. Unfortunately, there were no books left to benefit from the braewicker's delicate care. Mastad's systematic destruction of all writings was a grim effort to ensure the Word of God would not survive. His plan was brutally simple: to eliminate the one text he feared, he had to eliminate them all. Without the Word of God, many in the Realms were quickly losing their faith and moral compass, as evidenced by the thieving braewickers.

"Have you told them yet? Have you told any of them what we're looking for, or that Mastad will be trying to stop us at every turn?"

"Not exactly. I thought I'd leave that up to you," Beely answered.

"Me?!"

"You can do it."

Duly shoved his short, stubby fingers into his satchel, pulling out his dirty handkerchief once more. To Beely's relief, he managed to cover his mouth and nose before releasing a ground-shaking sternutation. "You know I cannot speak around more than two people at once—me being one of them!"

"You'll be fine. After the celebration, we'll all gather at my father's old studio in the cliff past the village. It'll be late, and no one will follow."

"That's all well and good, but I may not be there!" Duly scowled and quickly stomped away toward the celebratory crowd below. He loved food more than he despised people. Before the feast was over, Beely would inform him of the stash of Ognatia in her father's studio. There was no way he would pass up a supply of his favorite tea.

All those now living on the Wrens' land, as well as a few grifters who continued to live in the village, attended the celebration. The Twelve were also present. Both Beely and Max felt it was safe for everyone to meet, as no one had seen or heard from Mastad in many moons. There was little else for him to destroy, or perhaps he found some new, undiscovered virgin land to pillage. Whatever the case was, the evil pressing down upon them seemed to have recently abated.

Few outside their own circle knew them as the Twelve. There was no doubt in Beely's mind that Mastad would have undermined them all, had he known their affiliation with her and their true mission. He may have known something of what was happening—he had spies—but he could not have known everything.

The Twelve had been specially chosen to recover the Word and do whatever was necessary to end Mastad's rule—even at the risk of their own lives. They desired freedom, and they would die to bring it back. If the tides turned and Mastad's threats returned, they had a secret hiding place in the canyon cliffs where they could safely meet. For now, they would celebrate among the surviving remnant of Pixanese.

The sun had finally set, and the first moon had risen. Other than the glow from the moon and stars, bioluminescent organisms provided most of the light, yet the dark still prevailed. To everyone's delight, the taro-feathered gully birds arrived, providing just enough extra illumination for the festivities.

The Cogni-flora helped lift the bioluminescent organisms as high as their reach would go. With the near-total destruction of life in the Five Realms of Here, it was impossible to keep track of which species were surviving and which had become extinct. The glowing gully birds had not been seen in over a year.

It was a joyous sight to see them frolicking in the air and alighting on the shoulders of the guests. Johnny, try as he might, could not catch one—but his contagious laughter infected everyone watching his attempts.

The scent of freshly grilled meat permeated the warm night air. The aroma gave everyone hope that more successful hunts might be in their future. There were also plenty of other aromas—once common in every home—now freely wisping around the feasting guests. The air carried the smell of yeasty breads, sliced fruit, and steaming teas.

Johnny, in another failed attempt to capture a glowing gully bird, ran smack-dab into Beely. He was so slight, and she so tall, that he fell backward onto his rump. When he looked up, he saw a tear fall from Beely's eye. "I'm sorry, Auntie Beely, I didn't mean to hurt you."

Beely looked down at the boy and offered him her hand.

"These are tears of joy, darling boy. Even when Pixanese was rich in culture and had abundant, delicious delicacies, never do I remember such a beautifully blessed gathering as this."

The boy, now back on his feet, replied, "Of course not, my momma says rich folks don't appreciate hardly anything 'cause they already have everything."

"Your mother is a very wise woman. She knows the proverbs from the Good Book. One of them says, 'There is one who pretends to be rich, but has nothing; another pretends to be poor, but has great wealth.' With God, Johnny, you're never poor."

Before Beely could finish her sentence, Johnny had already run off after another gully bird. Fortunately for the gully bird, he was not nearly nimble enough to reach it with his sticky fingers. The glowing curiosity teased the boy—diving low, then darting up just out of reach. This game continued until it was time to give thanks for the meal. Johnny stood between his parents, tightly holding both their hands, his head bowed.

Maximilian waited until every head was lowered in preparation for the blessing. Just before he began, Reverie—Beely's eldest empachic—nudged Max's heel. She managed a sickly squeak—clearly a plea to be reunited with her friend. Max lifted Thai from his hip-pack and carefully placed him beside Reverie just before the start of his prayer.

"Dear God of the heavens, we thank You for the food You have provided and our very successful hunt. We thank You for keeping us safe amidst such darkness. We thank You for our Magistrate, Beely—for organizing and keeping us all together. We repent for any part we played in the evil that has overtaken this world. We humbly ask that You use us to fulfill Your will. We pray that our realms will be free once again. In the Lord's name we pray."

When he paused, everyone joined together, shouting, "Amen!" Max smiled at two of the most grateful attendees that night: Reverie and Thai. The two delicate empachics seemed noticeably stronger in each other's company.

The evening was indeed blessed. There was plenty of food, and there would be leftovers for days to follow. The joyful mood in the air was shared by everyone. The plants along the barely-trickling creek rustled their leaves in the waning light. The ferns brushed their feathery fronds against one another. The gully birds not only lit the night sky but they sang songs with sweet melodies no one could recall ever hearing before that night. Even the rays could be heard lowing softly in the barn.

Max found Beely back on the knoll, quietly contemplating the future of their village and its people. He saw sadness in her eyes. When blessings arrive during hard times, the sacrifices that made them possible cast a familiar shadow of sorrow.

Max gently stepped behind his wife and wrapped her in his arms. He pulled her close, then turned her to face his sympathetic gaze. Without a word, he took her hand, raised it above their heads, and led her in the dance of the two moons. Beely pressed her head to his chest, her other arm wrapped tightly around his broad shoulders.

She inhaled the familiar, comforting scent of the rays on his clothing. It would forever be a fragrant reminder that her husband had made it home. Her feet followed the rhythm of the drums below, her body surrendering to the strength of the man she was falling in love with all over again. She looked up into his eyes and whispered, "Can you hear them? Your rays are lowing in harmony with the gullies' song. I've never heard anything so beautiful."

Max placed his arm around Beely's lower back and dipped her so low that her hair brushed the dusty ground. He thought the harmony was simply coincidence—but as he lifted her back up, he said not a word. He felt the presence of God with them—a feeling his wife usually had, not he.

The beasts and birds were not the only creatures in harmony that night. Max had won back the love of his life—a love he would never betray, a love he would defend unto death. Just as he leaned in to kiss his bride, Thai and Reverie scrambled up the knoll, eager to join their two favorite people dancing in the moon's glow. Max winked at the two of them just before stealing a kiss.

The four of them looked up at the night sky as the second moon crested over the canyon wall. Members of the Twelve began to drift away from the celebration, slowly and quietly. They had an important meeting ahead. It was true that all was peaceful on the home front—but the meeting that night would stir unrivaled controversy once rumors of their intentions spread. No one would be pleased with the Twelve. No one.

Chapter 4

FIRST MEETING OF THE TWELVE

"What is he doing here?" demanded the chiropter. Before anyone could even attempt to answer his question, he added, "A giant among the Twelve! Not even one of the short, oafish giants but the overly tall, cunning giants! How can we meet in secret without getting detected by our enemies, with this big lug standing over us and everything else under the sun?"

Leopold, the chiropter, had a point. The giant was so large that he could not enter the meeting place. The door to the studio was left open as Zorian, the giant, held his massive head as close to the opening as possible. "I promise not to accidentally step on one of your demure little wings," said Zorian quite sincerely. "Or your tiny, frail ego, for that matter." This drew quite a chuckle from the others.

Leopold waved his wings and quipped, "And that breath! Whew, please exhale in the other direction!"

Francis was the first to come to Zorian's defense. Her large beaver tail twitched as she spoke. "Never before have I heard one of these tiny bats speak. Well, this one seems to be at no loss for words." Chiropters were not exactly tiny, but compared to Francis's eight-foot, nearly three-hundred-pound frame, most everyone seemed small. They stood up to three feet tall, with a wingspan just as wide. What they lacked in size, they more than made up for in tenacity.

Duly also spoke up for the giant. "I, for one, would trust a giant over a Mastadonian like yourself," he said, glaring at Leopold.

"How dare you insult me! I am a pure-bred chiropter. Neither my genes nor my limbs have been touched by that evil monstrosity from Okrad—or Mastad, whatever they are calling it these days."

"Nonetheless," Duly continued, "Mastad evidently used your kind to craft his cocktail of evil flying beasts—beasts that stole every last book from my library!"

Leopold did not miss a beat. "A braewicker, of all things, questioning the loyalty and uprightness of my kind. You were from a clan of lying thieves long before the Dry Death!"

"I was raised not as a braewicker, I'll have you know, but as a citizen of Pixanese."

Saint Elmo, Francis's husband, leaned over to his wife and

whispered, "A Glouscenshire doesn't fall far from the tree."

"I heard that!" shouted Duly toward Saint Elmo before releasing a thundering sneeze.

Cloy, the Mindalite, looked at Beely and remarked, "You see, this is why my clan is so clannish. You folks simply don't have the temperament to get along."

All Mindalites, almost without exception, had curly red hair, large freckles, and fair skin. They were a tight-knit and secretive clan with their own deep well—not even Mastad himself could find. The truth was, some of Mastad's Mastadonian warriors had located the Mindalites' well—but none lived long enough to report its location. Rumor held that one sip from the Mindalite waters would kill anything without crimson hair—and the Mindalites were the only redheads in all of the Five Realms.

Lira, a maker of Komas from Okrad, spoke. "Perhaps we should all just take a moment to pray. Let's invite the Holy Spirit to minister to this group before we begin. This is, after all, our very first meeting with all of us together."

Lira turned to the small young man beside her and said, "Malora, why don't you lead us in prayer?"

Malora was young by Five Realms standards—a mere twenty-six—and his boyish demeanor made him seem younger still. Beely had chosen him, not only because he was from the most distant village in the Realm of Many, but also because he was a frequent, welcomed visitor to the Empyrean Realm. To her knowledge, none of the other Twelve had ever been to the realm above the clouds—at least not by invitation.

It was a strategic move—but, as Propo had pointed out, also a risky one. "Malora is young, untested—mostly a mystery," he had said. Beely had countered Propo's doubts by asking if he could ride a ray to the Empyrean Realm himself—and convince a foghorse to join their cause. If he could, she would reconsider asking Malora to join them. No one ever doubted the loyalty or wisdom of a foghorse. Propo had been to the skyward realm, but had never encountered a foghorse. Foghorses, like the Mindalites, rarely interacted with outsiders.

A single curl of Malora's wavy, blondish hair grazed his forehead as he looked up with a radiant, wide grin that instantly captured everyone's attention. He leaned forward, peering out the door to acknowledge Zorian, who was quietly resting his chin on the railing. Instead of the prayer they had expected, Malora began to hum. After a moment, he began to sing:

> "Behold, how good and how pleasant it is for brethren to dwell together in unity! It is like the precious ointment upon the head, that ran down upon the beard, even Aaron's beard: that went down to the skirts of his garments; As the dew of Hermon, and as the dew that descended upon the mountains of Zion: for there the Lord commanded the blessing, even life for evermore."

The room fell silent. Francis thought she saw Saint Elmo wipe a tear from his eye, and Cloy, the Mindalite, subtly cleared his throat. They were stunned by the beauty of his voice. His angelic voice was the reason that the foghorses had become enamored with him. "Those in the Empyrean Realm never spoke—they only sang, and none more beautifully than Malora. As the mood in the room changed, Lira knew why. She was the only one who had ever heard Malora sing, as he called it, a prayer."

Beely sensed the room shift from doubt to quiet contemplation. Only moments ago, they had felt antagonistic and hopeless. Now the Twelve were ready to hear how they might help the Realms return to the freedom and prosperity they once knew.

Beely slowly made her way from the back of the room to the entrance. Leaning against the doorframe, she acknowledged Zorian, then nodded to Malora in thanks for his song. She spoke softly, confidently, and with conviction. "Not long ago, Eudox found me in this very place—my father's studio—overwhelmed by despair. I was desperately searching through my father's writings, before they were all confiscated, hoping to find the answers about what was happening...and what might become of our realms if the evil winds weren't quelled."

"Which one of you is Eudox?" Zorian asked. When he spoke, even though it was a mere whisper to him, the force of his breath caused a wisp of Beely's unbraided hair to fall loose. She brushed the stray strand behind her ear, thinking how blessed she was to be a part of such an eclectic group of souls.

"Most of you have met Eudox at one time or another, but of course Zorian rarely crosses paths with us smaller folk. Eudox was a friend of my father's, as was Propo who's standing next to him."

Eudox gave a slight bow in Zorian's direction. Propo lifted his arm, backhand facing outward, and with a quick twist of his wrist, greeted Zorian with a welcoming palm—the typical Pixanese greeting.

Beely continued, "Eudox—he wouldn't mind me saying—has been a grifter most of his life. And for good reason, which I'm sure he'd be happy to share with all of you someday, when there's more time. Propo was not only a friend of my father's, but he's been like a brother to me. He alone believed in me and stuck with me when almost everyone else considered me just another delusional Plotist."

She turned toward her husband and continued, "Maximilian, the mighty ray trainer, you've all met at one time or another. Duly, the braewicker with a conscience—as I like to say—has been the keeper of the Library of Truth for many turnings. No one before him had ever taken such good care of the books as Duly has."

Before he could stop himself, Leopold let out a disapproving grunt under his breath. It was not quiet enough to go unnoticed, however.

"What was that about?" Duly quickly objected to Leopold's snide slip.

"There are no more books—how good could you have been?" remarked Leopold.

Propo, wishing to have stayed out of the fray, felt compelled to speak. "You weren't there when hundreds of Mastadonians dropped out of the sky. Creatures that—whether you like it or not—carry the best part of your DNA, only modified and combined with other creatures to be stronger, bigger, faster, and even more ruthless. These abominations cleared the library of every book in less time than it takes you to find your dinner. There was nothing anyone could've done to save the books."

Beely immediately raised a finger to her lips. Duly was gracious enough to suppress his strong desire to verbally lash out at the bat. Perhaps it was the lingering reverberations of the beautiful prayer song still echoing that made him reconsider, but more than likely it was Beely's pleading eyes and Propo's heartfelt support.

Beely smiled in appreciation as she continued. "You all must recognize Saint Elmo and Francis—if not by their adorable faces or their long, flat, spectacular tails, then surely by the work

37

they've done in and around our once great rivers and lakes."

Leopold flapped his large wings and asked, "Wasn't it those two who worked with Mastad to enlarge the Lake of Entitlement by hoarding everyone else's precious water?"

Francis quickly responded, "It was called the Lake of Prosperity back then, and his name was Ankur—not yet the evil man we know today as Mastad."

Saint Elmo added, "That's what we do—we create oases where life can flourish. The Good Book says to work with all of one's heart as if unto the Lord—"

Eudox chimed in, "There was already an oasis in the Land of Mana. There was no need to divert even more water there."

"How were we to know the plans of Mastad? There has never been anyone like him. We thought we were helping," pleaded Francis.

"And perhaps you were," said Beely. "We have a strong ally in the Land of Indulgences. She's alive today because of the water reserves there. She will be a thorn in Mastad's side."

Zorian spoke as softly as possible, trying to keep his voice from carrying too far into the canyon. Even though they were meeting somewhat openly, caution was still necessary. "Yes, it is the beautiful Willow you speak of. There's no stronger ally to be found. If she weren't bound to the firmament, she would surely have taken one of our places here tonight."

Beely resumed the introductions. "Speaking of beauty—this is Lira, an artist, mother, and powerful loyalist." Lira gave a slight bow. "She risked her life in the very early stages of our battle. If we'd paid more attention to her, perhaps things wouldn't have ended up as dire as they are now."

"You give me too much credit," said Lira. "I'm here because of my son. He wasn't even born when any of this began."

She walked outside and stood next to the railing where Zorian rested his head. "And it is because of this gentle giant—breath and all—that my son is safe today. My son is living his best life under the protection of the giants among the Mara People. My son's father died before we made it to the Mara People. He gave his life for his family.

But now, my son has strong men to guide and teach him. He may never grow as tall as his teachers, but his great heart will make up for his lack of height. I know Ben is safe with the Giants. I will do whatever it takes to restore freedom—to bring back what we have lost. I can only hope the rest of you will do the same."

"Absolutely!" shouted Maximilian from the back of the room.

"I've lost countless family members and even more friends. I will see this through to the end!" exclaimed Leopold.

"I don't have many seasons left, but for as long as God gives me breath, I will fight," said Eudox.

Francis held tightly to her husband's hand and nodded for him to speak. "We were fooled by the evil one. We'll never be fooled again, and we'll do our part to see the springs restored to the way God intended."

"Since Beely asked for my help, I haven't hesitated. I trust her with every ounce of my being," said Duly.

"Is it true you don't believe in our God?" asked Leopold.

"I believe in her," said Duly, looking directly at Beely.

Beely noticed Duly's scrunched-up face and offered him a clean handkerchief. After he finished sneezing, she turned to Cloy. "Finally, you all must meet our Mindalite—Cloy. I bet none of you have ever met a Mindalite before."

Leopold could not help himself. "I've never seen anyone

so...red. It's like your hair is on fire."

Ignoring Leopold, Cloy shyly rose from his chair. "None of my people are happy about me being here," he said, looking down at the floor. "Aligning with the likes of you all."

"Then why have you joined us, Red Floopy?" asked Malora with his radiant smile. A red floopy was a bright red fruit that grew almost everywhere. It was not exactly an original nickname, but it stuck.

Cloy made eye contact with Leopold for the first time. "I am here because the Holy Spirit told me to come. I'm no fool; my people cannot stay hidden forever. If Mastad is not stopped, there will come a day when he will come for them too. We must all work together to end Mastad's illegitimate reign."

"And we will," said Max confidently.

"The prophecies foretell it," added Propo.

Beely nodded in agreement. "I am not an expert in the prophetic, but Propo has never been wrong. I'm not concerned about the 'when,' but the 'how.' The prophecies, when correctly interpreted, never fail. Yet, the defeat of Mastad does not guarantee restoration. It means little if we win the battle only to lose everyone and everything along the way."

"Where do we begin?" asked Zorian.

"I thought you'd never ask," answered Beely. "We begin by finding the painting. The painting will lead us to the Word."

Chapter 5

THE COST

"I want that painting!" yelled Mastad at his next-in-command.

Athaliah, once a beautiful and gracious woman engaged to a gentleman she loved dearly, had turned into a monster—a murderer—a lonely Mastadonian. She had willingly taken an injection created by Mastad's unscrupulous geneticists. The geneticists had spent many moons conducting experiments on various species.

The Mastadonian, the end result of those experiments, was a genetic mixture of the Mastadonian dog, the chiropter bat, various humanoids, and other more obscure creatures. The result was surprisingly successful, but the process was terribly painful, intrinsically unethical, and, more often than not, deadly.

Mastad's intention was to create invincible warriors impervious to pain and loyal unto death. He achieved nearly all of his goals. The Mastadonians were strong, frightening adversaries that protected their creator like the canines that were bred into them. Their bodies were shaped like large bats with incredible wingspans capable of flying long distances at great speed. Their heads, however, looked reminiscent of the dog they were named after: large, floppy ears, squashed pug nose, and large, round, deep-set eyes, all sitting on a neck obscured by a fold of useless wrinkles.

Although Athaliah was given a more advanced genetic drug than the other Mastadonians, she still struggled with her transformation. Her most challenging evolutionary adjustment was not her new wings or ability to fly, but rather her limbs. When her knees were bent, they pointed backwards while her feet pointed forward. Her claws made it easy to hang upside down, but they were terribly uncomfortable when walking.

She had to face the fact that she would never be normal again. She hated Mastad for turning her into such a wretched beast, yet she had to continue on as though still his loyal lackey. "We've looked everywhere for the painting, Prince Mastad. We haven't uncovered the smallest clue. I'm not entirely convinced such a painting even exists."

"Silence, you imbecile!" Mastad had become increasingly irritable since taking the genetic modifier himself. He had waited until the vaccine, as he referred to it, was safe. No one had died in at least twelve lunar cycles after taking the injections, compared to countless thousands during the more experimental phases.

His own transformation was incomplete: his skin peeled, his organs shifted, and blood and other fluids oozed from his pores, but most painful of all, his bones felt as though they were literally splintering and breaking apart inside a sack of skin he no longer recognized.

In truth, Athaliah was fairly confident the painting did exist. Unfortunately, she had poisoned her fiancé before discovering where he had hidden the miraculous artifact. If Mastad ever found out about her misstep, he would waste no time ensuring she met the same deadly fate. "Of course, we'll continue searching far and wide," she said.

"Do you have any idea what this painting is capable of?" He paused when she offered no reply, then continued: "Why would I expect someone of your level of incompetence to understand? I wish your ill-fated lover were still in my employ. Had he not met such an untimely death, I feel sure he would have discovered the painting's location. He was a smart young man. What he ever saw in you, I have no idea."

His occasional insults began as a method of control—but soon became part of his habitual discourse. He could not help himself. She bore his insults quietly, biding her time. She could kill her not-yet-fully-evolved cousin in a single, swift strike. The Prince, as he demanded to be called, was like a caterpillar in a cocoon; weak and vulnerable.

Yet, she needed him as much as he needed her. She did not know prophecy as well as Mastad. He possessed extensive knowledge of various religions. Furthermore, he commanded many loyal followers who were dedicated to him unto death. Athaliah could never rally followers herself; instead, she would use Mastad until she was strong enough to enact revenge. She hated her master, and seethed serving him. Yet serving no other, she served the one she hated.

"I apologize for my incompetence, sir. Please allow me to prove my loyalty. We will succeed."

Prince Mastad bit off a piece of molting skin from his upper lip. He then licked oozing pus from the corner of his mouth and appeared to almost smile. "That's my girl. That's why I trust you above any of these other fools."

He waved his disfigured arms toward the Mastadonian standing guard in his ghoulish throne room. The real reason he trusted her was that she was one of his only blood relatives still living, and he had groomed her from a young age. He felt sure she would never have the capacity to betray him. She had nowhere else to go.

"Isn't it time that you told me what's so important about this painting?" she asked.

Mastad looked down at his not-yet-fully-transitioned hand, which appeared mangled and was covered in a thin layer of web-like skin. He wanted to snap his fingers to summon a slave for a cloth to wipe the secretions draining down his face. Athaliah—having recently endured the same transition and knowing how aggravating it was to be unable to perform the simplest tasks—gently offered him the relief he so desperately needed.

She carefully wicked away the odorous fluid from her cousin's face. He was displeased by his protégé's forwardness, but when relief came, it brought with it a begrudging sense of thanks. He leaned forward on his bejeweled throne and whispered into her ear, "The painting is everything. It's the answer. It's the gateway to eternity."

"How do you know this? You've never even seen it."

He looked around; none of his Mastadonians were paying

them any attention, but he still whispered nonetheless. "I've consulted the prophets."

"What prophets would speak to those like us?"

"None that are still living," he chided.

"What is that supposed to mean?"

It would serve no purpose to tell her the truth, that once he got what he needed from them, he had them killed, so ignoring her question, he continued. "I've had visions. I know this painting exists, and I know what it can do; what it will do for me—for us."

Athaliah knew her cousin was more vulnerable than ever—otherwise, he would not have been indulging her curiosity. He had never before used the word "us," always speaking as if he alone were the beginning and end of everything. She knew he hated her. Why he loathed her so much, she might never know, but for now, she would take advantage of his weakness. Once he fully transformed into his new creation, he would likely never reveal anything of importance to her again.

"I need to know in order to help you. What is so important about this painting? No more riddles. No more vague innuendoes."

"The painting is a portal; it can transport a believer anywhere they wish to go."

"And are you a believer?"

"I can't fully explain it, but I know it to be true."

"Where would you go?" she asked.

"To the ones that don't believe we exist."

"Again with the riddles!" exclaimed Athaliah.

"Not so loud, girl."

"Just speak plainly." She dabbed his face once again with the cloth.

"There are more than the Five Realms of Here. There is a realm more whole than even ours."

"But how can that be? It makes no sense."

"The proof is in the painting."

Athaliah knew her cousin was a genius. She also knew that genius was a close relative to madness. "Assuming that everything you say is true, where in the realms would one begin to look for something as unassuming as a small work of art?"

"You will find it."

"How do you know this?"

"The same way I know the painting exists. What? Do you think you're here because of some special skill you have?" He laughed, but upon seeing her reaction, he quickly tempered his spiteful mockery. "You were chosen. Only the gods know why. You are destined to bring the painting to me."

"You saw that in a vision as well?"

Before Mastad could reply, the throne-room doors burst open with a crash. Two assailants, bows in hand, somersaulted and rolled into the center of the room. Neither Mastad nor Athaliah could immediately grasp what was happening; the intruders' arrows found their mark in the two door guards, killing them both.

The two remaining guards on the opposite wall barely had time to move before the skilled archers nocked and loosed two more arrows into the hearts of the warriors. Fortunately for Mastad, Athaliah had ascended into striking position before the second volley of arrows flew.

She descended so quickly upon the two assailants that they lacked time to nock another arrow. Athaliah landed directly between the attackers. She spread her wings wide, claws sliding just beneath their chins. When she retracted her wings, she sliced deeply into the soft skin of Mastad's would-be assassins. Their arms shot upward toward their bleeding throats—then they fell to the cold, hard floor before their hands could feel the warm life spilling from their bodies.

Two lone archers had managed to slay eight of Mastad's guards before Athaliah intervened, ending their failed mission to assassinate the ruler of the Five Realms of Here. Mastad was furious. The failure of his hybrid warriors to protect him was nothing compared to the betrayal of a conspirator within his own ranks.

There was only one vulnerable spot on a Mastadonian—a single precise shot to the lower belly could kill. The archers had been told exactly where to aim—to hit the heart. Never before had anyone attempted such a brazen assassination, nor such a bold attempt to take out the Prince. Earlier in his reign, someone had tried poison—but it only left his cupbearer ill for a few moons. This attack was bold, well-timed, and nearly successful.

It took a moment for Mastad to settle his nerves enough to speak without stuttering. It had been so long since he felt fear that he had forgotten its effects. When he spoke again, his words came measured—and cold.

"It was her. It had to be her," Mastad seethed.

"Beely wouldn't dare break the truce," Athaliah assured.

"I can't prove it was her, but who else?"

"There are a few scattered factions, Prince—perhaps it was one of them." Athaliah knew better—she had seen the small copper rectangles on the belts of the archers. It was a symbol associated with the Twelve—or so she had been told. She would not tell Mastad; she preferred to keep some things to herself.

"Perhaps. I want you to begin watching the Magistrate. Tell no one else. I want you—and you alone—to report back to me with any unseemly activities in which she may be involved."

"But what of the painting?"

"Is your feeble little mind only capable of doing one task at a time? Are you a small child that needs to be trained? If you can't handle the responsibilities the Kingdom of Mastad requires, perhaps I should install your replacement."

Athaliah froze in disbelief. She took a deep breath and held it for a moment, trying to suppress her anger. Then, surprising even herself, she laughed. She was sure the Prince flinched in response. Her reaction did not stem from humor, but from shock. Mastad never failed to surprise her with his astonishing lack of self-awareness.

She—his cousin and first in command—had just saved his life. She could not help but think that she had literally kept that leaky bag of skin with his useless limbs from taking an arrow to the heart. Yet he never looked back—even if it were just a few moments. He only ever looked forward. He never showed gratitude nor acknowledged good work. He found value only in criticism and torture.

Her abrupt laughter was simply an unexpected expression of shock. Yet she raised her head, stared hard into his cold, black eyes, and gritted her teeth. "Not only will I find the painting and spy on the magistrate, but I won't hesitate to save your life in between—whenever your other little dogs fail as majestically as these." She looked behind her at the dead guards.

It was the first time Athaliah had ever dared to chastise Mastad. He had made her angry many times before, but today was different. She had never saved his life until now. A few moments after her outburst, she began to tremble. She was not sure if Mastad could see her visceral reaction to his unbridled arrogance, but she vowed then and there that someday her revenge would hit him in the middle of his devilish soul—like a slow-burning brick of coal.

Chapter 6

FOLLOW THE RAINBOW

"He did a poor job of explaining things—an empachic could have done better," said Cloy.

"Empachics don't speak," said Duly.

"Exactly," said Cloy. He glanced down at Thai, the empachic resting near Beely's feet, and then up to Reverie, who Beely held in her arms. Both empachics seemed oblivious to the conversation—reinforcing his point.

The four of them—Cloy, Beely, Duly, and Eudox—sat in the studio several days after the first meeting of the Twelve.

Tensions were still high, but that was to be expected. If Mastad discovered the details of their plans—and most assumed he would—they would undoubtedly be targets for his wrath. By agreeing to work together—and against Mastad—they had essentially sealed their fates. There was no going back to the anonymity or the somewhat safer life they had once known.

"What is there to understand?" asked Duly. "I explained everything to the fullest extent of my understanding of the ancient prophecies." Duly took a sip of his Ognatia tea—it was the only thing that seemed to help alleviate his troublesome congestion, with the added bonus of soothing his nerves. His disdain for being around others was not waning.

"Therein lies the problem. We are using prophecy as our only guide—that can be a problematic task indeed," said Eudox.

"And all of you are relying solely on memory. We have no texts to consult. We're on a fool's mission!" exclaimed Cloy. His face flushed a deeper shade of red—as if all of his freckles had merged together.

"It's nice to have an optimist on the team!" barked Duly.

"Cloy is right," replied Eudox, rubbing his hand along his brow as he recalled his recent hunt and past encounters with Mastadonians. "We may all be doomed. We may indeed die having not achieved much—but to fight for freedom, even unto death—is that not better than to willingly concede? Pessimistic or not, he is correct. We may perish."

"Another optimist!" exclaimed Duly.

Cloy, pacing back and forth, took an arrow from Eudox's quiver. "The old man waxes poetic. Sure, his seasons have been many." He pressed the tip of the arrow with his finger and accidentally pierced the skin. He grimaced, but stifled his reaction, hoping no one noticed. "What is death to the dying?"

Cloy was referring to Eudox's advanced age.

Beely took the arrow from Cloy and put it back where it belonged. "Eudox may be the oldest among us, but he is stronger than most, both spiritually and physically. It was Eudox, the hunter, who helped secure sustenance for those in Pixanese. It was Eudox who knew prophecy well enough to warn my father—and later me—about the Dry Death. Everything he has told me has come to pass," explained Beely.

"So, tell us, Grandfather," said Cloy, looking directly at Eudox. "What's next? What does your keen memory of prophecy reveal in its ever-obscure language?"

"You are right, Red—I am an old man. Beely gives me far too much credit. I have lived long enough to see some prophecies come to pass, but that does not mean I am an expert," answered Eudox. "It is Duly who knows and understands the prophetic language better than anyone." Eudox glanced at Cloy's finger and discreetly passed him a cloth to stop the bleeding.

Cloy casually slipped his hand, wrapped in the cloth, into his pocket. "Am I—are we—to trust a braewicker who doesn't even believe in Yahweh? The Mindalites may live separately from our fellow believers, but our faith is as strong as any."

"The Bible, where the Word resides, is not of our world," Eudox said. "Yes, it applies to all of us, as there is only one Creator of everything, but realm prophecies are specific to the Five Realms of Here. I'm not sure one needs to believe in them in order to understand them."

Beely chuckled in response to Eudox's explanation, though she had not intended to be heard.

"Am I wrong?" Eudox asked Beely.

"Let me take this one," said Duly. "I have read nearly

everything that was made available to me. Floopy, please remind me to thank Malora for the fitting epithet. Floopy is correct when he says I am not a believer. I never have been—probably never will be." He turned to address Eudox who was sitting to his right. "I'm not even sure I believe in realm prophecies either. However, it seems that things have changed. I can't argue with the fact that eight out of the ten prophecies about Mastad have already come true. Statistically, it would be impossible to predict so much about one person thousands of turnings before his birth, were it not of divine origin."

"What about all the prophecies in the Bible? So many have already come true," said Cloy. "And by the way, floopy is not an epithet—it's a fruit." Cloy was not amused that everyone struggled not to laugh—including Duly, whom he had never even seen smile. "It's a stupid nickname. Okay?"

The levity was short-lived as Duly got back on point. "Time will reveal all. If the prophecies about the Messiah align with what's written, I may be forced to believe in the Word as well. When we still could read the Bible, I was up to over forty prophecies regarding the Messiah."

"How could you ever confirm Biblical prophecy? None of that takes place in our realm," said Eudox.

"Ah, that's where realm prophecies come into play. Our own prophecies state that messengers will come here from another world. The first messengers will not survive, but they will return the full Bible—both the New and the Old Covenants—to our realms," said Duly.

Beely sat quietly, observing from a far corner. None of what Duly shared was new to her. She and Duly had spent countless hours discussing their mission, the Word, and the realm prophecies. She studied the faces of Cloy and Eudox. Much of

53

this information was new to them, and she prayed they would not only understand but also believe in their mission—a mission rooted in the very realm prophecies Duly was discussing. She was pleased to see they were riveted on every word Duly spoke.

Cloy scratched his head with his good hand and asked, "I have a question—I apologize for interrupting, as you may address it later—but it was my understanding that our mission is to bring back a completed Bible, containing both the Old and New Covenants. How can that be, if indeed the New Covenant hasn't even happened in the Earthly Realm, yet?"

Eudox raised his hand in an informal gesture to take the floor. "I know that time here works much differently than in the other world. I don't know how or why—I just know it's different."

"This is true," Duly confirmed as he bumped into both Cloy and Eudox on his way to a tall bookcase. He snapped his fingers at Beely and pointed at a shelf out of his reach. Beely shrugged, but obliged. She brought down a small hourglass. Duly jumped up, took it from her hand, and promptly placed it on a desk. "These sands are from our realms. They fall as time passes, right?" Cloy shrugged, Eudox nodded, and Beely raised a brow. "Imagine if these grains of sand were so big they couldn't even be lifted in the other world—or too small to see—or so light they floated—or perhaps they held an energy or friction that made them go backward, stay suspended, or do any combination of things you could imagine." No one spoke a word. Cloy rolled his eyes. Eudox sighed, and even Beely looked a bit perplexed. Duly's face contorted as if he had just smelled a vulture's beak. "Let's just say, we're not bound by the same scientific restrictions as the Earthly World. We have ways of traversing time and matter that are, apparently, quite unique." Duly sat down in the nearest chair and folded his arms in frustration.

"Interesting," said Cloy flatly.

Duly remained seated. In a far less enthusiastic tone, he said, "It gets better. The prophecies tell of messengers—they are called missionaries in the other world—"

Eudox interrupted, "Missionaries? I've never heard that word. What does it mean?"

Duly continued, clearly satisfied to have regained their attention. "Until recent events, the Five Realms had no need of missionaries. Missionaries were—perhaps still are, or will be—sometimes it's all very confusing, even for me. Whatever the case may be, missionaries are specifically led to share the Good News with every tribe, village, tongue—and in our case, realm."

"Good News?" questioned Cloy.

Beely answered, "The Gospels—the Word of God—are often referred to as the Good News."

"Yes," said Duly. "Sometime in our future, a group of missionaries will deliver—bring back, if you will—the complete Word, both the New and Old Covenants, to our realms."

"When in the future?" asked Eudox.

Beely slowly made her way from the back of the studio to the front entrance. On her way, she glanced through the front window. She leaned against the wall next to the front door, after glancing down to make sure it was locked. Beely had felt that someone had been following her the past few days. She was not sure, it was just a feeling, but it had caused her to become more cautious. She listened for any unusual noises, but focused most of her attention on Reverie, whom she held close to her chest. An empachic could sense a stranger or nefarious activities from great distances, even through closed doors. What Duly was about to share was the most sensitive and important secret he had ever spoken.

Duly gave a knowing look to Beely as he glanced up at the same shelf where the hourglass had been. On it, hidden behind a board, sat a small clay model of a bird with long, straight, featherless wings. It had been given to him by a prophet. "Four humans from the Earthly Realm will arrive in a metal bird; a machine that flies, from what we can discern. They will somehow crash into our realm. They were missionaries on a mission in their own world, but what they unknowingly did was bring back the Word to ours. Mastad does not know or understand any prophecy that does not directly relate to him or benefit him in some way. He was too lazy to study them all. I am certain he knows nothing of it." Duly fondly remembered the last living prophet, not yet murdered by Mastad, that helped him decipher this most obscure and difficult prophecy.

"What Duly is telling you must remain between the four of us. Not even all of the Twelve know of this," said Beely.

Cloy began pacing in the overstuffed room once again. There were three desks and even more chairs, along with bookcases, side tables, and a random assortment of oddities either invented or collected by Beely's father. He had been gone for many turnings, but she could not bring herself to part with his belongings. "The future you say?" Cloy shook his head in frustration as he attempted to walk off his nervous energy without running into something. His frustrations increased as he was unable to accomplish either. "Ouch!" he exclaimed. His foot had landed squarely on what could only be described as a garbage container made to look like a tasmangular holding its two front winged legs open to form a receptacle for the day's trash. He looked down at the extravagant wood carving and asked, "What is that supposed to be?!"

"A beaver carved it for my father. Apparently, beavers despise tasmangulars," answered Beely with an apologetic tone.

Eudox, ignoring Cloy, asked, "How are we supposed to secure a book that hasn't even arrived here yet?"

"Excellent question," responded Duly. "In fact, it's the question of the day." Duly took a sip of his tea and gave Beely a nod to take over the discussion.

Beely sat Reverie on the floor as she walked to the center of the room. "Somewhere there is an ancient painting that I can only assume was left to us by an angel of the Lord Himself. Most who know of the painting, and that's not many, assume it can only transport the viewer to somewhere in the present. According to Duly and the prophecies, the painting can take one anywhere, including to the past and even the future."

Cloy, who had taken off his sandal to rub his throbbing toe, mocked, "So, we stand in front of this painting and tell it where we want to go?"

Duly addressed the sarcastic remark as he moved the tasmangular trash receptacle to the back wall, out of harm's way. "It's hard to say exactly. None of us have ever even seen this painting." Duly sneezed loudly from the dust under the wood carving. Beely promptly handed him a cloth from her satchel. She knew there would be more sneezing. "All I know is what the prophets have written. The painting resembles something different to all who look upon it, but it always has some form of a path or road. Once we find the painting—"

"And we will," interrupted Beely.

"Yes, according to the prophets we will find it. Once we find it, one or more of the Twelve must walk into it as if it were reality."

"I can't wait to see that," said Cloy.

Duly reached over and wiggled Cloy's toe, "I guess you better get to rubbing this little empy back to health, then. We have a lot of ground to cover." An empy was a cute name given to the small toe when children are just learning about things like toes and fingers.

Cloy pulled his foot back and scowled at the braewicker.

Duly continued, "The other thing specific to the prophecy in regard to the painting is the mention of a rainbow."

"What's a rainbow?" asked Eudox.

"In the Earthly Realm, according to the Word, it is a sign from God that He would never flood their world again. It is a colorful image that appears in the sky as an arch with lines of distinct colors," said Duly.

Eudox shook his head affirmatively. "Yes. Yes, I remember now. God wiped out all life in the Earthly Realm except for the animals and one family. That world had become reprobate, all were evil beyond redemption, if I remember correctly."

"Well, if Mastad had not destroyed all of the books, or if Duly had managed to hide a few, we might be able to reference them to find out exactly," said Cloy.

"If the small-minded were able to memorize and study, perhaps they would know without having to reference anything," snarled Duly.

Beely placed her hand on Cloy's shoulder. "I chose each one of you for your unique gifts and hard-earned skills. Eudox has proven himself a confident and successful tracker. Duly knows everything there is to know about realm prophecy, books, and the Word of God. You, Floopy, know the secret passageways of like no other. Your people have been in hiding for many moons. Not even Mastad has been able to locate your people. I can only assume the Mindalites have mastered the ancient canyon caverns and underground. Is this true?"

Cloy answered, "It is as you say."

"Excellent!" Beely exclaimed. "Now let's get about to finding where in the realms the Word is waiting to be found."

"What about the painting, should we not find the painting first?" Eudox asked.

"That task has been assigned to Propo, Lira, Malora, and Leopold."

"Where in the realms do we begin?" asked Cloy.

Duly had already begun dragging scrolls and placing them on the largest desk in the center of the room. "Here!" he pointed as he unfurled the scrolls.

They all moved in for a closer look. Eudox shrugged. "Where did you get these scrolls? I thought all writings and artifacts of this nature were destroyed."

"I just recently, with Propo's help, reconstructed these from memory. They are not perfect, but they should prove close enough," answered Duly.

Cloy shook his head vigorously in protest. "This is the most unwise thing you could have done. My people have remained safe because we have not been careless enough to harbor contraband. Surely you all know that Mastad commands the air, and with his blasphemous sorcery, he will find these scrolls in no time at all, if he hasn't already. We must destroy them immediately! These will lead him straight to us!" Cloy continued to shake his head while waving his hands demonstratively.

Eudox walked over and placed a reassuring hand on Cloy's shoulder. "It's going to be all right, Red."

"How is it going to be all right?" Cloy grabbed his pack off the ground and began looking for his things. "I've got to get out of here. I don't dare go back to my people. Mastad probably has his eye on us as I speak. What am I to do now?" Cloy was inconsolable

Beely grasped Cloy's hand and guided him to a nearby chair. He sat in a daze. Beely took a loud, demonstrative deep breath—a sound more for Cloy's benefit than her own. "We understand. Mastad will no doubt become aware of us very soon, if he hasn't already, with or without the scrolls. Maximilian, Zorian, and the beavers are keeping track of his every move."

Duly, although surreptitiously enjoying the Mindalite's nervous breakdown, offered a reassuring word. "Propo and I reconstructed the scrolls just before you got here. We need you to add your depth of knowledge to help us find ways to travel in secret. Your insight is invaluable. We will destroy them as soon as we have committed the most important parts to memory. That is, if we haven't committed you first." Duly's sarcastic comment acted like smelling salts to the Mindalite. Cloy exhaled fiercely. He slowly turned his head toward Duly and fired back with words so measured they sent chills down the braewicker's short spine. "If Mastad ever discovers the location of my family, he will discover you, one piece at a time. Commit that to memory."

Eudox stared down at the scroll on the desk without looking up as he spoke. "Come now, boys, let's not waste time. Show us what you know, Red."

Cloy, his faculties restored, stood next to Eudox and examined the map on one of the two smaller scrolls. Beely stood back and allowed Duly to point out the important details.

Duly stood on a chair and leaned over the table. "The

Magistrate's father—"

"Please stop calling me that," Beely interrupted.

Duly sighed dramatically. "As you wish. *Beely's* father had a theory about where the metal bird would land in our world. The prophet I consulted agreed. Look closely at this range of cliffs." They all leaned in for a closer look, jockeying for position over the desk.

"Who reconstructed these maps?" Cloy asked.

"Propo," Beely said with pride, "he worked with my father for countless seasons. They were very close. To my knowledge, Propo knew firsthand everything that my father wrote and theorized, including many ideas that never made it to paper." Beely unrolled the third scroll with Eudox's help, who held one end. "This is the list of the prophetic markers my father said would lead one to the Word when it returned."

Eudox read the first one aloud. "A rainbow will appear when doubt is most high. Follow the colors of the promise, and it will lead you to the location of the Word's return."

"How do we know that Propo remembered all the prophetic markers correctly?" asked Cloy.

"We don't, but I feel confident we have enough information. Many of these are based on prophecies of the Realms," replied Duly. "You've already seen the map on the smaller scroll, commit it to memory along with Malik's prophetic markers. Now, for the larger scroll." The two smaller scrolls were removed, revealing the larger one, already unfurled beneath them.

"I see," said Cloy.

"What am I missing?" Eudox asked.

Duly hopped off his chair and pushed it to the other side of the desk, maneuvering between Cloy and Eudox in the process.

"What Floopy has likely recognized is that this is a map of all the water that remains in the Five Realms." He climbed back onto the chair and placed his only wart-free finger on a small spot of blue.

"Whoever has made this map has put my people in jeopardy. If this map is discovered, the Mindalites will fight to the death to keep Mastad from taking over their well," Cloy seethed. Although he was not pleased, Cloy agreed that the scrolls were correct, as far as he could tell.

"The braewicker's finger rests upon the only source of water yet to be discovered by Mastad." Eudox stroked his thin, long beard thoughtfully.

Duly looked at Beely and smiled—an act so rare it caused her to flinch. "Well, these two might have enough sense to actually utilize the works before them!" he said.

Beely kept her gaze on Eudox. "You are correct, Eudox. That is the Mindalite well," she then turned to Cloy. "I apologize, Cloy, but when the map was reconstructed…we didn't think. We did what the task required."

"Which was?"

"We will be traveling far and wide, and we will need to know exactly where the water sources are, few as they may be. Not even the vines of a rubber plant could hold all the water needed for where we are going."

Eudox placed his arm around the smaller Mindalite and brought him close. "Well, buddy, I say we start committing this stuff to memory." He then picked up the large scroll and tore out the section that exposed the Mindalite well. He placed it in his mouth and chewed. "I guarantee you this, Red—unless this bit of scroll survives my hardy intestinal tract, no one, including Mastad, will use it to discover where your family lives."

Chapter 7

THE WOODLAND SHIRKS

Maximilian sat in a darkened cave with the beavers. Not even Thai was able to console him. He wished Zorian was still with them, as the giant always expressed hope even during the most difficult times, but leaving him to help guard the Shirks was an arrangement agreed upon by all.

A lone bioluminescent organism provided just enough light to reveal a tear welling up in Francis's eye. Saint Elmo had his head lowered in despair. The small wood carving he had been working on earlier sat unfinished in his lap. The intimacy of the small cave only encouraged the spread of emotions that Max struggled to contain.

Max stared at the stuffed pack lying next to Francis. The gifts were just one reminder of the support the Shirks had given them in their mission to find the Word and save their world. "They were the most skilled with a bow of anyone I ever knew," lamented Max.

"They will be missed," said Saint Elmo, finally looking up.

Francis placed a soothing hand on Max's shoulder. "They will never be forgotten. Wherever our story is told—"

"And it will be told," her husband assured.

"Yes, when our story is told—which is now also the Shirks' story—those two selfless archers will be remembered as heroes." Max bit the inside of his lip to keep his emotions in check.

Francis, not one to dwell too long on any unpleasant matters, let a few moments pass before broaching the next sensitive subject. "Is it time to talk about reuniting with Beely and the others?"

As if not hearing Francis, Max looked down at the ground and spoke in a near whisper, "It was just bad luck. The timing should have been perfect, but she was there." He looked up and said sternly, "She was not supposed to have been there. Athaliah is her name, more cunning than her master, and fully transitioned."

"The one who killed her own lover," added Saint Elmo, clenching his fist.

"Just a rumor," Francis added.

They were discussing the deaths of the two archers, who were slain by Athaliah during their attempt to kill Prince Mastad. There were some, other than the Twelve, who wanted to see Mastad's cruel reign end, but few who were willing to risk their lives in the process. Most of those who were against Mastad, such as the Mindalites, were simply hiding and biding their time, but not the Shirks—they were brave enough to face the danger head on, and their courage cost them their lives.

Max held Thai in his arms. The soothing purr of the frail empachic began to bring him some comfort. "I'm afraid my wife may have been right. This war we are fighting, against Mastad, will not be won by sword or arrow," said Max.

"I'll never get used to seeing a grown man coddle such a creature," Saint Elmo said, referring to Thai. Max nodded as if he might have agreed. Saint Elmo shrugged and asked, "What do we do now, Master of the empachics?"

Francis, sitting with her back against the cave wall between Max and her husband, slapped her tail hard against the stone floor. "I just had a revelation: Our task was to keep closer tabs on the evildoer and his cousin, Athaliah—but to what end? Our ultimate task is to protect and help one another, and we can't do that separated. We are better united as one, not scattered about."

"Francis, you may very well be correct," said Max.

Saint Elmo, who had just resumed his wood carving, spat out a shaving before asking, "So what is our next move?"

"I have prayed about this since we left the Shirks. Mastad has only continued to grow more powerful and cunning with each cycle of the moons. Francis is correct—we will be stronger if we stay together," said Max.

"After what happened today, you can rest assured Mastad will be watching all of us. He will want revenge for the attempt on his life," Saint Elmo added. "I agree with both of you, but I do think it was wise that Zorian stayed behind with the Shirks.

If the Mastadonians manage to find them, Zorian will protect them."

Max ran his hands across his face and through his hair. "So, it's agreed then."

Saint Elmo spat more shavings onto the cave floor, much to his wife's chagrin, and asked, "How do we find the others without being strung up on the death silk ourselves? Don't you think Mastad has his monsters searching both high and low for us?"

Max shook his head and gave a short laugh.

Saint Elmo looked astonished as he asked, "What in the realms could you find amusing about that?"

"The sacred silk of Okrad was once used to make beautiful works of art by the most skilled artisans. Now he uses the same material to make nooses to hang his enemies. Mastad has managed to twist everything beautiful into something ugly." Max walked to the cave entrance. "Excuse me—Thai needs some fresh air."

The beavers sat in silence for several moments.

"I'll go see about Max. You might want to clean up that mess while I'm gone," Francis pointed to all the wood shavings on the cave floor.

Saint Elmo moved his tail toward the entrance to halt his wife's exit. "Let him have a moment, dear."

She reluctantly nodded in agreement. "I suppose you're right. He feels personally responsible for the death of the Shirks. What more could I possibly say that would help?"

Saint Elmo looked into his wife's eyes. It was obvious they shared similar thoughts. Max had made a horrible miscalculation that had only created more problems.

Saint Elmo's mind drifted back to when they had first found

those who were usually so well hidden. He knew that the woodland archers could have stayed hidden indefinitely, but they had chosen to be found. They volunteered to fight, and they paid the ultimate price. His mind drifted further back to their journey to find the Woodland Shirks and the events that unfolded afterward.

"Are you sure they are still in these woods? All of the trees are dying or dead," whispered Saint Elmo.

Francis spoke as softly as possible, "I'm not sure of anything. I don't know if you have failed to notice, Elmo, but the last time we saw a healthy tree was many moons ago, and that was in the Land of Mana. Only the ones with deep roots could have survived this long without water."

"What makes you think the Shirks would be in this specific vicinity?" asked Maximilian.

Still whispering, Francis replied, "They shan't be far. This is where we, for too many cycles to count, traded our hand-carved arrows in return for their resin."

"Not just any arrows, mind you, these arrows were made of the hardest and finest wood a beaver could fell. They flew faster than any arrow even the archers themselves could craft," whispered Saint Elmo.

Francis added, "Not just any resin, I might point out. Many beavers used the resin of the Woodland Shirks to seal and preserve their most special works of art. Only the Shirks know how and exactly when to extract the golden sap from the majestic highland trees."

Zorian, failing in his best attempt to speak softly, asked, "Why did they need such specially crafted arrows?" Had there been any leaves left on the trees; they surely would have fluttered from the vibration of the giant's deep voice.

Before they had time to raise a finger to their lips to quiet Zorian, arrows rained down upon them from every direction. Hundreds of long pointed sticks whistled through the air at breakneck speed.

These were not regular arrows. Each flying spear had a strong thin rope attached to it. In a matter of minutes, the two beavers, Maximilian, and even the giant, were entangled in a mass of impenetrable chain-like fabric. Maximilian and the beavers, unable to balance without the freedom of their limbs, quickly fell to the ground.

Zorian, shocked by the speed and sheer number of arrows, stood frozen. It never occurred to him that the ropes, no matter the number, could be strong enough to hold him. That was until a group of archers rushed behind him, took hold of the ropes, and pulled Zorian to the ground.

The last thing anyone heard before the cheers of victory was the loud thud of a giant hitting the dry forest floor, followed by Saint Elmo's claim of a muffled groan from the giant. Of course, this would later be vehemently denied by Zorian.

After the celebratory dance of the Woodland Shirks had ended, several small Shirk children emerged from behind the thick leafless trees. After a few moments of tiptoeing around, the children giggled while nudging the four strangers lying bound on the ground. Francis was very perturbed at Saint Elmo for being unable to contain his own giggles as the children poked mercilessly at his ticklish ribs.

The tiniest of the children, a sweet girl named Audrey, pried her fingers between the ropes tightly strung across Zorian's face. She stared in awe at the giant's thick, long eyelashes until he abruptly opened his eyes and shouted with all the strength he could muster, "BOO!"

The little girl fell, rolled back a bit before landing on Zorian's belly. Surprisingly unfazed, she quickly crawled back up to Zorian's head and exposed the largest eyeball she had ever laid eyes upon.

"Get down from there right this instant, Audrey!" shouted the little girl's mother.

Zorian did not have the best view, but it was good enough to glimpse too many Shirks to count. The Woodland Shirks had been permanent residents in the High Forest of Pixanese for as long as anyone could remember.

Entire families lived high up in the canopies, and a few lived in the cavities of large hollowed-out trees, which often connected with underground tunnels following large roots. They had not been known to be particularly shy or combative. In fact, they were well-liked for being great storytellers with overly hospitable natures.

They would offer their best accommodations to weary travelers venturing through the High Forest, if and when the Shirks chose to reveal themselves. They kept the forest floor meticulously clean.

Until recently, they had only used the beavers' beautiful arrows in their forest games and when hunting their only source of food, the High Forest River snakes.

"Saint Elmo, is that you?" shouted the tallest of the Shirk archers.

Francis answered for her husband, as he was unable to speak with the children still tickling him. "Of course it's him. No one has a laugh like my Saint Elmo!"

One of the female archers by the name of Rosie shouted excitedly, "Francis! We haven't seen you two in ages. Free them, quickly," she called out to several archers standing nearby. They swung their bows and quivers over their shoulders and promptly began unraveling the strong thin ropes wrapped around the beavers. Max and Zorian were ignored, for the moment.

Still lying on the ground and struggling to catch his breath from the torturous laughter, Saint Elmo managed to speak a few words clearly enough to be understood. "What happened to your usual gracious welcome?"

Rosie's husband, Sam, made his way over to the Beavers and said, "Nothing in the High Forest is as it used to be, if you hadn't noticed, my friend."

Rosie pointed to the children and motioned for them to begin rolling up the ropes so they could be used again, perhaps for the real enemy the next time. She removed the hood from her head as she slid her arm around her husband's waist. "We are truly sorry for the poor welcome. We saw the giant and didn't take the time to identify the company he was keeping. Giants aren't trusted in these parts."

Max, still lying on the ground, bound tightly with ropes, said, "Our giant can be trusted. His name is Zorian, and he is on our side."

"Which side might that be?" asked one of the nearby archers.

"My name is Maximilian Wren from Pixanese. We stand against Mastad and all that he represents."

Another archer, standing on guard in case more intruders came their way, said, "Do you think it wise to speak against the great Mastad?"

"Off with his head!" shouted a Shirk further off amongst one of the many dead trees. The demand was met with uproarious laughter.

Another Shirk raised his bow toward the sky and released an

arrow. "With the mighty breath of enlightened air underneath our fletching feathers, we aim high toward victory's mocking call. It matters not whether we win or lose, 'tis the battle for good that is above reproof."

Maximilian, still bound and unable to rise off the ground, asked as loudly as he was able, "What is your name, poet?"

The little girl tumbled off Zorian and quickly made her way to Max, shouting as she ran, "That's my daddy!"

The little girl's brother yanked his overly exuberant sister back by her own small bow which clung tightly to her body. All Shirk children were given their own bows as soon as their draw strength was at least the weight of a normal sized empachic. Audrey's brother held her up in the air as her legs flailed wildly. "How many times have Mom and Dad told you to be wary of strangers?"

"Let me down right this instant, you big bully!" squealed Audrey with as much fervor as a sniblit stuck in a briar patch.

"My name is Thadius," said the poetic archer walking toward Max. "You can let your sister go now, Ticor." The young man, only a few turnings older than his sister, lowered her still kicking legs to the ground, but he did not let go until she stirred up so much dust that his eyes became irritated.

"Ticor, help free our two bound guests." Thadius pointed at Max and Zorian.

"Kids, this man is the husband of Beely of lower Pixanese. They had the most beautiful wedding that ever was and probably will ever be," said Thadius's wife, Nastra.

An archer by the name of Rodear, sitting high up in a tree, shouted down, "Beely? The one that betrayed us all? The one that negotiated with Mastad in order to secure water for herself while the rest of us were left to die?" His abrupt assertion prompted murmurs from the crowd that were quickly growing louder.

At this point Max was able to sit up, his upper body free from entanglements. "That's not at all what my wife wanted. She negotiated for all of Pixanese, both the valleys and the High Forest."

Rodear shouted down in response, "Look around you, the only green you will find here is what has been dyed into the cloth on our backs. The magistrate, as she is called, either failed miserably or more than likely never intended to help us at all. If only we had known what price the legislator required to save more than her own, we would have gladly paid it."

"You have no idea what you're talking about. Come down from your high place and let me face my wife's accuser," shouted Max.

Rodear jumped down from the limb on which he was sitting, grabbing a lower branch in order to swing himself within a few feet from where Max was awkwardly slumped on the ground still half entangled in rope.

"I have known no other home than where my feet have landed, from where my arms have swung, and from where I released arrows toward those who would see it destroyed. This was my father's homeland, his father's before, and his before. The most alive and lively place to have ever been was our home. My children now call our home the dead woods. They all want to leave, but where would we go? Can you answer that, husband of Beely, the traitor?"

Max paused as one of the children untangled the last rope around his legs. Max stood, keeping his distance from Rodear, and spoke as if he understood their plight. "There is no place to go. Not even in the valley of Pixanese below. There is no place where life is not bound by the injustices of an evil ruler whom we all allowed to slowly take over."

"How is that so? What did we Shirks have to do with making agreements and alliances? We keep to ourselves and let others be," said Rodear.

"I know the Shirks are noble and kind. My wife has always spoken highly of you. All of us in the Five Realms have existed peacefully for as long as our history has been recorded. But—"

"But what?" asked Rodear.

Zorian was still lying on his back, although he had been unleashed from most of his ropes. He lifted his head off the ground as he spoke. "It seems as though we all got caught lying down on the job. While you Shirks were hiding out in the woods, the rest of us were either overtaken by gluttony of the Glouscenshire or a belief that our own would be spared if we simply stayed out of Mastad's way. We were wrong. Those who aligned themselves with the Prince, those who hid from the Prince, those who ran from the Prince, and even those who made agreements with the Prince, were all wrong."

Rodear casually rosined his bow as he confidently looked up at Zorian. "Are you blaming us, giant?"

Zorian finally stood. The Shirks raised their bows and took a few steps back, except for Rodear who held his ground. The children ran behind trees. "No," said Zorian, "we are all to blame. The giants, both large and small, have always been few in number, but had we acted soon enough, I am sure we could have stopped Mastad.

Instead, we were lied to. The lies were beautiful to the ears of the giants. Promises of things we had never before imagined. A land we could call our own in the Realm of Okrad, with streams and lush gardens."

Nastra lifted her hands as she stepped in between Zorian and the archers with their raised bows. "Rest your arrows in your hides. These are our friends. Whoever is to blame for the fall, none is to blame more than Mastad. He is our only enemy. He is the one into which we shall release our arrows."

She paused before addressing Max. "Not all in the woodlands blame your wife. Rumors are no justification for further accusation." She looked back at Rodear. "My father knew Beely's father. He was a kindred spirit, and Beely, I know, is much the same." She announced with a loud voice so everyone in the dead woods could hear, "You are all welcome here."

After the four visitors were freed from their bindings and all introductions were made, the daylight had nearly vanished. It was decided that instead of heading back to the valley, the foursome should spend the night under the protection of the Shirks.

The Dead Woods came alive at night in ways that might not be appealing to unsuspecting travelers. In fact, one of the Shirk children recently discovered an aggressive yellowish-grey moss that had never before existed in their part of the forest. Ticor had accused his sister of stealing food just a few days before the visitors arrived. He only later deduced that the food had actually been devoured by the moss.

Ticor called the new addition to their forest floor the smothering moss. Anything left to rest on top of it for more than a few minutes would eventually be completely covered and consumed by the seemingly innocuous ground cover. There were other strange happenings in the forest; any visitor should beware.

The village of the Woodland Shirks was some distance away.

After following the Shirks and their families for the better part of a day, they came upon a trail so narrow that they had to walk in single file. On either side of the trail were large boulders stacked so high that those below could barely see the sky.

The boulders were once covered in ancient carrier vines. It was believed that this was the place carrier vines originated and were eventually spread to other areas of Pixanese by the roofa bird, even as far as the Realm of Many. Carrier vines needed centuries to mature. Their beauty was heralded for their many bright red, purple, and sometimes yellow flowers. Their strength was legendary, as not even a sword crafted by the greatest metalsmith could slice through their seemingly petrified exterior.

But thirst is cruel and can take down far more than an army of swords ever could. The vines still held onto their anchors to the heavens, but they were naked and their grip was weakening. It was a sad sight not fully appreciated by those unfamiliar with the rich history of the forest.

Once through the narrow trail, their hosts led them around trees that were once so green and glorious that even the air radiated a shimmering shade of jade. The trees on this side of the trail were much larger and taller than the ones before it. Yet they too, like the carrier vines, had lost all of their leaves and sat profoundly naked, stripped of their honor.

Bark futilely hung onto trunks and branches, but their days were numbered as the smothering moss waited patiently below. The branches still reached skyward forming a thick canopy over the forest floor. Neither Francis nor Saint Elmo had been this far into the High Forest. Even they, artisans of timber, had never seen such fine specimens. Francis could only imagine how dark it must have been before the waterways were choked, denying leaves their right to return. The only living thing now was the moss scavenging the dead and decaying material slowly falling from above.

"Where will you go when the very trees themselves begin to fall?" asked Francis.

Nastra, holding up the rear, answered Francis, who was having a hard time traveling such a great distance on land. Francis and her husband had gained considerable weight since their work had dried up. "These trees are made of strong fibers. They took centuries to form, and they will not lie down anytime soon. The canopy will continue to cover this forest until we are long gone, I suppose."

"I have felled many a tree in my day, and never have I seen such beauties as these," said Francis.

"Interesting, isn't it? The very things that have provided us shelter and protection from the elements are at the mercy of our hands, and in your case, teeth. We completely consume that which gives so freely—even the very air that we breathe," said Nastra, offering her hand to help Francis.

Francis waved Nastra's hand away. "When I can't traverse down a gnarly path on my own, I will retire to my lodge and never be seen again!" She squeezed in between two tight boulders with a sigh of relief. "My Saint Elmo would agree with you. He actually says a prayer of thanks before every tree he fells."

Francis' labored breathing did not go unnoticed by Nastra. "We have arrived, my friend. Our village is just past this next bend."

"Thank the good Lord above for little mercies. I don't think I could have gone another minute without a rest," said Francis.

Nastra nodded and sighed compassionately, spurring Francis

to remark, "Don't you worry about me, though. Put me in a river and I'll swim circles around any of you tailless folk." For added flair, she whipped her tail on a large rock. The unnecessary demonstration threw her balance off and left her lying flat on the ground staring up at Nastra in surprise. Francis' eyes were as wide as saucers, and Nastra could not help but burst out laughing. After a short moment, Francis joined in, laughing at her own clumsiness.

The others had already arrived in the village of the Shirks. It was a harmonious mixture of nature and craftsmanship. The homes were not too unlike the tree houses in the village of Pixanese, except the Shirks only lived in the trees. They had no cave dwellings nor did they construct ground structures. Everything was high up in the air amongst the tallest trees.

Even without leaves and flowers, once so common, the tree houses themselves were beautiful, ornately designed, and crafted entirely of natural fibers. Francis had joined her husband, and both were speechless, standing back-to-back in the center of the village.

The others thought it a curious sight that the beavers stared up at the houses as if paralyzed. They were in awe. Beavers were great artisans and well-known for creating masterpieces out of anything from wood, but what they saw before them was otherworldly, and it was an entire village.

Francis slowly pointed up and spoke slowly. "The sides...They've interwoven branches as if they were threads of silk."

"The base of every structure and the bridges connecting them have been crafted from boards cut, or perhaps carved, into curves and angles most fluid, as if poured out like water. The time it must have taken not only to make those cuts of wood but to place them together in such organic symmetry," said Saint Elmo.

"The ornate draping of vines intertwined into so many ethereal shapes," added Francis.

Those that had not joined the other Shirks in initially subduing the unannounced visitors, were now looking down from their balconies. Some had stepped out onto the bridges to get a better view of the new arrivals. In all, for an ancient clan like the Shirks, there were surprisingly few of them. Max estimated that there were no more than three hundred in total.

Sam, the husband of Rosie and the most skilled archer amongst his people, smiled as he approached Francis and lightly punched her on her furry shoulder. "If you think this is something, wait until tonight."

Rosie waved to those up in the trees, and a few in the hollowed-out trunks, to come out and join them. "The night is nearly upon us. We shall prepare a meal for our guests and afterward discuss the state of the Realms."

The Shirks needed no direction, as each of them had their skills, specialties, and roles in the clan. They immediately began setting up for a grand feast. A small fire was started in the middle of the open area in a large contained pit. Fires used to be large and on top of the ground, but now that the forest was so dry, care was taken that no ember should escape freely.

Others set up tables and brought out wares for cooking and eating. Audrey and Ticor rolled out small logs for their guests to sit upon until accommodations were made. The other children, about ten total, giggled as they stood around Zorian. Every time he made the slightest move they would scream and run only to return until the next move he made. This would continue, to the amusement of Zorian, until dinner was served.

Even though the food and drink were not what they would have been before the Dry Death, the welcoming spirit of the Shirks was unsurpassed. Francis was captivated by the musical skills of the children when she heard them play their various stringed instruments. Max and Saint Elmo enjoyed the storytelling of the elders. Zorian, perhaps the most entertained of all, could not take his eyes off of the dancers. He was tempted to join them, but Max made him reconsider for safety reasons. A giant dancing amongst little people was an accident waiting to happen, he had said.

Toward the end of the spirit-filled night, when the last story of the oldest elder was recited, and the children were safely tucked in their beds, Sam, Thadius, and Rodear met with the four guests to discuss which of them would travel to Okrad.

Armed with the intel that Beely had gathered when she herself met with the Prince, the skilled archers could end Mastad's takeover with one perfectly aimed arrow. It was not necessarily something the other Twelve, specifically Beely, had considered, but Max was desperate. He could not entrust fate to a painting that may never be found. He had to act and act fast.

Sam, Rodear, and Thadius fought over who would make the journey to Okrad. Maximilian was proud of and humbled by such brave men. He wanted to go with them and argued vehemently for it, but they all insisted that he needed to stay with the Twelve and that his skills were not appropriately matched with that of the archers. Instead, Francis chewed three sticks from which the archers would choose; the shortest of the three would remain behind and take care of their families should they not return.

When Max eventually came back into the cave, Saint Elmo's thoughts of the Shirks drifted away. But the one thing he would never forget was who had drawn the long sticks. Sam and Rodear's strength went far beyond their muscular arms and legs. There was no such thing as a pacifist Shirk.

Sam and Rodear spoke with their wives, hugged their children, and left the only home they had ever known to defend everything they loved and held dear. Now, Saint Elmo hid out in a dark dismal cave with Francis and Maximilian, grieving about what went so wrong and praying about what to do next.

Mother
and
Daughter

She sighed and did not bother to look up as her foot landed on the first of many steps. Her hand traced the rough bark around the spiral staircase while climbing the knotty, ancient picalo tree. With each new step, Beely flashed back to old memories—some pleasant, others not so much. It was unknown if anyone would be home. She was not there by invitation. Between the memories of her childhood and questions she had for her mother, she considered turning back. The silence between her and Marybah had lasted an age, and she vowed she would never be the one to break it.

The climb up the giant picalo tree seemed longer than it should have been, but perhaps apprehension was making her feet heavy and slowing her pace. Beely loathed the idea of admitting she might have been wrong—wrong about blaming her mother for her father's death, and wrong to have ended their relationship. Yet the only way she could face her mother was by considering the possibility that she herself had been wrong all this time. Maybe—just maybe—her mother was not guilty of being a horrible person.

"Why would anyone live up so high in a picalo?" Beely mumbled to herself.

The late afternoon air was cool, but the perspiration on Beely's face suggested otherwise. She looked up for the first time. She did not have far to go. She paused, then slowly leaned back until she was completely seated, just a few steps short of her destination. She wiped the moisture from her skin with a cloth usually reserved for Duly, for when he had one of his sneezing fits. Her forehead tensed at the thought that she would not be seeing Duly—her friend and sounding board—for quite some time. She brought a braid forward over her shoulder and smoothed it with her palm. It was Marybah who had taught her the traditional Pixanese braid interlaced with copper. It was one of Beely's first memories with her mother—one of the few good ones.

"Are you planning on coming the rest of the way up?" Marybah asked.

Beely could not see her mother. She assumed she was standing on one of several balconies on the first floor of her enormous treehouse. Beely was directly underneath the spot where the spiral staircase led into the grand entryway. Her mother had probably been watching her all along. Beely ascended the final steps and even managed a faint smile as her head cleared the opening. Except where the trunk of the tree blocked the view, her eyes swept the entire first floor before she made it all the way inside. Marybah was nowhere to be found.

"Mother?"

"I've been waiting to hear that word for what seems a lifetime. I honestly didn't think it would take this long." Marybah emerged from the other side of the tree trunk.

"What made you think you would ever see me again?"

Marybah walked confidently over to a large open balcony and signaled for her daughter to follow. "You're a believer, of course. I don't mean someone who just believes in God, but someone who abides in Him. Your devotion, trust, and love for God were evident even as a child. Somewhere along the way, you made the decision to follow Him and you never turned back."

Beely joined her mother on the balcony overlooking the nearly abandoned village below. "What do you know about being a believer?"

"Be kind to one another, tenderhearted, forgiving one another, just as God through Christ has forgiven you."

Beely raised a brow. "That's from a letter that Paul wrote to the Ephesians."

Marybah stepped in front of her daughter and placed two fingers on her chest, slightly left of center. "It's also in there. Forgiveness is in your heart, my child. Sooner or later, you were bound to forgive me." She sat down in her swingsong chair and began packing her pipe.

"That's typically presumptuous of you, Mother. I don't know why I'm surprised. But you're wrong. I wish I could say it was

God that made me come here today. The truth is that it was for a much more selfish reason…"

"Go on, you have my undivided attention." Marybah took a drag from her pipe and blew the smoke away from Beely.

"I didn't want to die with the regret of not having made amends."

Marybah set her pipe down and joined Beely at the balcony railing. She chuckled ever so slightly. "God is so deep in you that you can't even tell where He ends and you begin."

Beely, ignoring her mother's comment, stepped back inside the living room. She walked around disapprovingly. She was only on the first floor of the multitiered treehouse, yet the furnishings were exquisitely lavish. She could only imagine what the rest of the house must look like. She sat in an ornately carved chair and ran her hand across the silk cushion.

Marybah smiled proudly. "A beaver family carved the wood for those chairs. Beautiful, aren't they? The silk is from Okrad."

"It seems you have prospered quite well at a time when most everyone else is suffering," said Beely. "You've even managed to gain body mass. From where—or should I say from whom—are you getting your food and supplies?"

"This," Marybah gestured toward her body, "runs in our family. It won't be long until you too add a little body mass." She returned to her swingsong, hoping her daughter would remain seated for at least a few more moments. She gently leaned forward to retrieve her pipe, careful not to cause her swinging chair to sing. Despite what Beely thought of her, despite whatever evidence her only child held against her, and despite their complicated history, Marybah loved her daughter. She had always loved her daughter. She took a drag from the pipe, and exhaled before asking, "So, have you forgiven me?"

"For what?"

"For all the things a daughter harbors against a mother who simply did her best—the best she knew how."

"How can I forgive someone who doesn't even seek forgiveness?" asked Beely, who had finally stayed in one place for more than a few seconds since arriving.

"Dear, Bee. I do want forgiveness, but I think you and I have entirely different ideas about what for."

"Let's start with the most obvious. Divorce was almost nonexistent in Pixanese before you left my father. Not only did you crush his spirit, you made me a pariah."

"I didn't leave your father, nor did I divorce him. He left me."

Beely shook her head in frustration. "You're lying."

"No, I'm telling the truth, but there's more to it... He wanted to end the marriage because I was unfaithful. He wanted to shield you from my improprieties. Neither of us could have foreseen how judgmental the community would be—or how it would affect you. But one thing we did right was never to speak poorly of one another. It seems he honored our agreement by keeping my indiscretions a secret."

"Why are you telling me this now?"

"You are an adult now—a married woman yourself. You know how hard marriage is. Your father's reputation is well established, and I couldn't possibly harm it. It's time you knew. Isn't that why you're here? You were never one to take the easy way. You forgave me a long time ago. You've been a believer far too long not to have reaped the benefits of your faith."

"Who was it?"

"Knowing who will benefit no one," answered Marybah through a smoky haze.

Beely could barely speak; her mouth suddenly felt as dry as sand. "Was it Mastad?"

Marybah nervously moved away. She walked over to the bar opposite where Beely sat. She placed both hands on the edge of the counter and stared into the reflective glass in front of her. "I will never call him by that name. He will always be Ankur to me... I knew him even before I met your father."

Beely stiffened, staying rooted to her chair. She put her hand to her mouth as if that might halt, or at the very least delay, the need to retch that was rising from her stomach to her throat.

Her mind raced. Maximilian had once mentioned seeing a picture of Ankur while visiting Marybah. Somewhere along the way, Beely had suspected, but she had never said it out loud or given the outrageous idea more than a passing thought.

"Please tell me you are no longer involved with that monster..."

Suddenly, the full truth hit her like a swinging door. Her face drained of color, and she could barely breathe. When she finally regained control of her emotions, she continued, "Now everything makes sense. Of course—how else could you have continued living like this? He gives you everything—food, furniture from the best artisans, even the finest smoking herbs."

"Mastad keeps you. And whether you call him by that name or not doesn't diminish the truth of his evolution into something unrecognizable: Prince Mastad, a genetic mutation of his own evil imagination."

Marybah turned around and laughed. "No one keeps me, dear. I abhor the creation he has become as much as anyone. Ankur simply honors our agreement, the same as he honors yours. I'm just a woman, dear, what would you expect me to have done?"

86

"In case you've forgotten, I'm a woman too. What scheme did you concoct with him? You must have some power over him, because he certainly didn't honor my agreement."

"Oh, but he did. Trust me. Neither you nor Pixanese would be here now—even in the lowly state into which it has fallen—without Ankur's agreement with you. Pixanese would have been overcome with the Dry Death just like every other kingdom."

"How do you know so much? Am I to believe you are innocent in all that has been happening?"

"Your father was right about many things, Bee. I know you thought I considered him nothing more than a Plotist, but that's not where our disagreements began or ended. Your father was right about Ankur. I may not have known the extent to which he was correct, but now I do. He was a visionary, your father."

"You don't get to rewrite history, Mother… Anyway, I'm not sure I care about the details any longer. All I care about now is how to stop this evil monster from permanently destroying the Five Realms. I came today not only to say I forgive you, but also to say goodbye. I will die before I let Mastad complete his desolation of all that is good. Unless God deems otherwise, I will fight him all the way to my grave—and I'm not alone. If anything you've told me thus far is true—if you do love me—you will tell me what his weakness is."

"That's why you really came here today, isn't it?"

"It doesn't matter why I came. What matters is how I leave."

"That's why I wanted you to marry Maximilian. Ankur needed Pixanese—"

"Wanted? Wanted me to marry Max? You manipulated every single thing up to the moment of the actual wedding day!"

"Oh, come now, dear. That's a bit dramatic, wouldn't you say?"

"I wasn't completely naïve back then. I saw much of what you were doing—coordinating our first meeting, somehow convincing his parents that the Rembres were a worthy and noble family despite a divorce and a Plotist for a father. When I found out you were responsible for most of the wedding costs, I knew. But why? What was it about the Wrens?"

"You honestly don't know?" Beely remained silent, and Marybah continued. "The land, of course. The Wrens were not fools. They might not have believed everything your father espoused, but they knew he was a brilliant man. They also believed in the Word, as you know, and they were counted among the most faithful in all of the Realms."

Beely shook her head in dismay. "Oh my, I'm a complete fool. Of course—the land. But how did you know the spring was under their land?"

"Your father told me."

"And you told Ankur."

"Of course not. I left that up to you. Whether or not you made the right decision to tell him where the spring was located, only time would tell. It was the only major spring—other than the Mindalite spring—to which Ankur could not gain access. The spring had been capped off and diverted many centuries ago, and very few knew of its existence."

"Other than the Wrens and you."

"Other than your father and Wrens who had long since passed away. Not even Max's parents knew about the treasure beneath their land."

Beely ran to the sink and leaned over it, breathing heavily. She swallowed hard, and the moment of sickness passed. "I made such a terrible mistake telling Mastad about the spring. It was the worst decision I have ever made. I will spend the rest of whatever days remain trying to set things right."

Marybah came behind her daughter and rubbed her back. "You were always the hardest on yourself. Mikalo and I never needed to discipline you, even as a young child—you took care of that all by yourself. But you're not a child any longer, and there are greater powers at play here. Realm prophecies have never been wrong. It was not just about the spring, Beely. It was about you. The spring was just part of a larger puzzle."

Beely sighed and did not immediately respond as too many thoughts bombarded her mind all at once. She wanted to ask more about her parents' relationship. It seemed that so much of what she remembered of her childhood was distorted. She knew, however, that there was no time to look back. She had to concentrate on the here and now.

"What agreement did you make with Mastad? If you're not still romantically involved, why would he continue to help you?"

"It wouldn't be prudent for me to tell you that," answered Marybah.

"Prudent? You've just told me that much of my childhood was basically a lie. If you have any information that could help us stop Mastad, then you need to tell me now. You owe me that much."

"What I owe you is the truth, and I have told you the truth— as much as you are ready to hear. I will not tell you something that would surely get us both killed."

"You mean something that would get you killed?"

"My dear daughter, Ankur is not a man to be trifled with. There is nothing he doesn't know or can't quickly find out about you and your band of misfits. If you become a serious threat, he won't hesitate to kill you all in the most public ways possible. I don't doubt that's exactly what he's waiting for."

"What more could he be waiting for?" asked Beely.

"Not everyone is eating his adulterated fruit. There are many—not just your 'Twelve.' There will come a time when a remnant of the strongest and most resilient will rise up against him. He will want to make examples of his adversaries who remain after his purge. He's been planning his reign for a long time."

"Why not just kill us now and save himself the trouble?"

"There are still things he needs. I would ask you to stop your pursuit of Ankur if I thought it would make a difference, but I know you are your father's daughter. No one can stop you once you've made up your mind. I will do everything in my power— which diminishes more and more each day—to keep Ankur from harming you."

"You speak out of both sides of your mouth. If you aren't still involved with Ankur, how could you offer any protection?"

"Only time will reveal the answers you seek. If your God is real, you need only trust in His ways. I cannot give you what is not mine to give."

"I would ask you to pray for me—for all of us—but I'm afraid to ask who you would be praying to!"

Beely walked over to her mother and gave her a long embrace. Looking directly into her eyes, Beely spoke the last words she considered her mother might hear from her. "Even so, the one and only loving Creator God wants you. I pray that you will someday believe in Him, Mother. I want you to know that saving the Five Realms of Here was never about saving a place, but about saving souls."

She gave her mother another firm embrace, and as a tear rolled down her cheek, she thanked God for His wisdom. Her bitterness, anger, and all the malice Beely had held against her mother melted away. Only with God was such a thing possible, thought Beely.

What Beely would never witness were her mother's tears—heavy with ages of unspoken regret—as Marybah watched her only child descend the spiral staircase of the listless picalo tree. From the balcony, hidden just out of sight, she followed Beely with her eyes until her figure vanished into the abandoned village below.

Marybah had not truly known loneliness until the moment she could no longer see the braids she had once woven into her daughter's hair.

C h a p t e r 9

THE
COLLECTOR

(Long Before the Twelve)

The bat followed Nicholas for many days and across much territory. He had seen more of the Realms in the last few cycles of his life than in all his previous cycles combined. He disliked traveling in daylight, but he found ways to remain hidden—often tucked beneath the eaves of deserted structures, or, most recently, stowed under a carriage, as Nicholas's preferred method of travel was by a quixsor-drawn carriage.

A quixsor was anything but quick, despite its name. They were awkward-looking beasts, primarily used as pack animals. These bluish-grey creatures were hairy, heavy in the hindquarters, and often sported a long, sandpapery tongue that hung from their mouths. What they lacked in speed, they made up for in surefootedness and strength.

"Slovenly" was what Leopold once called them, until he got to know one up close and personal. He had grown fond of the loyal, gentle beast. His name was Arnox, and he was not only kind enough to keep Leopold's presence a secret from Nicholas, but his low, soothing hum gave Leopold much comfort in strange lands, far away from all those he loved.

"I suppose he's here to tell Ankur he's quitting."

Arnox could not tell whether Leopold was making a statement or asking a question, so he offered a noncommittal huff in reply.

Leopold had clung so neatly to the quixsor's bridle during most of the trip that the casual onlooker would never have detected he was there. It helped that his fur matched the color of the leather straps. He was much more noticeable now, with his wings partially open as he perched atop the beast's head. "Surely you must know why he's here, Arnox. Didn't he tell you?"

Arnox huffed once more before replying in his dry, excruciatingly languid fashion. "Sir Nick does not speak much of late, as you know. He is rather depressed, I would say. I think you're correct in your assumption—he's come to quit the Prince."

"Well then, this is a meeting I can't miss. See you soon, my friend," said Leopold, as he lifted off Arnox and into the air.

Chiropters had been disappearing in great numbers. Entire families were missing without a trace. This was why Leopold had been assigned by his elders to follow Nicholas. The chiropters had reason to believe that Ankur, or some group or person associated with him, was capturing their kindred.

Leopold was not the only chiropter sent on such a task. There were others assigned to follow Ankur himself and many of Ankur's workers. There was even one assigned to follow Athaliah. Their mission was to find and free their fellow bats.

Of course, Leopold knew without a doubt that Athaliah had no knowledge of any such crime against the chiropters. She was a loyal friend and would never harm any of them. The elders, however, demanded that they leave no stone unturned. Chiropters were in danger, and they had to find out who was behind it.

Leopold flew toward the unassuming quarters of the most talked about man in recent memory. It seemed, to Leopold, that Ankur's influence was trickling into realms he had no place influencing. Those in Okrad had known and appreciated Ankur for his contributions to their realm for many seasons, but it was strange that he was now reaching out into other realms.

Leopold flew directly to the front entrance and clung to the smooth peach-colored stone next to the door. Nicholas had already entered a few moments earlier, and there was no one else around. The whole area was eerily quiet. Even with the door closed, he found that there was sufficient room to squeeze over the top of the thick wood door.

Once inside, he paused to listen for movement or voices. He heard shuffling on the west side, and he heard two voices to the east, one of which belonged to the man he had been shadowing for three straight days. The other voice sounded familiar, but he could not quite put a face to it.

He then moved closer to where the tense conversation was taking place. Leopold flew quickly down the long hallway, keeping as close to the top corner as possible. Even though the walls were dark in color, matching his own dark body, he avoided fully opening his wings so as not to be seen. There were no windows and not much light.

It only took him mere seconds to find the room. As luck would have it, the door was closed. He was just about to squeeze in, but stopped when he recognized the other voice was none other than Athaliah. Athaliah was no stranger to chiropters, and she would undoubtedly spot the uninvited guest.

Before he had time to think of another way in, the door opened. Leopold quickly darted behind a large vase on a table in the hall. He was completely obscured, but could still see through the dark glass vase with his superior scotopic vision.

Athaliah stepped out of Ankur's office, closing the door behind her. She leaned against the wall and absentmindedly used her overcoat to absorb the sweat from her palms. She then wiped what might have been the beginning of a tear from the corner of her eye.

Her purpose for the abrupt exit was much more diabolical than simply concealing her emotions. The passion she once had for her first and only love had been replaced by hatred. Athaliah had learned that hate had much simpler objectives than love.

She reached into the lining of her jacket and retrieved a capsule of white powder. The small capsule had been hidden in a pocket next to her heart for days. She had not been certain if she would ever have a chance or the will to use it, but once she stared into the face of betrayal, she could not stop herself.

Athaliah had taken the capsule out of its hiding spot no less than three times in the hour before her once betrothed was due to arrive. She brought the encapsulated poison into the light one last time. It was odd, she thought, that something so small and seemingly insignificant could hold so much power.

A servant with a tray of refreshments startled Athaliah, who quickly cupped the pill in her hand, effectively hiding it from view. "It's alright, put the tray on the table, and you may go." Without saying a word, the servant nodded, set the tray down on the table with the vase, and quickly left.

Athaliah watched the servant turn the corner before she twisted the capsule she was holding in two. She was careful not to lose any of the powder inside. If the poison became airborne, it might find its way into her lungs.

She slowly turned the first half of the capsule upside down and watched as it disappeared into Nicholas's favorite drink. She turned over the second half and waited until it, too, completely dissolved. She was utterly unaware of her hissing as she stirred the cup of revenge. She was also unaware of the voyeur watching her every move.

Leopold could only assume that Athaliah was up to no good. Yet, he could not be certain what the white powder was: a truth serum, an incapacitating agent, or even perhaps a deadly poison.

In either case, Leopold was not there to save anyone. He was not a friend of Nicholas, and he had only known Athaliah in passing. He was no friend of humanoids, and by all accounts, the chiropters might be better off with one less of them. They had become somewhat suspicious of all creatures, but especially those like Nicholas, Ankur, and Athaliah, since the disappearances.

After Athaliah returned to Nicholas, with tainted drink in hand, Leopold's thoughts quickly moved from the white powder to the words being spoken on the other side of the door. Words so important that Leopold placed himself in a position of potentially being discovered.

He would not have thought the proposition of being found

out so dire only a few short moons ago, but now, nothing was clear nor safe. Things were changing, and all that had been taken for granted was now being chased after with reckless abandon. He dug his sharp claws into the soft wood as he clung to the door, listening to every syllable.

"This information was too sensitive to send by courier," said Nicholas before a short pause. "Tell Ankur that I have located the painting, the one he most wanted to find. I have it hidden away in a safe place."

"Where?" asked Athaliah.

"No, information about things of any consequence is for his ears only."

"Excuse me?!" exclaimed Athaliah.

"You heard me. I have the painting, and it's hidden. Only I know where it is."

Leopold tensed up, loosening at least one of his claws, as he sensed that someone on the other side had moved very close to the door.

"My cousin won't be happy with your insolence. Tell me where the painting is." Athaliah sounded desperate. She was almost pleading.

What was it about this painting that was so important? Leopold would not find out anytime soon. The door was moving, and so too was he—back the way he came; so smooth and quick, not even the servant at the end of the hall detected his escape.

It was not long before Leopold discovered something else. The white powder that Athaliah was so fascinated with turned out not to be a simple agent meant to incapacitate. It was indeed poison—a very strong poison as shown by the short amount of time it took to leave its victim breathless and cold.

Nicholas's last breath was a choked gasp, his body slumping to the floor with a soft thud, eyes wide but unseeing. Although the chiropters no longer had a need to worry about Nicholas, Leopold would recommend that they quickly expand their covert operations.

Why would Athaliah want to kill one of her own, and what could be so important about a painting? It was well known that Nicholas was a collector of antiquities, but it did not seem to be a profession that should have come with deadly consequences. Yes, everything was changing. Death and disappearances were becoming as commonplace as the chiropters' nightly aerobatic dances.

Arnox was heartbroken by the collector's untimely death. He had been Nicholas's traveling companion for a long time. Nicholas had never requested Arnox to cease humming or to speak faster when questioned, like other coachmen in the past.

Leopold wanted to rush home and tell the others what he had discovered, but his more compassionate side dominated. He would see to it that Arnox made it home—not alone, but with a friend. It would only be two days' travel south, and then Leopold would fly by night with a message that would surely change the elder chiropters' plans as well as his own. Leopold was about to embark on his most important and greatest adventure, even if he did not quite yet know what that would be.

Chapter 10

THE KALIDESCOPE

Propo held a tiny tool in one hand and a small, ornate brass kaleidoscope in the other. He carefully removed the outermost lens as Lira, Malora, and Leopold looked on curiously.

"Mikalo and I invented this before anyone believed the Realms would be thrust into the chaos and devastation we are experiencing today. Mikalo was convinced—and I was too—that we would need this."

He eased several multicolored gemstones from the brass cylindrical tube. "Mikalo didn't just read the prophecies; he studied them and came to find enough evidence to believe them—as did I." He laid the three gemstones on the table and glanced back toward an old wooden cupboard.

In anyone else's home, the cupboard would have been filled with dishes and utensils, but in Propo's simple one-room dwelling, it held an assortment of tools, test tubes, and other oddities.

Propo looked toward the bottom of the cupboard and called out, "Come and show yourself—there's no need to be shy." When no one came forth, Propo bent down and rapped his knuckles on the floor.

At that moment, an adorable creature no larger than a man's fist scurried out from behind the wooden shelves. Its oblong head was covered by a hard green exoskeleton, much like that of a beetle. Its bright yellow eyes were quite large and bulbous. The rest of its body was brown and furry, resembling a miniature empachic. It made no sound other than a few short, unintelligible squeaks. None of the others, apart from Propo, had ever seen one before.

"What is that?" asked Lira. "It's strangely delightful." She bent down and held out her hand, but the little creature retreated.

"It's all right," Propo assured her. He tapped the floor again, and it cautiously returned, stopping just out of arm's reach. "I call it Twoknocks. I'm fairly certain it's either very hard of hearing or deaf, but it does respond well to vibrations—two knocks on the floor usually do the trick."

"Where did it come from?" asked Malora.

"The only place they're known to exist is beneath the arms of a willow tree." A sudden hush fell over the room. There was only one willow tree that they knew of remaining in the Five Realms of Here—and that was Willow herself. "Yes, it has been on a very long journey from the Land of Indulgences. It has been hiding and protecting something important for quite some time."

Leopold flapped his wings and leapt from the back of a high chair to the corner of the table just above the mysterious visitor. He stared down at the odd little animal. "What could that small, helpless creature be protecting, and where in the realm would the simpleton hide it?"

"I thought you'd never ask," said Propo, wearing the broadest smile any of them had ever seen on him. "All right, my little friend, it's time to put all the pieces together. You may release the final gemstone." He knocked on the floor again and then held up one of the gemstones.

Lira gave Malora a quizzical glance, while Leopold looked at the door as if someone else might enter. When no one did, all eyes moved back to the diminutive guest. They watched it closely as it turned its backside toward them. It then lifted its furry hindquarters and excreted a small, shiny stone.

The sparkling pink gem pinged as it struck the floor. Everyone stared at the oddity until Leopold fell back on the table, spread his wings as wide as they could go, and let out a loud burst of laughter.

He laughed so hard that the bioluminescent lights above flickered. Malora clutched his stomach in an uncontrollable fit of mirth. The laughter spread like a contagion to Lira as well. Propo, despite his usually stoic demeanor, erupted in loud chortles. Meanwhile, the little creature with the very important deposit turned around and bashfully lowered its head.

"I think we've embarrassed the little tyke," said Propo. The small creature rose onto its hind feet, squinted its eyes, and scowled before scurrying off back behind the cupboard.

Propo took a few steps forward and knelt down to retrieve

the small gem. He polished the stone with the corner of his garment before speaking one last time to its keeper. "Thank you for taking such good care of the keystone. You've kept it hidden well from those who would use it for evil, and for that, we will forever be thankful."

The others looked on as Propo took the stone back to the table where he had disassembled the kaleidoscope. He placed the newest stone into the tube first. He then followed it, one by one, with the other three gemstones. With the small tool in hand, he secured the glass lens back in place, and then raised the instrument to his right eye.

"Hmm," Propo looked puzzled.

"Hmm?" repeated Lira. "What does it do? What's so special about the stone?"

Propo beamed as he looked at the completed kaleidoscope. "Mikalo and I are simply agents of the Most High. Sure, we can manipulate raw materials to make a kaleidoscope such as this, but we are not supernatural. We cannot make water come from stone, or turn a staff into a snake, or walk on water."

Propo continued, "The pink gemstone is the miraculous touch of God. That is the stone that will allow us to see the other miracle... the painting."

Malora echoed Lira's question, "Was there a secret message written on the stone?"

Leopold, having reassumed his position on the top rail of the tallest chair, stretched toward Propo to get a better look at the scope. "Let me see, let me see."

Propo held the scope in front of Leopold. "Be very careful with this. It's the only one of its kind, and it cannot be replaced."

Leopold took the one-of-a-kind instrument in his winged

hand and proceeded to examine different objects in the room through it. When Malora came into view, he paused and said, "I don't see anything unusual—just the same old boring views as before."

"That's because you're not looking at the right thing," said Propo as he took back the scope. He lifted it to his eye for one last view before wiping it off with a soft cloth and placing it carefully in a solid wooden box.

Lira shrugged her shoulders and asked, "What's with all the mystery? What's it for?"

Malora interjected before Propo had a chance to answer, "Isn't it obvious? That's how we are going to find the painting. We look through it, and it will guide us to its whereabouts."

Propo raised his brow and said, "You're not completely wrong, Malora. I wish it were as easy as that, however. This is only utilized for confirming we have the correct painting after it has been found."

Lira tapped her finger on the box a few times before asking, "How does that work?"

"The painting we are looking for is not what it seems. A regular painting is only two-dimensional. Our painting is of a much higher dimensional space. It offers a fourth dimension, possibly more. This is not visible to the naked eye, however."

"Excuse me—what does a fourth dimension consist of?" asked Leopold.

"In theory, alongside the three spatial dimensions of length, width, and height, the fourth would add time," answered Propo.

Lira, now rubbing the box with her hand, asked, "So this kaleidoscope allows us to see into the fourth dimension?"

Leopold flapped his wings and landed right next to the wooden box. He looked up at Lira. "Why are you stroking the box so? It's not a living creature." He turned to look at Propo. "Or is it?"

"Of course it isn't living. The painting, however—I'm not so sure."

"What's that supposed to mean?" asked Leopold.

"The painting is a miraculous work of art. It has qualities beyond our comprehension. The kaleidoscope will be able to see into the painting, revealing its depth far beyond that of a two-dimensional object."

"If we can see into the painting, into perhaps another place or time, then we know we have the painting of miracles," said Leopold.

"That's one way of looking at it. Mikalo was sure that with the scope's help, there would be no mistaking that we had the right painting."

"That's all well and good, but it would help if we had something to first help us find where it is," said Lira, whose gaze had not left the box.

Leopold abruptly flapped his wings, startling Lira, and finally breaking her fixation with the now boxed kaleidoscope. He flew over to the only window in the small cave dwelling, landing on the sill. "I know who last had the painting. It has been hidden from both Mastad and Athaliah. They have no idea where it is."

"Do you know who has it now?" asked Malora.

"Of course not, but at least I know that it has not been destroyed, and I have a good idea of where to begin looking."

"Do tell," said Lira.

At this point, everyone was seated at the table. Leopold flew back to the chair railing and explained all that he saw and heard so many moons ago, when Athaliah made her first kill. He told them about befriending Arnox the quixsor and following

Nicholas in search of captive chiropters. He explained that he never personally discovered the fate of his missing brethren, but he had overheard talk about the fate of the infamous painting. All of this had taken place just before Athaliah poisoned her once-betrothed. He lamented the fact that he never imagined the discussion of a painting would be more important than witnessing the murder of an innocent man.

"Are you sure they were discussing the same painting?" asked Lira.

"It had to have been the painting we are after; no other painting would be worthy of being the last words a man would ever speak," said Malora.

"According to Leopold, Nicholas wasn't aware he had been poisoned. He wouldn't have known the painting would be the subject of his last words," added Propo.

Lira nodded in agreement. "Which brings me back to my original question. How can we be sure they were discussing *the* painting?"

Propo inhaled deeply before answering. "We can't know for sure. Yet, it would be logical to assume there is no other painting of such great importance, and it would be the only object worthy of discussing at such a meeting."

"Precisely," added Leopold. "Furthermore, Nicholas must have known there was something special about the painting, but how would he know this without the special keystone and looking glass?"

"Whoever he took it from must have told him how important it was," said Lira.

"Who is to say that he even took it? Maybe he left it where he found it," added Malora.

Propo addressed Leopold, "Are you sure nothing else of

importance was said?"

"Nothing of importance. Nicholas said he would only tell Mastad of its whereabouts. But if you ask me, Nicholas wasn't about to tell anyone where that painting was."

"He had to have told someone. People just aren't that disciplined to keep such a secret all to themselves. I hate to admit it, but I could not keep such a secret. I would have told someone. Not just anyone though, someone that could make sure it was protected or used for good," said Malora.

"I agree with Malora. Also, if this collector knew the painting was so important, he would have needed help keeping it safely hidden," said Lira.

"The best way to keep something hidden is to confide in no one of its whereabouts," said Propo.

"He told someone, I just know it," said Malora.

Everyone fell silent as they contemplated the most important question before them—everyone but Leopold, that is.

While Leopold was honest about what he had overheard between Athaliah and Nicholas, he decided against telling them that the chiropters had spent much time and energy searching for the elusive painting themselves. They never found it, but after analyzing all the information, Leopold had narrowed down its location to three probable places.

While the others were thinking about who had the painting, he was thinking about why he was withholding such important information. Leopold had not even told his fellow chiropters what he had learned. Perhaps, he thought, it was the last thing he had all to himself that made his life meaningful. He had no mate, no children, and no real place within the chiropter autocracy. If he gave away the probable locations of the painting, what would he have left?

"What's wrong, Leopold?" Lira walked over to her friend and gave him a light scratch on his nose. "You look far more troubled than you should. We're all together now. We'll find it."

Malora smiled and gently rubbed Leopold on the back. "God made sure that we would have each other, and each of us has something special to offer. We'll find the painting. I know we will."

Leopold swallowed hard and fought back tears. He was not the emotional sort, but the moment caught him off guard. He was not prepared to actually like these people, but more importantly, he was not prepared for them to like him.

"I must say, Leopold," said Malora, "You're a lot softer than I would have ever imagined."

That was enough to change Leopold's emotional response from tears to a jolt of laughter. No one had ever called him soft before. The others had a good laugh as well, after they too confirmed that yes, Leopold's very light coat of fur was quite soft.

He protested every stroke and pet, eventually flying to the top of the bookcase to escape their hands. Lira, however, could tell by Leopold's reaction that he had been starved for physical touch, and she would make sure to give him more during their journey together, whether he protested or not.

Chapter 11

THE YOUNGEST BROTHER

With two moons crossing in the night sky, there was usually enough light to help travelers find their way, even in Okrad's most uninviting terrain. This night was an exception. It was one of the darkest in Mastad's many recent late-night outings.

A thick haze of dust hung over the once-lush, green countryside, obscuring the glowing moons. The self-proclaimed Prince of the Five Realms of Here welcomed the dark. He reveled in the shadows that others feared.

His transformation was almost complete, and his newfound scotopic vision was a welcome addition to his increasing prowess. For the first time in his life, he could see clearly, even though the Realms had never been darker. He also recently discovered that he could manipulate sound waves to aid in his navigation. This specific skill no doubt came from the chiropteran genetic contribution to his manufactured hybrid DNA.

Mastad inhaled deeply. It was the first time he had been back to the cave since his transformation. The veins underneath his new skin undulated with powerful surges as he exhaled with unbridled confidence. He was a new man—if a man is what he was. He was one of a kind. A new creature. A creature of his own design.

There were others, made in his image, but they were less than Mastad. No one was given as much of the genetic-altering drugs as himself. Mastad made sure that he would be the strongest and most imposing of all of his creations.

He arrived at the remote cave with no one but his loyal Mastadonian. The opening was so small and obscure that even the most observant passersby could miss it. Mastad was the only one who knew about the cave and where the mystical seven doors were located.

The doors had been deep in the mountainside for many ages. He discovered them in his youth, quite by accident—or so he had thought. Evil, it has been said, is never embraced by accident, but only when someone heeds its call. Evil constantly beckons any ear providing a welcoming harbor.

The doors themselves were not evil, however. Once, long ago, it was believed that each door opened to places of beauty, peace, and abundance. Over time, more and more beings began to abuse the goodness of the doors. There were those who used the doors to become rich and powerful. Others relied on the doors for all of their needs and became complacent and lazy.

After countless ages of abuse, the doors became harder and harder to find until they had all but disappeared.

The few who did manage to find the doors discovered that they had become corrupted. There was one door, and only one, that remained good, but interestingly, it was the door most overlooked.

When an unsuspecting soul fell prey to the evil lurking behind the deceptive doors, it became forever trapped in a lie. The door most traveled through allured seekers with visions of immense prosperity. One of the doors promised never-ending youth, and another, beauty everlasting.

The door most captivating to Mastad brought visions of power, fame, and unceasing adulation. Each of the corrupted doors devoured those who simply peered over their thresholds. The misguided souls who ventured through the open doors faced an eternity of hopeless, inescapable misery.

Mastad dared not look into the door he most admired a second time. Usually, it only took one curious glance, and the onlooker was lost forever, but Mastad was special. He was saved for something more. The door, or perhaps something or someone behind the door, needed Mastad to remain exactly where he was. Still, Mastad never tempted fate; he never looked through any of the doors again.

The cave got darker the further Mastad traveled. After successfully maneuvering through the darkened tunnels, he began to see the now familiar faint light that led him to the place he had discovered so many turnings ago.

The closer he got to the doors, the brighter the light became. His Mastadonian, usually quite bold and fierce, was becoming more timid with each step. When he finally made it to a large cavern with a very high dome, the faint glow that oozed from the cracks of one particular door was enough light to illuminate the entire cathedral-like room.

Mastad dared not look directly at the light's source. His dog whimpered and retreated to a far corner opposite the doors. They both had witnessed more than one unsuspecting soul's inability to control his or her impulse to enter into the place of no return.

Altogether, over the seasons, Mastad brought eleven people to the cave of the doors. One by one, he lured them, and one by one, he witnessed them disappear, never to return. He turned his back toward the glowing rectangle and gently rapped upon the wood with his knuckles.

"Hello?" he called softly.

"I am here," said the Shining One.

It was uncommon for those on the other side of the doors not to entice and welcome visitors with unwavering veracity. Yet, not once did the Shining One even ask Mastad to look upon him. They were both very familiar with one another by now.

"I need your help, Shining One," said Mastad.

The Shining One's voice resonated richly in the hollow cavern, angelic and almost hypnotic. "How long must you continue to drink milk? When will you partake of the rich fare I have to offer? I will not always be here to help you. The doors come and go when and where they please—you have been told this. There will come a day, soon, when the doors will be lost to you. It is my will that you achieve all that you desire before this happens."

"I understand. But would I not be a fool if I failed to honor the time that you are here and available for counsel? The idea to abolish the Five Realms of Here, making them into one

Kingdom, was yours. Taking away the Word and controlling the resources has brought those remaining here to their knees. You were right, Morning Star; chaos has served me well. I come here seeking more wisdom from the greatest mind I have ever known."

"You come here groveling, and you secretly hope to usurp me someday." He laughed, but Mastad thought it sounded like instruments of harps and bells.

"This world of yours is merely a stepping stone to a plan that has been evolving since time began. You are nothing more than a figment in a dream that has been slowly seeping into the reality of every hardened heart. You are a fool."

Mastad, still turned away from the door, noticed that his Mastadonian raised his head only to quickly cower back down to the cold cave floor. The light in the cavern had increased, and Mastad was sure the door, to all of his hopes and dreams, had opened a little more. Still, he did not dare look to confirm his suspicion but waited for the Morning Star to continue.

"I am well acquainted with dealing with fools. I am the one that will see you through to the end, but my patience will not endure forever."

"If not understanding your riddles makes me a fool, I must admit, you know your audience well."

"Why have you come here on this night?" asked the Shining One.

"I trust that your knowledge of the prophecy of this world is as great as that of your own," said Mastad.

Harps and bells emanating from inside the door, ringing out into the cavern once again. "This world? I am increasingly invited into this world. There are few boundaries I cannot cross. The thoughts of created creatures easily come to the dark places in which I flourish. I know this world better than you who reside here, and you would not find all that I know to be agreeable in the least. The truth is not your friend."

"All I want is to complete the work we started, but the threat against me is increasing, and I am no closer to finding the painting than when we first began."

A violent wind swirled around the dark cave, stirring up a cloud of gritty, dry dust. Mastad could taste the dirt as he inhaled. His dog whimpered as it scampered over to him, kneeling before his master.

The voice behind the door deepened. "I cannot do everything for you. I have given you all that you need. The painting must be found. What about the young girl I led to you? The destruction of her betrothed was a wise choice. I can feel her heart growing colder with each passing day."

"Athaliah, I can trust. She has proven worthy and useful on more than one occasion, but even she has not been able to find the painting."

"What would you have me do?"

"I need more time, and I need more power to defeat my foolish but unrelenting foes."

"Your transformation looks to be complete. You are a new creation, twentyfold stronger. You have wings capable of flight. You have enough to conquer all of your adversaries."

"I need more. If I am to finish what we have started, I need more of what you have to give."

"One more gift I will grant you."

"Thank you, great Morning Star."

"Any willing soul that would open itself to you can be ruled by you."

"What does that mean?"

"You will be able to possess any willing creature. But you can never inhabit more than one at a time. And you must be invited, but have no worries, there are more willing fools than there are stars in your sky."

"And you think the ability to possess will lead us to the painting?"

"The alternative is death for you and all of your kind. I will not tolerate failure," said the Shining One.

"I've asked you this before, I will ask you again. Why don't you just find the painting yourself?"

"I have answered you before, and I will not answer you again. I am not of this realm, nor am I a figment. It is only because of the weak in my world that I can influence yours. The battle of the mind is far greater than a field of soldiers wielding swords and shields."

"Once I find the painting, what then? How will a simple painting secure my authority in the Five Realms of Here once and for all?"

"Your prophecy foretells visitors from my world coming to save yours," he said. "How they come is a mystery. But how they escape involves the painting."

"Save my world from what?" Mastad absentmindedly patted his dog on the head. The Mastadonian eventually lowered his head onto his master's foot.

"From you, of course."

Mastad did not quite know how to take this new revelation. Part of him was honored that he was actually mentioned in the sacred scriptures of the Realms. He felt empowered and important. The other part of him was disturbed that he was on some type of prophetic radar. Either way, he assumed prophecy was nothing more than a guess about the future. The work to be done was the same. Knowledge of the future changed nothing, as far as he was concerned.

"You are telling me that not only do I have to battle the remnant here in my own world, but I am going to have to fend off warriors from yours as well?" Suddenly irritated by his dog, he lifted his foot, effectively pushing the loyal dog back to the corner of the cave.

"Yes, but fear not, they are mere children, and their faith is even less than yours."

Battles were nothing new to Mastad; he was the youngest of eleven brothers. By the time he was born, his father relied on his other sons to help their youngest find his way. They were all bigger, stronger, and more resilient than their little Ankle Biter—a nickname that Ankur, now known as Prince Mastad, despised.

His mother's attempts to shield and protect her wee son caused more harm than good. His brothers resented him for the favoritism and for the gifts his parents showered upon the less-than-worthy son.

Ankur the Ankle Biter became well-equipped to manipulate every situation to his advantage. He became surprisingly skillful in the art of deception, which caused even more resentment among those aware of his flagrant disregard for loyalty and honor.

He once convinced the entire township that his brothers schemed to destroy the village's ancient silk industry, intending to take full control of all production. It was a completely fabricated story that succeeded in shocking the villagers. A kingdom that had never known scandal before Ankur's birth was now at the mercy of a bad seed. The brothers saw Ankur slowly working to become the sole heir to their family's estate—

an estate worth more than any other in Okrad.

Before anything could be done to curb Ankur's habit of causing division and doubt in the kingdom of Okrad, a series of strange disappearances rocked the township to its core. Eleven family members vanished almost overnight. His parents, in the end, found some solace in the fact that their youngest son, Ankur, was spared whatever fate befell their other children. When the dust settled, they at least had one son remaining.

What they never found out, before their own untimely, suspicious deaths, was that their favorite son discovered that each of his brothers had their own unquenchable desires. Ankur took his siblings to a place that promised them what their hearts most desired. He took them, one by one, to the Cave of the Seven Doors. He watched each brother as they looked into the doors of false promises. Not one of them chose the door of truth; the lies were far more tempting.

Mastad had gotten what he had come for—more power and more answers. It was the last time he would see the Seven Doors or speak with the Shining One until he accomplished all of his goals. He did not know it at the time, but he would see the doors one more time before his days in the Five Realms of Here were over.

As he was about to leave the caves, he noticed his dog cowering, yet still desiring his master's attention. Mastad felt a tinge of guilt for pushing him away.

"Come," he called. The dog rushed to his side, and Mastad knelt down to give his only friend a hug. The dog's tail happily hit the sides of the narrow tunnels until they reached the open air. Refraining from striking the dog for its annoying joy was the most restraint Mastad had shown in quite some time.

Chapter 12

THE DEPTHS
OF FAITH

Before the winds of change and the Dry Death, creatures rarely traveled outside of their own realms, other than to the Library of Truth, which could always be reached with relative ease. It was not until Mastad plundered resources, poisoned entire villages, and killed anyone who stood in his way that survivors were forced to seek refuge in strange unfamiliar lands.

There were few maps of the Realms, and even those were not always useful. To find something that had been lost or hidden in the Five Realms of Here would be an insurmountable task for even the most faithful and the most resourceful. The Twelve had varying degrees of faith and few resources, but

117

together with their unique gifts from the Holy Spirit, finding the painting went from unlikely to possible.

Underground, deep in the tunnels, dark caverns, and beautiful cave cathedrals of the Five Realms lay paths that connected one realm to another. It was arguably the safest way to travel, and it was the way that Leopold insisted upon taking. Both Lira and Propo had been praying and fasting for days before they agreed to Leopold's plan to lead them through the underground mazes. Malora thought it made perfect sense, for no creature was better equipped to traverse the caves and tunnels than a chiropter.

"It's nice of Leopold to scout out the tunnels before us, don't you think? I've heard rumors of all sorts of strange things down here." Malora hesitated before continuing. "Leopold thinks it's safe, but I'm not sure. First of all, it's really dark, even with our luminaries."

He spoke to no one in particular. In fact, he did not expect or want any answers. He simply found comfort in talking. Neither Lira nor Propo were bothered by his chatter, which had pretty much continued nonstop since Leopold instructed them to wait until he returned. Malora's voice was comforting, whether he was singing or simply talking. Eventually, he did ask a direct question: "Have either of you had friends or family go missing down here?"

Lira and Propo were seated on a part of the tunnel wall that jutted out just enough to uncomfortably accommodate two people. Lira gave Propo a look, signaling him to respond to the youngest of their small group. Propo obliged, more out of boredom than obligation.

"I gather, dear Malora, that Leopold is simply saving us a lot of time and energy by selecting paths in which there is less likelihood of having to backtrack—or, worse, encountering creatures of unknown allegiances. I would not have ventured down here without the guidance of a chiropter. They are experts in the tunnels. We are in good hands."

"Unknown allegiances? You mean Mastad has his Mastadonians down here too? Surely not." Malora's gaze darted anxiously between the path ahead and the shadows behind them.

"Probably not," answered Lira without looking up. She continued to weave strands of bioluminescent plant vines together. "Mastad has nothing much left to gain by scavenging what's left of these caves and tunnels. Everything has fallen under his control. What could it benefit him to be down here?"

Malora eased his way over to Lira and picked up one of her bioweaves. "You're really good at this."

"I should be. I've been weaving my entire life." She lifted a vine and twirled it in the air. "In their own way, these aren't too different from the silk of the Okrad caterpillars."

"There is one thing those in power fear more than anything," said Propo, referring back to Mastad.

"What is that?" asked Malora.

"Losing it," answered Propo.

Lira paused braiding for a moment. "So, you think Mastad is still on guard, protecting his interests?" asked Lira. "But from whom?"

"From us," answered Malora.

"The youth is correct. The Twelve are mentioned in the prophetic writings, and Mastad has been made aware of all prophecy that involves him. This I can assure you. He is many things, Mastad, but he is not naïve," said Propo.

"You may as well put a target on our backs. You both realize that none of us are getting out of this alive, don't you?" Malora's anxious glances from one side of the tunnel to the other had now evolved into him aimlessly pacing back and forth.

Lira took Malora by the arm and asked, "If you honestly think that, why would you have joined us?" She then placed a bioluminescent weaving onto his head, adjusting his blond curls until the glowing halo sat just right. While it cast little light in the tunnel, it effectively distracted Malora from his anxious pacing.

Malora reached up to feel the crown of lights in his hair and smiled at how much better he could see. His smile did not last long. "I'm good as dead either way. I'm not like the rest of you. I have no influence. My people were poor long before Mastad took over. I mean, don't misunderstand me, we always had food and shelter, but we never lived high up in majestic picalo trees, or in fancy cathedral caves like the Pixanoans. We utilized the ancient creeks for water but had no access to the inexhaustible underground springs. My people were never going to survive this apocalypse."

"The people of Pixanese are known as Nectarions," replied Lira.

"That's not what my people call them. They will always be Pixanoans to us," said Malora.

"I'm curious," said Propo. "How did you make it all the way to the Empyrean Realm? That's quite a feat for one without many resources."

Before Malora had a chance to answer, Leopold returned. "I saw your lights several turns ago. Is it really necessary to be...so bright?"

"You must take into consideration that our eyes are not as

adjusted to these dark caves and tunnels as yours, Leopold," said Lira. Not only had Lira made a crown of light for Malora, but she had also woven bracelets for herself, and embellished Propo's walking stick until it resembled a lightning rod.

"The three of you together resemble a glowing trio of marauders. It's not very becoming," sneered Leopold.

Malora sighed. "It's practical, not a fashion statement. I, for one, would like to see my fate before it arrives."

"Very well," said Leopold, "I have a bright bit of news myself. Follow me, and I will tell you all about it."

Leopold could have quickly flown through the passageways, but he knew that those following would be unable to keep up with his pace. Instead, he slowly hovered just above the ground while he led the way. Since his wings completely covered his thin legs and small claw feet, the others assumed he was walking, but millions of tiny, hair-like cilia moved in unison to keep him lifted off the ground.

Lira thought Leopold was quite graceful. Malora thought his gait looked creepy. The chiropter was very thin and only stood a little over three feet tall when fully erect, creating an interesting tableau when gliding in stride with his companions.

Propo moved past the others to speak directly to the chiropter. "What news do you have for us?"

"Did you know that this is not really a tunnel at all?" asked Leopold.

"Huh?" responded Propo, clearly confused.

Leopold tilted his head to the side. "Caves are naturally occurring, while tunnels are not."

"Okay... why is this important?" asked Propo.

"There are so many things that defy explanation. Tunnels like these are too perfect not to have been made by someone...or something," Leopold said, pointing up. "Look at those protruding stones. Not only are they beautifully colored—I'm partial to the golden-amber ones—but they are polished; not one has a sharp edge. Yet, no one made them. These tunnels are as old as time itself."

"I could ask how you know this, or I could ask what difference it makes," said Propo.

Leopold smiled. "Both worthwhile questions, but we'll focus on the latter—"

Propo quickly interjected. "God made them. That's true with everything. That's what is written in the ancient texts."

Leopold quickly opened his wings and flew up to the ceiling. He then hung upside down directly in front of Propo. Lira and Malora caught up to them, and for a brief moment all three just stared at the hanging bat before he eventually spoke. "Have any of you figured out why Beely chose us to look for the painting? Did you think it was because we have special tracking skills?"

Lira was the first to offer a response. "A good leader will always help the lower ranks avoid temptation. Propo is a scientist; he believes in evidence and not so much the miraculous. If the painting does exist, it would be the most miraculous thing any of us have ever seen. Malora, although he has a youthful exuberance and an angelic voice, is terribly insecure. And you, the talented acrobat, have an entire species to avenge."

Malora's frustration could be heard in his tone. "What does anything you are saying have to do with the painting and why Beely chose us?"

"None of you will go into the painting once it's found. Propo doesn't have enough faith, Malora doesn't have enough courage, and Leopold has perhaps too much of both," she answered.

Propo seemed intrigued by Lira's deductions. "And what of you?"

Leopold let go of his perch and righted himself on the ground below. "Lira... Well, she is quite brave, and probably has enough faith, but she would never enter into a painting that might take her away from her son, whom she loves more than life itself, unless she was sure of the outcome."

"That still doesn't answer the question," said Malora.

"The painting is in safe hands with us. Such a powerful thing, one that defies time and space, in the wrong hands could be disastrous. Yes, all of us were chosen, but all twelve have unique weaknesses, wants, and desires. We struggle to do what is right, but the painting is not as great a temptation to us as it might have been to the others," said Leopold.

Propo was impressed. "I didn't take you for being so wise. As close as I am to Beely, I'm not sure I would have deduced as much. However, I think you may very well be correct."

"Useless observations if we don't find the painting," added Malora.

"We'll find it. Have a little faith," said Leopold as he resumed his walking-like hovering.

"You left us waiting for quite a long time," said Lira. "What did you discover up ahead?"

"It's more about what I failed to discover," answered Leopold.

"Do you hear that?" asked Malora, hearing strange noises emanating from one of the adjacent pathways.

"I don't hear anything," answered Propo.

"Shh. Malora is right," said Lira. Lira placed her hands on the tunnel wall, then took Propo's hand and placed his palm on the smooth stone.

"The vibrations of many feet," said Propo.

To Leopold, it sounded as if a thousand tiny feet with overly long, sharp claws were rapidly descending upon them, yet he kept that bit of information to himself. Leopold flapped his wings and became horizontal to the floor before anyone had a chance to inquire about the eerie sounds. "Do your best to keep up. Secure your water skins and run!"

He flew fast, but not so fast that the others would lose sight of him. "What's happening?" shouted Propo as he secured his light-stick with his belt.

Leopold kept flying but looked back toward the others. "The subterranean river is no more; it has gone completely dry. It's the worst-case scenario for us. There is still life down here— very thirsty life. Only one thing will quench that kind of thirst, and at the moment, we're the only ones that have it."

He shouted one last instruction before increasing his speed. "If you lose sight of me, turn to the right at the next intersecting passageway."

Understanding the cruelty of the Dry Death for those above, the foursome knew those below would be even more desperate. So they ran, but the sounds of a thousand blood-thirsty creatures kept getting louder and closer.

Propo, the oldest of the group, began to lag behind. Lira kept her position just between Malora and Propo, but she, too, could not sustain such a fast pace for much longer. At first, she could only think of what the hideous creatures chasing them must look like—sharp teeth, long, nimble appendages, and dark, beady eyes.

The next moment, her thoughts were consumed with her son. She could not fall prey to a murderous, evil horde. Her son needed her to prevail. Even if she never saw her son again, she had to make sure he had the opportunity to live and love as a free man like all those before him. She ran without another thought of what might or might not happen to her, unable to ignore the burning in her lungs and the ache in her heart.

Malora, the youngest and most fit of the three, had lost sight of Leopold. He assumed the worst—that the chiropter betrayed them all unto death. In fact, Malora thought the chiropter had probably planned it this way from the beginning. He had the sinking suspicion that the bat knew all along where the painting was and wanted it all for himself.

Beely was wrong about Leopold, thought Malora. Perhaps their underground guide would use the painting in some way to go back in time and kill Mastad before any of his own kind could be captured, murdered, or mutilated for Mastad's sick experiments. Malora's mind raced, but not as fast as his feet. Whatever was chasing them was no longer under the influence of old realm standards of treating guests with love and kindness. This was the new realm, and these creatures were thirsty and angry.

Lira raced forward, and just as she was about to lose sight of Malora, he stopped cold in his tracks at the intersection. Surely, he had heard Leopold's directions to turn right.

Lira paused for an entirely different reason. She leaned forward, placing her hands on her knees as she tried to catch her breath. To her surprise, Propo was right on her heels, grateful for the reprieve as he loudly sucked in the stale cave air.

"What's he waiting for?" asked Propo.

"I don't know. Maybe he forgot which way to go," she mumbled, more to herself than to Propo. She then yelled to Malora, "Go to the right! Turn right!"

When there was no immediate reaction, she turned to look behind her. Whatever crazy horde was after them had not yet caught up, but they were undoubtedly very close—if the dirt and dust falling from the top of the tunnel was any indication. Lira began to run toward the intersection, followed closely by Propo.

Just before they reached the turn, Malora stepped to the left. Lira screamed as loud as she could, "No! That's the wrong way. Go to the right—the other way!" But it was of no use; before they could get to him, Malora disappeared down the tunnel to the left. She heard the loud clacking of his sandals quickly diminish. Lira paused, ever so briefly, at the crossing before joining Propo to the right.

As they ran, Lira thought she could no longer hear anything following them. She was not certain, however, since her own breathing filled the narrowing tunnel. She and Propo ran, not knowing where they were going. The bio-lights only illuminated a small distance ahead. They were running blind, plunging into the darkness, praying the path was clear.

Lira was once again in the lead. Propo was on his second wind but still trailing behind; he would not be able to run much longer. Fortunately, he would not have to. He heard a loud thud directly ahead. Lira cried out as if someone or something had knocked the wind out of her.

He slowed down cautiously, no longer able to see the bio-lights on Lira's wrists. His own light staff was far too dim to be of much use. He walked slowly, squinting to engage every optic nerve. He could not hear any footsteps other than his own. Suddenly, his foot gave way, and he fell into a pit in the tunnel floor, landing knees first. His fall was softened by Lira, who tried her best to keep him from hitting his face on the hard ground.

Leopold quickly replaced the trap door, effectively hiding the three from the dangers above. "We are safe," he said softly. "There are many secret hiding places in the tunnels; you just have to know where to look. We will continue when those chasing us have either given up pursuit or ventured far away from here."

"Where is Malora?" Propo whispered, brushing the dirt from his pants.

"He went the wrong way; he turned left at the crossing," answered Lira.

"Shh." Leopold waved his wings until everyone quieted down. After a moment, he said, "I know what must have happened."

"What?" asked Lira.

"The desperate cave dwellers must have followed Malora; he led them away from us," he answered.

"Do you think he did it on purpose?" asked Propo, seated on the ground and appreciating the reprieve.

"Doubtful," answered Leopold. "He could not have known they would follow him or that they would not split and follow us all. In his frightened state, he simply made a crucial mistake."

"A deadly mistake, more than likely," added Propo.

"We can't leave him—we must go and find him," pleaded Lira.

Propo shook his head. "We all knew the risks we were taking."

"I am sadly forced to agree with Propo. It wouldn't be prudent to look for him at this time. We have a job to do, and we must succeed. We cannot allow Mastad to locate the painting—he would use it to seal the fate of the Realms forevermore."

Leopold paused, carefully picking a few specks of dirt from Lira's hair. He then gently lifted her chin with his hand. "We chiropters have a sixth sense, and mine is telling me that Malora has not been killed. God is with him, and the youth will live many more cycles of the moons."

Their faces were well lit in the small hiding spot under the tunnel floor. The bio-lights glowed brightly. Lira could see the sincerity in Leopold's eyes. It was the first time she noticed how beautiful the chiropter was, now that they were face to face.

His eyes were curiously brown; all this time, Lira had assumed they were black. Whether it was a stereotype—secretive cave dwellers with dark eyes—or just a preconceived notion, she was not sure. His fur was rich and shiny, the color of soft, glowing fire. His short snout and fairly large ears were darker and really quite cute, thought Lira. He was a handsome fellow, she fondly concluded.

Regardless, Lira was persistent. "But what does success matter if we lose our compassion? We can't leave him behind."

Propo shook his head grimly. "Dear Lira, Malora has most likely already succumbed to a fate that no one, not even the Creator Himself, could remedy."

Lira could not help but show her disappointment. "There is a verse: 'Have I not commanded you? Be strong and courageous. Do not be frightened, and do not be dismayed, for the Lord your God is with you wherever you go.' As you, of all people know, Propo, the Word of the Creator applies to all of His creation. Even in our Realms."

Propo spoke measuredly as he slowly repositioned his legs. "Is that an admonishment, Lira?" Lira was unsure whether Propo was uncomfortable in the small, tight space or uneasy with her sentiment concerning Malora.

"I'll let scripture speak for itself. I will agree to whatever we decide together. I pray that the Good Spirit will lead us to the right action. Where two or more are gathered in His name, there He will be also." Lira paused, then looked back at Leopold. "You do believe in the Holy Word and in the One who inspired it, do you not?"

Leopold considered her question as he listened for any sounds above. When he heard nothing, he responded, "I am perhaps somewhere between the braewicker, Duly, and Beely. I have a very hard time reconciling our status as a secondary creation. The Word you quote is not realm scripture but rather for those from the other world."

Propo quickly interjected. "That is simply not true. We are part of God's creation. Nothing—no thought, no deed, anywhere it may be—is outside the purview of the one and only Creator God. The Word is complete and affects all, no matter the realm or the world. The difference, my dear Leopold, is that our own prophetic scriptures do not apply to those of the other world; they are specifically for us and us alone. The two are not to be confused. The Word of God, both old and new, is complete and whole within itself."

"So, what are we? That's the age-old question for those conflicted like me, who want to believe. I mean, I do believe—I do. It's just hard to accept that I might be nothing more than a tool for the others—others living in a place I have never been and perhaps could never go," said Leopold.

"May I say something?" asked Lira.

"Of course," answered Leopold.

"I think of myself as a servant of the Most High. I am here to serve His will, not my own—whatever His will may be." She paused, carefully choosing her words. "Perhaps you are correct, Leopold. Maybe we are secondary—figments—as some call us, but what difference does that logically make? Even in the other world, where the Christ will walk, every believer is a servant of the Most High, if they are truly believers. The way I see it, we have an important role. We in the Five Realms of Here are loved, we are meaningful, and we are just as much a part of His creation as any other—albeit perhaps less than some and maybe a little more than others."

Propo could not help but smile as he listened. It was the first time Leopold had seen the usually stoic and often nervous man show joy.

Propo, still smiling, responded excitedly, "I never considered what you just said. Logically, it makes no difference whether we are figments or something other. We are part of the creative mind. No matter how large or how small our part may be. And if that is true, we must do the Creator's will. We must glorify the Lord wherever and whenever. That is what I intend to do. That is what Beely intends to do. And I do not want to speak for Lira, but I know that is what she also intends to do."

Lira reached over and squeezed Propo's shoulder. "Yes! I do. That's what I have taught my son. We are always to glorify the Lord—the Lord is worthy."

"I can see your point," said Leopold. "Who am I to question where I stand in the hierarchy of God's creation? Even the lowliest servant of the greatest King could never lower himself more than the King of Kings."

Lira looked astonished. "You got that from what we just said?"

"That's so much more profound than any way I could have said it," said Propo.

Leopold smiled. "Yes, I do have a way with words, don't I?"

"Well, that just ruined the moment," jeered Lira, after which both she and Propo erupted into laughter.

Leopold joined in their laughter before abruptly placing a wing over his mouth. "Shh, we mustn't be too loud—there could still be scouts up top."

Lira took a deep breath and nodded. "So, what do we do about Malora? I think there will be a heavy price to come if we don't help him."

"I agree with you, Lira." Propo rubbed his chin. "No good will come of this. I also agree with our guide here. We can't jeopardize our mission. I pray that God will watch over Malora, but I fear we must continue until we find what we came here for."

Lira hung her head low and sighed. "Okay, we go on without Malora. I too pray that God looks after him and forgives us if we are making the wrong choice."

Propo looked at Leopold and asked, "Now what?"

"Not far from here there is a tunnel leading to the home of a special friend of mine. His name is Arnox, and he is a beast of burden just outside the Realm of Restoration. He is both trustworthy and loyal. It only occurred to me, fairly recently, that Arnox might be the only one who knows where the painting is, as he was the last one to see the collector alive."

"Who is the collector?" asked Propo.

"The collector is the one who was betrayed by Athaliah. Some say that he betrayed her, but if one considers murder the ultimate betrayal, then the matter is settled in favor of the woman scorned. The collector was under the employ of Ankur, whom we now call Mastad. He was commanded to gather all the important artifacts, including the painting."

Lira asked, "Will Arnox tell us what he knows?"

"I cannot be sure; it depends on how much he understands about the current state of affairs and how his family and friends have been impacted by Mastad's reign."

Leopold pushed the top of their hiding spot just enough to look out. He then looked back down and spoke just above a whisper. "I'm confident that even if Arnox knows nothing of the painting, he will still be able to give us information on where the collector went just before and after he was poisoned."

Leopold then squeezed through the opening. Once on the other side, he lifted the covering and ushered the other two out. Lira looked down at the lights on her wrists. "These bioluminescent vines are beginning to lose their vigor. I'm not sure how much energy they have left."

"Don't worry. We haven't far to go, and if they go completely dark, I will lead you the rest of the way. Let us hurry in case there are any others looking for us."

The eerie sounds of scavengers were no more. They were safe, for now. What none of them realized just yet was that Malora was the last one to be in possession of the kaleidoscope. Even if they found the painting that Nicholas, the collector, might have hidden, they could not be sure if it was the actual painting that held the power to turn the tide of the evil winds of change. At every turn, it seemed as though Mastad was one step ahead of the Twelve.

Chapter 13

NO GREATER LOVE

Since the first clandestine meeting of the Twelve, no member had ever returned to the Wren home. Sooner or later, Mastad would come after them, so they all agreed never to return in order to keep the refugees living there safe. Beely, Eudox, Cloy, and Duly were planning their next move while hiding out at Marybah's.

Still, Beely kept tabs on the remnant in Pixanese. She felt it was her duty to render aid if ever it was needed. Without the influence of the Glouscenshire, more shelters were built, water and food were painstakingly rationed and stored, and everyone

133

fervently prayed. The Nectarions who had memorized much of the scriptures before the Word was purged taught them to others, and not a day went by that worship did not take place, or so the roofa-birds reported.

Beely could not have been prouder of her fellow Nectarions. They would be the ones to restore Pixanese to its former glory when Mastad was eventually defeated—or so she hoped. As it turned out, she was wise for having stayed clear of the encampment and her people. Not much time would pass before Mastad retaliated for the attempt on his life.

As far as he was concerned, any agreements made with Beely in the past were now null and void. He had no verifiable proof that any of the soon-to-be-fabled Twelve were responsible for invading his home and killing his Mastadonian guards, but both he and Beely knew there was no other group as capable, organized, or motivated.

The moons had crossed and disappeared behind the canyon walls. It was a dark night under Marybah's picalo tree. The wind steadily rustled the leaves as the ancient tree creaked and moaned. It was the only tree in the now-abandoned village that was getting any water. Marybah made sure the foundation and support for her beloved home got just enough water to sustain it until Mastad unblocked the springs.

No one knew when—or even if—Mastad would restore the flow of water once he had complete control. But why would any sensible conqueror let his spoils completely go to ruin? Yet, as Marybah knew all too well, Mastad had never been sensible.

Her guests had settled in for the night, leaving Marybah alone on the top floor. All of the earlier discussions brought back memories of the very first time she met the man she refused to call Mastad. It was before Beely was born and during a very rough time in her marriage to Mikalo.

She saw Ankur standing on a boulder, gazing across the creek just outside the village of Pixanese. She knew immediately he was not from her realm by the clothing he wore. His pants were unlike the tunics and robes she was familiar with. He wore black boots with leather straps that went almost to his knees. His shirt—the only loose-fitting thing on him—still managed to handsomely frame his broad shoulders and muscular chest, but it was his dark, thick hair and meticulously groomed beard that she remembered most.

"I may not see you, hidden behind the ferns; I may not ever meet you, but the scent you are wearing will feed my imagination long after you have departed." His deep, eloquent voice caused her heart to skip a beat. Her instincts told her that she should quickly depart without looking back, but instead, she could not resist engaging the charismatic young man.

"Who are you?"

She never forgot his answer: "I am the one who will lead the Five Realms of Here into the Age of Enlightenment." It was not what he said that Marybah dreamt about that night—it was how he listened. She dreamt of how he listened to her that very first day, the way he looked at her, the way he touched her heart. Like all things Ankur, every word from his lips proved to be lies—but in her dreams, as that night, Ankur spoke only truth. If only real life had been as beautiful as her dreams.

Unlike Marybah, Cloy had a hard time sleeping. The gentle swaying of the picalo tree was foreign to him, and the lingering, woody aroma of Marybah's pipe was inescapable. He missed his family and was consumed with worry for their safety. He could not shake the feeling that Mastad would discover the Mindalites' well—and then the Mindalites themselves. He had sent a messenger back to warn his loved ones, but even that worried him. What if someone was watching him? What if someone followed the messenger?

The ruddy young Mindalite stood on his bedroom balcony, the faint glow of a few distant stars still visible. His room was completely dark with all of the bio-lights placed in their sheaths. He found some comfort holding Reverie in his arms. He was not too familiar with empachics, but what the others said was true: her vibrations soothed his nerves like the Balm of Gilead.

He was sure she must have sensed his sadness to venture all the way down to the second floor of Marybah's treehouse. The other guests, Eudox, Duly, and Beely, were in bedrooms higher up in the tree.

The wind eventually calmed, and the treehouse and village below were as quiet as they had been since they arrived at Marybah's several moons ago. He stood on the balcony, remaining as still as possible, immersing himself in the solitude. Reverie, sensing he was better, jumped down and disappeared into the dark room.

The silence allowed him to think and soon inspired him to pray. He lifted his hands toward the night sky and gave thanks to God. He thanked God for the tiny, beautiful flowers that bloomed faithfully each cycle in the meadows where he had lived. He thanked God for the chatty dragonflies that often visited during the full moons. He thanked God for all the wonderful meals with his family and the warmth and comfort of their home amidst the winding creeks. Before the Dry Death, there was no place as magical as the Mindalite meadows.

Cloy sat down on his bed and continued to give thanks. He also asked for protection for his family. He prayed that evil would be defeated once and for all. He prayed that God would use him for good in the struggles to come. The prayers lifted his entire countenance—even the smoky residue of Marybah's pipe no longer bothered him.

He continued silently praying until he was interrupted by a small thumping sound near the stairwell. He looked, but could see nothing in the dark. He wrote it off as Reverie bouncing up the stairs. There were no doors in the typical treehouse—just stairs with small, partially enclosed landings. There was another thump, followed by a young girl's giggles.

Cloy knew someone was there with him, but even when squinting, he could not see anything. As he fumbled his way to the tabletop to unsheathe a light, he heard someone whisper, "Shh."

"Who's there?" he asked.

His question was greeted by more giggling and more shushing. When he finally drew his light from its sheath—after more fumbling—he was shocked to see his wife standing behind his young daughter. Her hands were holding the excited young girl by the shoulders as she pushed forward in an attempt to embrace her father.

His daughter grinned from ear to ear, and his wife—with her beautiful red curls—could not have looked more delighted. It had been many moons since he had seen his family. He could not move his feet—or his mouth. He was the most awkward-looking figure—utterly bewildered. Before he could move or speak, the young girl had wrapped her arms around her father's legs.

"Daddy, Daddy, I've missed you so much!"

Cloy, finally able to move, knelt down and lifted his daughter off the floor. He swung her around and embraced her with a hug as if she were the last living soul in the Realms. "I love you too, my little meadow flower."

Capy was small for her age; her bright red hair loosely framing her cherub-like face. With his daughter in his arms, he looked astonishingly at his wife. "What—"

"We had to see you. I couldn't bear to hear her cry herself to sleep one more night," said his wife. Bailey was young, radiating strength and optimism. She was never seen without a smile covering her freckled face.

Cloy gently placed his hands over his daughter's ears and whispered to his wife. "But we spoke of this. It's far too dangerous for you to venture out, and this jeopardizes the entire clan. What if one of Mastad's spies had seen you?"

"We have the elders' blessing, and we took every effort not to be seen. There is no one better at staying hidden than a Mindalite. The messenger you sent assured us the path to you was safe and undiscovered."

Cloy attempted to scold his wife again, but she gently placed two fingers on his lips to quiet him. "Dear Cloy, we are here. We love you. Just enjoy the moment." She kissed her husband and wrapped her arms around both him and Capy. It was a strange feeling—he had always placed family first. That was why he had agreed to defend the Five Realms from a tyrant determined to destroy every last person he cared about. Yet he had never felt as complete as he did in that moment. Embracing his family felt like a dream. The moment was euphoric—a feeling that was too good to be true.

And it was.

He was still lying in bed—he opened his eyes, awakened from his dream. It was still dark. An overwhelming sense of dread and sadness at the sudden loss of his loved ones enveloped him. It may have only been a dream, but it seemed real. They were gone, but he was not alone.

He heard an unfamiliar sound—one that had only recently shattered the serenity of the Realms: leathery wings brushing against a large, hairy body as they opened and closed. Cloy's nostrils recoiled at the sweaty odor of a beast that knew only death.

Before he had time to reach for a weapon, the Mastadonian warrior was on top of him. Its claw-like hands wrapped around his throat, silencing any attempt to cry out a warning to the others. Cloy struggled for breath—he could feel the creature's claws puncturing his skin.

His mind raced with many thoughts—chief among them, his dear Bailey and sweet Capy, whom he knew would never see him again in this life. He refused to succumb quickly, driven by a desperate need to warn the others of the evil intruder—or intruders, as the case might be.

The creature pressed down even harder on his throat. He reached up with his one free hand and tried to punch through the thin membrane of the monster's wing. His arm flailed as he scratched and tore at the impenetrable webbing. Cloy stood no chance—he was not a warrior. He was a husband, a father, a believer in good, and a follower of a loving God.

His last thought, before closing his eyes forever, was filled with peace. There was irony in finding complete peace at the most violent moment of his brief life. He rested in the knowledge that God knew this moment would come—it came as no surprise to the One who loved him most.

Cloy need not have worried about warning those above him. Reverie, whom Beely almost always kept near her side, sensed the danger coming before it arrived. A Mastadonian's smell might be dreadful to any ordinary person—but to an empachic, it was overwhelmingly putrid. Reverie alerted Beely—jumping up and down in an uncharacteristic frenzy.

Beely, Duly, and Eudox occupied two floors above Cloy's. Marybah was just below the top deck; the others one floor below her. Beely awoke Duly, and together they met in Eudox's room. Eudox had not yet gone to bed. He was quick to assimilate the information relayed to him.

"You and Duly must get out of here—quickly," whispered Eudox.

Duly managed to suppress a sneeze before responding. "There is but one way out of here that I know of, and that's down—down where the evil is rising." He nervously scrambled to gather a few essentials, placing them in his satchel.

"Besides, we can't leave Cloy. What will become of him?" Beely pondered more than asked.

"Whatever is upon us did not take the stairs. I have them set with traps and warning signals," said Eudox.

"How did they get in, then?" Duly asked—then answered himself: "Oh…it's those hideous flying creations of Mastad's."

"I'm afraid so. I don't know how many there are or which floors they occupy. You'll be lucky to escape alive." Eudox retrieved a weapon from his rucksack.

Beely responded with concern. "Don't you mean we…we will be lucky to get out of here alive?"

Eudox ignored her question. "Beely, do you think the ray would hear your call if you made it to the rooftop?"

Duly answered for her. "That creature loves her. He follows her everywhere. I guarantee you he's not far."

"Joshua does not follow me," said Beely.

"Trust me, he does," whispered Duly. "He's always somewhere near; I've seen him myself on many occasions—"

140

Eudox interrupted, "We don't have time for this—the two of you must go up, and he will fly you both to safety."

"And what of you?" asked Duly, fumbling with his pajamas. He wished he had worn his tunic to bed. He would never again be unprepared for battle, no matter the hour.

"And what of Cloy and my mother?" asked Beely.

Eudox had never appeared more solemn or serious to either Beely or Duly than he did at that moment. "If Cloy is still with us—"

"Still with us?" Beely exclaimed in a forced whisper.

Duly cut in, "He's right, Bee—we haven't much time. You must listen to his plan." Eudox continued, just as solemnly as he had begun. "A ray can only carry two normal-sized people at most."

Beely looked at the braewicker and said, "He's not a normal-sized anything. My ray can carry all of us."

Eudox shook his head. "Your mother is a little more than normal-sized, and I'm afraid I must stay behind to keep anyone from following you." Just then, a muffled sound came from the floor below. Duly flinched at the sound. Eudox placed a comforting hand on his shoulder before continuing. "I don't have time to argue or convince you—just get up there and pray the ray is nearby. Someone must continue leading this fight, and at this moment, that someone is you, Beely."

Without saying another word, Beely threw both of her arms around Eudox's neck and squeezed hard. She reluctantly followed Duly, who had already made it halfway up the stairs— somehow managing to throw on a cloak over his nightclothes. Marybah seemed to know what was happening. Without saying a word, she handed her daughter a small package, which Beely quickly placed in her shoulder bag. Duly nodded to Marybah and then made it the rest of the way up the stairs to the rooftop balcony.

Marybah took hold of her daughter's arm and spoke earnestly: "I'm sorry for my part in this. I have made so many mistakes—but you...you are my hope. I should have never believed a word Ankur told me. I fear he used me from the very beginning, but there was one thing he did not count on—that was you. It was because of me that he learned about your father and the many secrets that might otherwise have been hidden from him. I failed you and Mikalo in so many ways. There's more I need to tell you—I just don't know where to begin—"

Marybah hesitated, hearing a loud crash below them. Beely watched the stairwell as she spoke. "You can tell me later. Come with us, Mom."

"How? I'm in no shape to flee—I would only hold you back."

"Max has trained the strongest, most skilled rays. If the one who's loyal to me comes, he can take the three of us someplace safe," Beely said.

"Even if that were possible—and my doubts prevail—I have prepared for such a day when assassins might come."

"You knew they were coming?"

"Dear, I didn't even know you were coming—or that we'd be reconciled. I only ask that, no matter what revelations come your way, you'll forgive me. Find it in your heart to understand that any secrets I've kept were only to protect you. Find Maximilian, and fight the battles to come together. The two of you are stronger as one."

Beely took the first step upward—then turned, asking one last question: "Will I see you again?"

"I don't know, Bee. There's so much more I need to tell

you—but if you don't hurry, I'm afraid all will be lost." Marybah turned toward the stairwell, then glanced back and yelled, "Go!"

Beely turned and rushed up the spiral staircase to the top floor. She would later lament that she had not told her mother she loved her or that they did not embrace, but theirs was a complicated relationship in the best of times, let alone the worst. After a brief look around, she found Duly hiding beneath a small wooden table. Had she left him, she was sure he would have been the only one to survive—no one would ever think to hide in such a place. It was the sneeze that gave him away.

Beely leaned over the railing of the rooftop and called out, slightly above a whisper, the name she had given to her husband's most loyal beast. "Joshua." Realizing a whisper would not carry—but anything louder would give them away—she looked to Duly for help.

He shrugged. "What do you expect me to do?"

"Pray," she said earnestly. Then, into the dark night, she called out the name of her ray—not once but three times: "Joshua…Joshua…Joshua!"

"Well, if the evil bats were confused about our whereabouts before, they're certainly not now!" Duly exclaimed, eyes fixed on the spiral staircase's opening.

Moments before Beely and Duly made their way to the top of the stairs, Eudox crammed every object he was able to move into the landing on his floor. He could hear the creature below pushing its way through. He had just enough time to position himself in the far corner.

The Mastadonian tore through the rubble faster than Eudox expected—but he was ready. He drew his sling tight, confident in his weapon. The first thing Eudox saw was the crazed, hate-filled eyes of the killer. The creature was fast and wasted no time in coming toward its prey.

Eudox took a breath, aimed at the evil beast's head, and released the stone. The moment played in slow motion as the smooth, round missile sped through the air until landing right in the center of the assassin's forehead. The sound of the invader's skull cracked as the stone penetrated deeply into its flesh.

The creature still made it several more paces before falling face-first a foot away from Eudox. The victor exhaled while his hands remained frozen as if the stone had just left its sling.

He never saw the second demon enter from the open balcony. It crept silently behind Eudox, who had his sling pointed in the opposite direction. He felt a sudden wash of warm air hitting the back of his neck. Eudox was an old man, but in the time it took to draw a second breath, he was fast enough to drop his sling and pull a dagger from his belt. The knife would not save his life, but it would save the lives of his friends. As he fell, he raised the dagger, slashing the wing of the deadly beast, rendering it flightless.

What happened to Marybah would not be known for some time—and few held hope for her survival. As for Beely and Duly, their escape was truly a divine spectacle. Joshua—the ever-loyal Brorayding—heard his call and responded with such speed that even Duly could not deny the miracle.

The night was calm, yet Joshua's vast, powerful wings stirred the air with such force that Duly cowered, covering his face. Beely had never stood directly beneath such a majestic creature. In the cramped rooftop space, she dragged Duly by the cloak to Joshua. The only way aboard was via one of his pectoral wings, which lay flush to the ground like a magical carpet.

Beely stepped onto the thick, wide, triangular wing. Reverie, who had followed them up the stairs, bounded over to the ray and leaped into Beely's arms. Beely had never seen the little girl jump so far before. She tucked her into her rucksack before reaching back for Duly, offering her hand to help pull him aboard.

Although physically able, he was terrified of flight. With gentle coaxing—and a reminder of what Mastadonians do to their enemies—Duly scrambled over to Joshua's horn. Holding on tight, he sat and offered a silent prayer to a God he didn't believe in. Beely stood behind him, pressing him against the great horn with her full weight. Her warmth and confidence reassured him; Reverie's soothing vibrations helped further. Duly relaxed and vowed to get an empachic of his own someday.

"Take us to safety, Joshua," said Beely. She rubbed her hand on his thick hide and patted him reassuringly. Joshua, with two riders and a little empachic on his back, lifted his wings and pushed through the air with emboldened strength.

They ascended straight into the night—no roll, no yaw. When he completely cleared all obstacles below, Joshua flapped his huge wings, pushing forward with great speed. Although secure, Duly felt butterflies in his stomach. In different circumstances, he might have enjoyed it, he thought.

"Hang on tight, Duly—you haven't seen anything yet!" Beely urged.

Joshua climbed higher and higher until the small village below looked like a child's doll house. Beely and Duly never saw the demonic ogres who struck down their friends; Joshua flew too fast for pursuers. Beely knew they were safe the instant they took flight. Nothing could match a ray in the sky—not even the prince of the air himself.

145

Still, the stakes had changed, and danger was far from past. She held a quiet truth in her heart: the Twelve were in danger— Cloy, in all likelihood, was the first to fall. In their brief time together, he had been young, honorable, unwavering in truth. She had never met anyone so loyal to family. His death, and their loss, would not be in vain. She'd also come to deeply admire—and even love—Eudox. Apart from Propo, he was her last link to her father. She would never be the same Beely. Now, she was more determined than ever to bring Mastad and all who followed him down.

Chapter 14

DULY'S VISION

"I apologize for being a possible nuisance in light of your graciousness in hosting me while Beely looks for Maximilian..." Duly paused, reconsidered asking the same question yet again, but in the end, he could not help himself.

It was the fourth time he had asked Willow, and he was running out of original ways to phrase his queries. "How are you so certain that Mastad won't find out that I'm here?" He placed his hand over the upper left corner of his lip in an attempt to halt its involuntary twitching.

He had not slept a wink since Joshua and Beely dropped him off in the Land of Mana under the care of Willow. Willow tried her best to make Duly feel safe after the recent trauma he had suffered from losing his friends. Her limbs had woven a soft hammock for him to rest upon. The mushrooms that grew along the tall, winding surface roots—usually quite chatty—remained silent the entire night.

Willow's leaves shielded Duly from both the cool breeze and the morning light. While Duly pressed Willow for a fifth time, the brown rounds polished his sandals, making them shine like new. "Do you have a secret power over Mastad? Am I invisible to him under your canopy?"

The mushrooms could not shed tears, but they drooped for Duly. The brown rounds' bright green tops had turned a sickly shade of pale yellow. Everyone under Willow's arms was sad for Duly.

Willow was a very patient soul. She struggled to find different ways to address his concerns, hoping that she might eventually convince him that he was safe.

"Mastad no longer sends his minions to collect his Glouscenshires. He has no more use for the Land of Mana. As long as you remain under my branches, there is no danger of anyone seeing you. The only one who would cause problems is the old, stiff—"

"Ekrad Oren? The tree in the middle of the orchard that made the bargain with Mastad? I'd like to take a hatchet to that old tree!" grumbled Duly.

"Yes, that one. He is barren and sullen. He speaks to no one and receives no visitors. Many birds and other creatures of flight come here for water, but none alight on his limbs or bring him news from outside the garden."

"How have you managed to live here, in the same garden as him, for so very long?"

Duly's new inquiry brought a moment of unexpected levity. The mushrooms giggled, and the brown round with the crooked ear smirked. It was a dragonfly that swooped down in front of Duly's face and replied, "What kind of trees do you know that walk from place to place?"

Two mushrooms stopped giggling just long enough to echo in unison, "Place to place."

There were now several dragonflies, a couple of brown rounds, and too many mushrooms to count, all making Duly feel very silly indeed. "Of course trees can't walk. I know trees can't walk. It was what we scholars like to call a rhetorical question," said Duly.

"Rhetorical, he says," repeated the dragonfly as it buzzed near Duly's face once again. On its way back, it whispered in his ear, "Scholar, he says."

Willow finally interceded on Duly's behalf. "All right, everyone, settle down. This is no way to treat our honored guest." Willow's leaves rustled, and all the critters quieted down before she continued. "This is my home, and it is where God planted me. I am ever so grateful for my place here in the garden. No home is perfect, but God has His reasons for where He plants all of His creatures—including you and me, as well as the old tree in the center of the garden."

Duly made his way back over to his hammock and promptly buried himself deep under the soft leaves. He said nothing for a moment, then sighed. "Willow, I know you believe in God, and you believe the Earthly World—where the others exist—is real. But even if they are real and even if God is real, why should we care about them? What difference do they make to us and our realms?"

"Duly, you don't need to believe that they're real. If you believe that *you* are real, then they matter," answered Willow.

"I don't follow your logic." Duly attempted to sit up in the

149

hammock but rolled out onto the soft dirt. The mushrooms turned their mushroom heads and tried very hard not to giggle again.

"My young braewicker, have you not learned by now that love is all that matters? The greatest thing of all is love. You may have no faith, and you may have little hope, Duly, but if you have not love, then all is meaningless. I'm not talking about loving yourself or loving that which brings you joy, I'm talking about loving others. You have not learned how to love others—especially those who can give you nothing in return, those who are less than you."

"What makes you think that? I love plenty!" exclaimed Duly, still struggling to sit in the hammock.

"No. If you did, you would understand what this battle for the Five Realms of Here is all about. Sure, you may be fond of Beely for giving you a home. You may have sacrificed your time and efforts for the place that once housed all of your books, but true love is reserved for living beings. Books may have brought you entertainment, knowledge, and joy. Yet, sacrificial love may bring you nothing but the knowledge of knowing that what you did was right."

Willow's limbs parted to allow a few more rays of sunshine through.

"I resent your observations, Willow. How do you know what I have or have not sacrificed? I gave my life for the Library of Truth. I dedicated all of my energy into taking care of your God's Word and helped to make sure that anyone who wanted to read about Him could do so."

A breeze gently rustled Willow's leaves, refreshing all under her canopy. "Yes, your life's work has been noble and appreciated. But books do not love, dear one."

"If you say I don't know love, who am I to argue? How can one who has never known love ever know when or if they have ever loved? I'm not saying you are correct in your assumption of me; I'm just saying—how could I prove otherwise?"

Duly finally managed to balance himself in the plush, green hammock. Truth be told, the limbs were constantly counterbalancing his fidgeting by gently tightening around his short, plump limbs to keep him from spilling over once again.

"I need no proof," said Willow. "Yet, would I be a friend if I did not encourage you to find the greatest treasure ever known, if I knew exactly where it was buried? Duly, you have the capacity to find the greatest treasure that can never be stolen from you, never be erased, never be burned or misplaced. A treasure that will embrace you for eternity. If the treasure is real, do you want to find it? Do you even want to look for it?"

"Of course—how could I not, if there is such a thing, yes, I would want to find it."

"Lie back down in my branches and let my leaves cover you. Be still and listen."

Duly did exactly what Willow asked of him. He sank deep down into the hammock, feeling more branches and more leaves slowly, gently cover his body. They were warm from the sun. Once Duly was still, the branches gently rocked him back and forth. He could hear nothing around him except his own heartbeat.

He began drifting as if into sleep, but this was something different. He was not sleeping as he knew sleep. He drifted further and further into a vibrant dream-like state until he found himself somewhere unfamiliar. He stood beside a tree that looked just like Willow, only much smaller. A strangely built house, made from materials he did not recognize, sat nearby.

He then heard voices to his right, and he saw several people. They were strange, yet familiar. They did not see him, for Duly was only a figment in their world. He watched and he listened with intense curiosity.

Two children, a boy and his slightly younger sister, ran in and out of the weeping branches of the tree. Seth broke off a small branch of the tree and chased his sister while thrashing the wiry limb as if it were a sword. Seth was tall for his age, with a tan complexion, striking blue eyes, and wavy light brown hair. He looked equally athletic as he did studious.

His sister had long blond hair and large blue eyes. It was obvious by the way she looked at her brother that she admired him. She was a bit of a tomboy, wearing faded overalls and a backwards baseball cap, like her brother. Their grandmother, Azora, was busy planting flowers along the front of the house until she heard yet another branch of her beloved willow tree being snapped off by one of her grandchildren.

Azora slowly got up from her knees with the support of a nearby lawn chair and promptly walked over to the kids. "Now listen here, you two young'uns. If I hear another branch snapped off my tree—that never did one little thing to the two of you—I will not only make y'all go to the early church service tomorrow morning, but I'll also see to it that we stay for Sunday school afterward."

Seth ran up to his grandmother and gave her a one-armed hug. "We're sorry, Grandma. I forgot how much you love this tree. We won't break another limb…promise."

Azora incorrectly assumed Seth and his sister, Melissa, did not like Sunday school. In fact, they loved going to church with their grandmother and doing art projects with the church teachers. What they did not like, however, was going to the early

152

service.

Azora eyed her grandson skeptically and then smiled. She adored her grandchildren. Their trips to visit her in the country were the highlight of the year. "That tree was here long before us, and it's likely to be here long after I'm gone."

By this time, Melissa had joined Seth and her grandmother. "Where are you going?"

"Don't be naïve, sis. Grandma's old." Seth's blunt response did not faze Azora. She was an old, hard-working southern lady, as forthright as they came. Seth came by his candor honestly.

"He's right, Melissa. I'm not long for this world."

Melissa tilted her head like a curious cat and asked, "What does that mean?"

Seth was quick to answer. "It means she's going to die soon."

Melissa's countenance immediately sank, her lips slowly turned down, and her eyes began to swell. "Take that back!" she cried as she punched her brother's arm.

"Melissa, I'm not dyin' anytime soon, God willin', and it's not nice to hit your brother. Apologize to him right this instant."

"Yes, ma'am." She turned slightly toward her brother, squinted her eyes, and looked down at her feet. "I'm sorry...but what you said wasn't very nice."

"The truth is, none of us know how much time we have to spend with one another. I reckon I have a little less time than the two of you. Really, we all ought to consider we're not long for this world." Azora slowly worked her way back over to the lone lawn chair next to the front porch. The kids followed.

"What world are we long for, Grandma?" asked Melissa.

Again, Seth responded before Azora had the chance. "That depends on how naughty or nice you've been. If you're nice, you get to go to heaven and be with God. If you're naughty, you go directly to hell. And whether or not you end up living in heaven or hell, it lasts a very, very long time."

Azora managed to sit in the flimsy yard furniture without tipping it over. Part of her wanted to chuckle at Seth's response, until she realized that he was not trying to be funny. "Well, son, if that's what you've been taught in the big city about the Gospel, let me be the first to inform you that God and Santa are not one and the same!"

"What's the Gospel?" asked Seth.

"Good Lord, have mercy on my soul and your father's too. That's who I blame for your ignorance—your father. What is the Gospel? Heavens declare!"

"It's exactly his fault, Grandma, because Daddy don't believe in God," said Melissa, who was promptly kicked on her big toe by Seth as he tried to shut her up.

"Shh," Seth tried to stop his sister from igniting Azora on a tirade about their "unrepentant father," as Azora called him.

"Dear children, if I've told you once, I've told you a hundred times, nobody loves you more than Jesus. Jesus is God, and he died on the cross for you because he wants to live with you forever in the place known as heaven. A home far away from here. You can't be good enough to go, and you can't be bad enough not to…only your faith in Jesus can bring you to the home that lasts forever."

It was perhaps the hundredth time Azora had told her grandchildren about salvation, but it would be the first time she specifically mentioned the unseen world. "We wrestle not against each other, mere flesh and blood, but against powers and rulers of the unseen world, and mighty powers of this dark world, and against evil spirits in heavenly places."

Melissa stared blankly at her grandmother. Her eyes grew wide, and she said, "Wow. That sounds crazy, Grandma. How are we supposed to do all that stuff?"

Before Azora could give a thoughtful answer, Seth had managed to distract his sister with a large bug he found crawling up his pant leg. "It's a walking stick, look, Sis!" But before she had time to get a good look at the six-legged bug, he took off running back under the tree. She chased quickly after him.

"Let me see. Let me see," she shouted as Azora watched them disappear under the willow branches.

By the time Melissa caught up to her brother, the bug had escaped. Melissa began to pout. She was quite fond of walking sticks, and they were nonexistent around their house in the city.

"Don't worry," he assured her, "We'll find it again, or maybe a different one. Help me look. It was here just a second ago, maybe it's still here, somewhere close."

The two of them looked all around, but fortune did not prevail. Seth eventually found something else to distract his sister. "Look at this, Sis."

Melissa sat next to her brother, under the tree, as he carefully used a small twig to dig up a rusted piece of metal. "What do you think it could be?" she asked.

"It's hidden treasure, of course," he said. Once he had freed the object from the ground, he brought it closer to his face and blew off the remaining dirt.

"It's a key," said Melissa.

He gave the copper-colored key to his sister. She polished it with the corner of her shirt and brought it up to her face. "It's definitely a key, but I've never seen one like this."

"I have," said Seth. "But only in books."

"What kind of books?"

"Books about the Roman Empire."

"What's the Roman Empire?"

"Something really old, just like this key." He answered.

"I wonder what it opens?"

Seth abruptly took the key out of his sister's hand. When she tried to get it back, she fell face first into the hard ground. Seth pocketed the key as he knelt down to help her up.

"I'm sorry, Sis. I didn't mean for you to fall." When he reached over to help her up, she pushed him away. She scooped something up with her hands and held it close. "Whatcha got there?" asked Seth.

"It's the sticky bug," she said in between sniffles. She stuttered as she said, "I...I...smu...smu...smushed him."

Seth gently held her hands in his and slowly opened her fingers one by one until he could see the insect. One of its legs was broken, and it was not moving. He knew his sister well enough to know she would not be fooled by trickery. There was no way to convince her that the bug was still alive. So, he did the next best thing a big brother could; he officiated his very first funeral.

It took a while for Seth to find just the right tissue paper and ribbon. With the help of Azora, the small cardboard casket looked quite fancy. Azora said a sincere prayer, making sure everyone bowed their heads out of respect. Melissa was encouraged to give the eulogy which—once it was explained to her what a eulogy was—became the best made-up life story of a walking stick ever recited in Garland County.

Duly watched it all. He spent what seemed like days peeking into the other world, though it was merely a few moments in his own. He was oddly smitten with the family that lived next to the willow tree in the peculiar looking house.

He would never be able to explain the effect the vision had on him. He deeply wished he was more than a figment so he could actually interact with the people from the Earthly Realm. He never stopped thinking about them long after the vision ended.

Duly looked down at the loamy soil beneath his bare feet. The dirt felt soft between his short, stubby toes. He held onto the hammock that was still hanging under Willow's canopy and asked, "Is that what's happening right now, in the other world?"

"It was your vision, not mine. I don't know what was shown to you or why, but what I do know is that the time here and there is not the same."

Duly took a moment to contemplate what Willow had said and then changed the subject. "I hear you're one of the wisest, if not the wisest, beings anywhere in our realms."

"I am old, and I have existed for a long time. My roots go deep, and my branches stretch far into the sky. But wise? That is not for me to say. If the way I have lived and the things I have said bear fruit someday, then perhaps, then I might think…yes, I am, or perhaps I was, wise." Willow's leaves rustled.

Duly looked up and around at all the hanging branches. It was quite roomy underneath Willow's canopy. Sunrays trickled down from above, creating the perfect amount of natural light. It felt like a home, if not for him, certainly for all the mushrooms, brown rounds, and other little creatures living there.

"I heard that you sometimes create an image of yourself when speaking to others."

"Not of myself exactly. I can form a dreamlike reflection and sometimes I can manage a tableau that loosely mirrors those I'm speaking with. What you see now is my true image."

Duly reached up and ruffled a few low-hanging branches. The muscles in his face began to relax, and the edges of his lips even curled upwards as if they might eventually form a smile. "Whimsical limbs, flirty little leaves, curvy roots, and a gnarly trunk that feels delightful beneath my hand—quite beautiful just as you are."

"Thank you, Duly. My description of you might not be that much different."

The mushrooms giggled at the thought. "You know, I've never met a braewicker before," said Willow.

A brown round interrupted, squeaking as it rolled a large purple fruit toward Duly, which he immediately recognized. In the process of reaching for the delicious treat, the hammock teetered, and he fell to the ground, face first.

The mushrooms burst out with riotous laughter, as riotous as little fungi could. The short, awkward braewicker had the worst balance of anyone they ever saw.

"How nice that the soil that feeds you is as soft as the feathers I usually sleep on at home." He sat up on his knees and brushed the dirt from his clothing before taking his first bite of the purple fruit. "Home…I guess I have no home now," he said remorsefully as he finished standing.

"The Library of Truth was never meant to be a permanent residence for you. Have you no other home?"

"I haven't thought too much about any other home. I suppose my home will never be far from Beely, though I'm not sure Beely herself has one anymore… The Realms may never be the same—if they survive at all… Thank you for the vision you allowed me to see, Willow. I know what we are fighting for now. I will be more than a figment. I will show you someday that I know what love is."

Willow gently wrapped two thick limbs around Duly. He looked down at her branches and soon realized that she was giving him a hug. "These cynical little fungi are going to start calling you a sniblet-hugger," he said.

The time he spent with Willow was short, but it was some of the most peaceful hours of his life. He never sneezed nor coughed under her branches. It was because braewickers, or sniblets as some called them, lived under the ground and toiled in the dirt. They lived not in houses, caves, or libraries.

It would not be long until Duly once again toiled in the dirt, but he might never see Willow again after that day. Like Azora in the other world, he felt he and the other remaining Twelve might not be long for this realm, but for now, he had work to do—and very little time in which to do it.

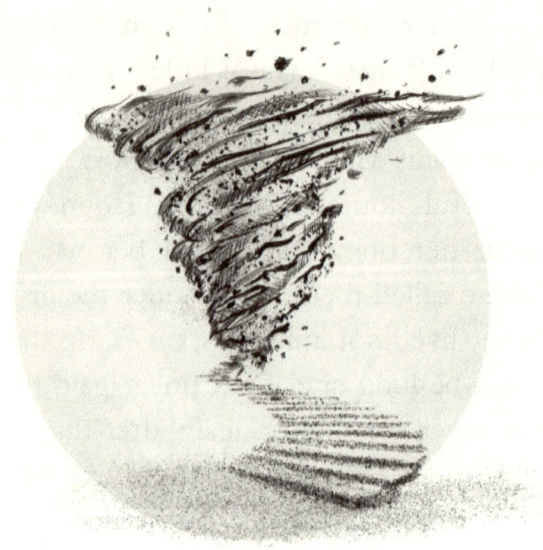

Chapter 15

The Prince of the Air

"Why did you have me meet you here?" asked Athaliah.

Mastad looked up into the air. "I'm considering this place for my new fortress. What do you think?"

Athaliah looked at Mastad. Then, turning in a slow circle until she faced him again, she asked, "Why?"

"No one and nothing around for as far as the eye can see." He was right; the entire area was free of any settlements. No one had ever lived there. It was not a place—even if there were a spring—that was hospitable to life. The few trees that

160

survived the Dry Death had been cut down to fuel Mastad's tyranny. There were few plants, no visible animals, and no creatures of any sort.

Athaliah stared down at the sterile ground. "Seems as good a spot as any, I suppose."

"Not down here." Mastad pointed up to the sky. "Up there." Mastad seemed more annoyed than usual. Athaliah had learned not to question his mood; it only intensified whatever was bothering him.

"You're going to build a tall fortress that reaches into the sky?"

"You will never get anywhere with that limited imagination of yours. Can't you dream bigger than tall buildings made by the hands of weaklings?"

She shrugged, which seemed to make him even more irritated. He bent down and scooped up a handful of dust, throwing it into the air. At first, the dust simply spun around, gathering more grains. Before too long, it turned into a small, howling tornado. The sand had formed steps which led into the devilish whirlwind.

Athaliah stood back in awe, one wing raised to shield herself from small stones that hurtled toward her. She was truly impressed. Was this ability due to Mastad's genetic alterations, or did he have some greater sorcery? She wondered if she too might someday be able to command the wind.

Mastad walked up the first few steps, the wind hissing with each one. He suddenly stopped and looked back down, as if he had forgotten something. As she tried to make sense of what he was doing, he was already back in front of her. The whirlwind, with its steps of sand, slowly dissipated.

All the while, Mastad's eyes kept darting about—left, right, then back again.

"Don't you hear it?" He frowned and shook his head in frustration. His large ears drooped as if they were trying to block whatever noise was bothering him.

Athaliah proceeded cautiously. "Hear what?"

"That excruciating noise." He paused as if she might acknowledge the intrusive sounds, and when she did not, he continued. "The singing. A thousand voices—no, a million—all shrieking blasphemous songs to Him!"

He bared his canines and clenched his teeth. "I must get away from that incessant noise."

It was never clear to Athaliah what Mastad was hearing. Those in his inner circle no longer spoke of the voices in his head. Those who had spoken of it—before he had them killed—thought he was going mad. They said he heard the voices of the saints singing praises to the Lord God.

Athaliah did not believe in God.

Mastad yelled to Athaliah in an attempt to be heard over the voices. He refused to believe no one else heard them. "I will build my home in the sky where the wind will drown the voices out."

Athaliah said nothing. She had no idea if he was serious or just venting his frustrations. His parlor trick with the dust and the wind looked nothing like a fortress. Perhaps he had figured out a way to suspend a structure in the sky. Maybe he was just trying to frustrate her with ridiculous nonsense—it would not have been the first time.

Either way, she did not care. Mastad grew more peculiar as the Realms continued to deteriorate beyond recognition. He had fully transitioned into the creature of his own making—the strongest Mastadonian of them all. He had conquered the Five

Realms of Here, and now it seemed, he was indeed going mad.

Athaliah's lips turned upward into a smile. She covered her mouth with a part of her wing so Mastad would not grow curious about her own mental state. She had one last job to do for her cousin, and after that, she would find a place far away from Okrad and Mastad.

But Mastad was much stronger now, forcing Athaliah to bide her time and her hatred until the opportunity to free herself came. She would continue to serve her master, but she had not come to indulge his whims or delusions. She was there to report on their progress.

"I have good news, Prince."

"I'll be the judge of that," he barked.

"Two of the Twelve have been exterminated."

"And what of her?" He was referring to Beely.

"She was not one of them. She escaped with the help of one of the great flying beasts. Their flight is as stealthy as ours; they are fast, strong, and difficult to track."

"I should have dissected those ridiculous-looking creatures, along with the chiropters. The Realms should have been purged of those…what do they call them…broraydings?"

"Yes. There are not many of them. Their numbers have always been few," said Athaliah.

"What of her mother, Marybah?"

"She was not harmed, per your request."

"Find the others, and Beely will be nearby. When they locate the painting, bring it to me, and then kill them all."

"Even Beely?"

"The prophecy says she will find the painting; it does not say she will keep it. I need her to find it, so that I may take it from her. After that, I don't care what you do with her. She is of no use to me, and she will have no power or followers to cause me any further consternation."

"I have it from a trustworthy source that some in the group are trying to find a Bible. It is not just the painting they are looking for. What do you know of this?"

"They are wasting their time. The Word has been eradicated. It no longer exists here; it is an impossibility." Mastad shook his head, as if to clear water from his ears. The noises inside were getting worse. He then raised his wings and lifted into the air, flying high into the sky. Athaliah watched for a moment and then followed. She found Mastad hovering. "Do you hear it?"

"I hear nothing but the sound of the wind and our wings," she answered.

"I do not like that they are wasting my time searching for a lost book that does not exist. It is time that could be spent on locating the painting."

"What would you have me do?"

"There is nothing you can do about that. But I do know of something else that would make you worthy of your designation."

"Yes?"

"Those woodland archers, from the High Forest…"

"What about them?"

"Kill them all. I want them ended for what they tried to do to me. Not one of them shall remain."

"Your wish is my command, Prince."

Mastad spread his dark black wings wide and rotated them one hundred eighty degrees at his shoulders. He retreated backward as his wings repeatedly traced a figure-eight motion. Athaliah was amazed at how quickly he had adapted to his new wings and his ability to fly. She hadn't even realized, until she

164

tried it a few moments later, that she too could fly backward. Without saying a final word, Mastad did a backward roll, heading toward the center of Okrad. He left her hovering without so much as a farewell. Her disdain of him would never wane.

She hovered for a few moments before rotating her wings and then repeating the same figure-eight motion as demonstrated by Mastad. Her body smoothly moved backward. It was both disorienting and oddly exhilarating. She never would have fathomed having such a skill, had she not seen it with her own eyes.

Her beloved chiropters, whose genetic coding was stolen and manipulated, were not able to fly in such a manner. She could not help but think about what other secret skills her cousin had cultivated. The thought aroused a sense of fear within her. Mastad purposefully demonstrated his abilities as a show of superiority. He would only do that, she reasoned, if he too was fearful of her.

She had little time to contemplate the possible implications of Mastad's machinations. Athaliah needed to keep her focus on their remaining adversaries with the added chore of exterminating the Woodland Archers.

No one had her interests or well-being in mind; not her own cousin and certainly not the remaining members of the Twelve. She was alone, and if she was to survive, she had to stay one step ahead of them all.

Chapter 16

ADRIEL

Joshua's sleek emerald-grey body glistened in the sun as if water was cascading off his leathery coat. Beely understood why her husband was enamored with these majestic creatures; they were beautiful in a way that touched the soul.

It was not just Joshua's physical appearance she noticed, but the way he moved. When changing directions, he did not simply turn, but rather wrapped his wings around the air as if caressing a long-lost friend. His tail did not whip around aimlessly, but instead moved in the same rhythm she felt undulating throughout his body. When he took a deep breath, she could feel the expansion of his lungs, and when he exhaled, the sound was like a thousand winds blowing gently through the trees.

"Why do you not always feel as safe as you feel right at this moment, dear one?"

Even though they were thousands of feet in the air, the voice coming from behind her was clear and commanding, as if it belonged to someone casually walking by her side. She turned to her right, and she could not believe her eyes.

The creature next to her was some type of bird that Beely had never seen before. It was completely white. It had feathers like the Roofah birds, but its eyes were round, and it had no discernible neck. This was the largest flying creature she had ever seen, with a wider wingspan than even her ray, Joshua. Yet the profound presence beside them made no sound as it effortlessly followed along beside them.

Joshua did not appear in the least bit concerned by such a formidable creature flying so close. Perhaps, Beely thought, Joshua and the other rays had met this creature on one of their many skyward adventures. Either way, Beely felt secure as long as she was with Joshua. She knew nothing bad would happen to her.

She stared deep into the large, round, golden eyes of their visiting neighbor and asked, "Who are you?"

"My name is Adriel."

"Which realm are you from? I have never seen anyone like you before," Beely asked.

"I am not from your realm or any of the five realms you know," he answered. His wings were so large and strong that he seemed to almost glide next to the ray, while Joshua, with his heavier load, had to work his wings much harder.

"Are you joining us? Are you here to help fight against the evil that has overtaken these realms?"

"I have always been near, as many of my kind have, but while we may intercede from time to time, it is not the will of the One who has always been that we should be more than we are. On this occasion, I am a messenger sent to minister to one of God's chosen."

"Obviously you know how desperate things have become, or you would not be showing yourself. Forgive me, but time is a luxury we no longer have. If you are not here to join us in battle, I'm not sure how you could be of much help." After Beely said this, Joshua bucked lightly, causing Beely to lose her balance. She took hold of his horn, and her shoulders dropped. "I spoke unwisely, and most of all, ungraciously. Please forgive me, Adriel." She patted Joshua's back and added, "With this guy underneath me, I will find my way."

"You, Beely Rembre, were given so much, yet you took so little."

"I don't understand."

"What did your father teach you? What was the one lesson that he repeated every day, while all the other teachings changed with the seasons?"

Beely took a moment to reflect. A knowing smile slowly overtook her face. "To pray."

"And?"

"He always read the Word, every day," she said, still smiling.

"Yet, you have not done enough of either. The Word should not be gone from your world, and that is not the fault of the one pursuing you."

"Whose fault is it then?" Beely's smile faded, and she sighed because she knew the answer.

"The fault is yours," said Adriel.

Beely's countenance immediately changed, her shoulders sank lower, and her eyes dropped to the ground. She was not surprised by Adriel's directness, but she was disheartened. "Yes, I know." She paused and ran her hand along Joshua's smooth coat before looking back at Adriel. "I don't know where or when or even why I lost my way."

"The Word would not have been lost had you committed it to your heart. Did you know that in the other world, God's chosen people often memorized the inspired scriptures? The Word could never be taken away from them, but I fear times are changing there as well. The Word is not hiding; the people are no longer looking." Adriel lowered his head and dove down toward the ground. Joshua followed, remaining by his side, as if he knew it was his place.

"Don't worry, dear child, He did not send me to condemn you. You must have confidence that the way will never be lost. You are His, and you will never be taken from Him. I am here to remind you that your faith in Him will be your victory."

"Is my faith enough to save the Realms?"

"Faith is enough to save anyone, but your faith will be tested far greater than you could ever imagine. You must remain strong, and you must endure."

Beely felt Reverie pushing on the flap of her satchel. Reverie had not been herself for days and nights. Without the routine delivery of her medicine, she had become weak. Beely gently rubbed her head and took her out, holding her in one arm. "This little girl is Reverie; she is quite ill. I bring her with me everywhere, even when I ride Joshua."

"I know this one; she has brought much comfort and joy to you."

"How could you know such a thing?"

"I know many things. She has much life left in her, you need not worry."

"No, I'm afraid you're wrong. The Roofahs told me she will die soon."

Adriel hooted loudly. The hoots mimicked a type of laughter. Beely flinched at the loud outburst and was unsure what it meant. Before she could ask, Adriel nodded and said, "Hold her up toward me."

Beely hesitated, but it was obvious by Reverie's squirming that the empachic wanted to get closer to the great bird. Beely wrapped one arm around Joshua's horn to keep herself steady while she lifted Reverie with the other. Beely was saddened at how much weight Reverie had lost from her illness, yet it made it effortless to raise her up over her head.

Her fur flowed wildly with the wind, but Beely's grip was sure. Reverie was as confident as ever, enjoying the wind as well as the view. Adriel eased closer until the tiny empachic and the great bird came face to face.

When the two touched, a faint, warm glow lit the faces of both creatures. Adriel rubbed his pale bill on the frail empachic just before gently pulling out one fine hair from Reverie's head. The glow stayed with Reverie as Beely lowered her back down into her arms.

Beely looked back to Adriel with a tear slowly rolling down her cheek. She watched as he released part of Reverie, still aglow, spiraling upward out of sight.

"Fear not, God knows every hair on your head. Take good care of her, she has much work left to do," Adriel said.

Beely, upon later reflection, was not sure who Adriel was talking to.

Reverie immediately started to vibrate more than she had in many cycles of the moons. Beely pushed the hair back from her face, revealing Reverie's eyes. The cloudy grey had given way to the vibrant green of her youth.

"Is this why you came, to heal Reverie?"

"Do you think you yourself are a figment, Beely Rembre?"

"I don't think it matters what I think, if I were to think about it at all, which I don't."

Joshua began descending toward a tall, singular monolith on a shallow plateau along the canyon wall. They had arrived at their destination. Adriel followed.

When they were all on the ground, Beely slid off the great beast, taking special care with Reverie. She watched Adriel carefully walk to the plateau's edge and look down at the canyon floor below. Adriel twisted his head, cautious not to slip.

Beely looked at him curiously. "For someone who can fly, why do you look terrified? It's not as if you could fall to your death."

Adriel hooted with laughter once again. "I like to imagine what life is like for those with more limitations than myself. One day, there will be those who will fall from this very spot."

"Really?"

"Yes, many, actually."

"No, I meant, do you really like to imagine such things?"

"I do. It's a fascination I have. To imagine what life would be like with so many limitations. Life is often dangerous. Do you know the 23rd Psalm? It is contained in the Old Testament."

Beely shrugged. "I'm sorry, I'm not sure."

"You will need to know who God is now more than ever. You have lost two, and you will soon lose more of those allied with you. You think we have seen the worst, but the Prince of the Air has only just begun, and he will not stop until he finishes."

Reverie poked her head out of the satchel, and Beely pulled

her as close to her heart as possible. Her loud vibrations caused Beely's eyes to widen as she relaxed and took a deep breath of fresh air. Reverie squeaked joyfully as she showed off her miraculously renewed strength by effortlessly jumping to the ground. Beely poured water from her carrier vine into a small cup, which Reverie quickly lapped up while Adriel recited scripture.

> *"'The Lord is my shepherd; I have all that I need. He lets me rest in green meadows; He leads me beside peaceful streams. He renews my strength. He guides me along right paths, bringing honor to his name. Even when I walk through the darkest valley, I will not be afraid, for you are close beside me. Your rod and your staff protect and comfort me. You prepare a feast for me in the presence of my enemies. You honor me by anointing my head with oil. My cup overflows with blessings.'"*

"My father recited those verses many times. I didn't know it was called the 23rd Psalm. He, like you, had them committed to memory."

"I need you to do as your father did. I need you to hide these verses deep in your heart, where they will never be lost or stolen."

"I will… and we will find the painting and bring back the Word. I don't know these messengers spoken of by the prophets, but I will do everything in my power to make sure we are ready for them when they come."

Beely paused to look out over the vast canyon. "Have you been to this place before, Adriel? I know my father was here. Why did he not think to leave a Holy Book in this place?"

"I have not been here. But I have known of its existence.

Your father was wise, but he did not know everything. What he did know was that prophecy states that the Word would return with those from where the Christ lived—where the very Word Himself would lower Himself to human form, die, and conquer death."

Beely remained silent for a moment as she picked up Reverie's empty cup. She watched as the now energetic empachic playfully teased Joshua by pouncing on his tail. Beely walked up to Adriel, shaking her head in frustration.

"What am I supposed to do?"

"I am only here to show you that you are not alone. You have been chosen to fulfill the prophecy, and you only need to believe."

"And what if I am just a figment? What if that's what we all are? Will it make any difference what anyone here does?"

"I thought you didn't think about such things." Adriel walked over to the monolith as its shadow began to spread.

Beely followed him. "I don't, but others do. They say that is why Mastad is so angry. He wants to take over the other world where the two testaments were written. He will not settle for being less than the chosen ones."

"All I will say is what you already know and what Mastad will never learn. It all begins with the imagination. The manifestation of what becomes starts in the mind. What happens in the Realms—the good and the bad—all of it matters. 'We capture their rebellious thoughts and teach them to obey Christ.'"

"God has made Himself known to me. I cannot depart from that. He is good. All that is good, in thought or in deed, comes from our Lord. I will always serve Him and Him alone. So, if that's what you came to find out about me, now you know."

Adriel opened one of his wings and pulled Beely close until they were nearly face to face.

"I resemble what is known as an owl in the other world. They assume I am wise because of my heightened senses and my ability to see through darkness. Truth be told, I am no wiser than any other who seeks the Lord with all of his heart and mind. You will not see me again until all has been accomplished. The journey is as important as the arrival, and everything works for good for those who love the Lord. You must remember these things when all seems lost."

"Why can't you stay with us?"

"We all have our paths. Mine has already been determined, and yours is yet before you. Your love for others and your love for the Father will light your path."

"I understand," said Beely.

When she bent down to pick up Reverie, she noticed the monolith's shadow was almost fully formed. She and Reverie would need to cross over it and into the secret hiding place soon. She looked back up to find that Adriel was near the edge of the plateau.

"One last thing, it may seem odd, but you must make sure it gets done."

"If I can, of course."

"Have the beavers build a small boat and place it in the shadow place. The Messengers will be in need of it when they come."

"I know so little of these Messengers; can you tell me more about them?"

"You know enough. They have their mission and you have yours. Bless you, dear one. What you need to know is that His faithfulness, no matter what comes your way, will keep you forever under His wings."

Beely watched as the great white owl lifted off the small canyon wall and soared through the air. She heard him, quite some distance away, call out with one last hoot. This hoot sounded not like laughter but like a trumpet—an announcement of the coming battle.

Chapter 17

DECIMATION AND DELIVERANCE

Three nights had passed since the Roofah bird brought the worst possible news. Two fathers—beloved husbands and cherished members of the close-knit Shirk clan—would never be coming home. The loss was devastating, yet the Shirks seemed resilient.

As Zorian waited for the ceremony to begin, his thoughts drifted to Max—the one who had insisted they find the Shirks to seek their support in defeating Mastad. He could still hear Max's voice as they entered the High Forest: "If we don't get to Mastad first, he'll kill every last one of us. I'd end his life tomorrow if I could—but I can't do it alone. And I sure can't

176

do it with two three-hundred-pound beavers and a giant so tall you can see him coming from another realm!"

The Shirks, with their unmatched archery and stealth, were their best hope—and everyone knew it. But Zorian also knew Max's urgency wasn't just strategic. He was afraid for Beely. Whatever Mastad had against her, it went beyond his lust for power—it was personal.

A voice snapped Zorian out of his thoughts.

"He should be here," said Rosie, the wife of one of the fallen archers. She was perched on a low tree limb just above Zorian—so close that he flinched at the sound of her voice.

"He has lost many loved ones as well," said Zorian. "Too many to count. Maximilian is a good man; if he could have been here, he would have."

"He asked you to stay behind in case Mastad retaliates, am I right?" Rosie asked.

"You are." Zorian tried his best to speak softly. He did not want to cause any distraction from the upcoming funeral. "I promise you, Rosie, I will remain here as long as necessary to help protect you all."

"We are strong enough to protect ourselves. We should never have allowed outsiders into our village," she said remorsefully.

The wind, with no leaves on the trees to slow its flow, blew Zorian's hair into his eyes. He brushed it back, only to have it fall onto his face again. "Max made a mistake. He knows it."

Rosie held onto a branch as she leaned over toward the giant. "Let me see your hand." Zorian lifted his hand up in front of Rosie. "Or in your case, a finger will do." She rubbed an arrow along his finger. "It's tree resin mixed with other woodland oils. Good for many things. A little goes a long way, even for a giant."

He looked at her with his brow furrowed and shrugged, "What do I do with it?"

"Rub it through your hair and it will keep the wind from blowing it about. It will help you look a little more presentable for our memorial."

He smelled the resin on his finger and then rubbed it onto both of his hands before massaging it into his unruly mane. "Sticky."

"That's the point…What about you? Do you have any loved ones wherever it is you come from?"

"I have a wife and several children; the youngest is almost fully grown. They are with the other giants amongst the Mara People."

"Why do you do this? If time is limited, why not spend the last of it with your family?"

"I do this for the same reason as the other eleven as well as your husband and Rodear. We do it because it is the right thing to do." Zorian's nostrils flared, and he looked back toward the village. The smell of roasted meat filled the air. It had been a while since he had eaten a good meal. The Woodland Shirks were even better at hunting than Max and Eudox.

"There is always much food after a ceremony. I think they made extra," she said.

He smiled. "If you haven't noticed, we giants don't eat any more than you small folk."

"But you eat more than greens; you do eat meat, yes?"

"We love meat."

Rosie stood up on the limb to get a better view of those preparing for the ceremony below. "I don't buy it."

"Really, it's true. We don't eat as much as what most people think."

"No, I don't buy it that you just do it because it's the right thing to do."

"That's because you don't believe," he said.

"Believe? In God?" She paused a moment and sat back down on the branch near Zorian's head. "How did you know?"

"It's impossible to know the heart of another; only God knows the heart. Yet, I think if you believed, you would know that the truth is worth fighting for. It's really all that we have. None of us are long for this world, Rosie, Mastad or not. If there is no God, none of this would matter, and you are correct, I would not be here with a Woodland Archer whispering into my ear from a tree. I would be home with those whom I love and with those whom I would never see again when this life is over…if I didn't believe."

"I admire you as I admired my Sam. He had so much faith."

"It would have only been a matter of time before Mastad's warriors found you, whether we came or not."

Rosie stood up on the thick branch for the last time and looked out over the hill. "We'll never know, now, will we?" She said nothing more. Zorian was not sure if his comment angered her. He wished he had never said it. When he looked back, she was gone, having left to join her family, he assumed.

A traditional ceremony was given for Sam and Rodear. A final farewell without the bodies of the deceased was a first for the Shirks, and it only helped make an already heartbreaking occasion worse. Traditionally, the deceased would be cremated and their ashes released with seven arrows over the hill to a place known as the Never Ending. Even without the ashes, the bows were still bent.

Though the trees were no longer green and there were none

of the usual hillside flowers, the memorial was the most beautifully profound Zorian had ever been a part of. Several hundred Shirks stood in solidarity with a confidence and serenity that should not have been. Only people who believed in an almighty, wonderful God could face such loss so valiantly. They played their stringed instruments, and they sang in harmonies that echoed throughout the dead woods, rumbling deep into every nook and cranny.

As the Shirks plucked the strings of their wooden instruments, Zorian felt the vibrations resonate through his chest like a quiet storm. Rosie, in the crowd below, glanced back and caught the giant wiping away a tear just before it fell. He clenched his fists, forcing his emotions inward—after all, a weeping giant was never a welcome sight.

As the first seven arrows took flight, the Shirks sang:

"From dirt we come, through air we go. We
feed the roots and help the woodlands grow."

The somber cadence only deepened the ache in Zorian's heart. He longed to gather everyone present into a single, fierce embrace. Instead, he bowed his head and whispered a prayer: that he might be strong enough to help these people when the time came.

Even if Zorian had lived long enough to tell what happened after the ceremony, he would have kept it forever to himself. The gentle giant would have only shared the virtuous things. He would have described how the arrows sailed high into the air and far over the hill. He would have told how the songs and music touched his soul, and how his respect and love for a people he had just met gave him new resolve to fight Mastad even harder.

He would have shared the beautiful stories about his new friends, the Woodland Shirks, but he would have never, ever told anyone what happened a few days after.

All of the Shirks were thought to have been exterminated by the heartless Mastadonians. There were not supposed to be any survivors, and that is what the Mastadonians reported back to Mastad. They did not lie to their master; they could not have known that the smallest of the Shirk children were safely hidden away. No one ever knew how they found the village, or the details of how the merciless murderers desecrated the Shirks, killing almost every one of them. The details would have been too horrid to share, and the only survivors were too young to remember.

Mastad, in his unbridled fury for revenge, wanted all of the Woodland Shirks killed. Had the Dry Death not forced the Shirks to dig a deep pit to contain their fires, he might have gotten his wish. Max knew that it was only a matter of time before the Mastadonians found the village, and that was why Zorian volunteered to remain behind to help protect them.

The night the village was raided, Zorian had very little time to react. They took out the Shirk sentinels so quietly, that there was no warning. It happened just before bedtime when most of the children were still with Zorian. The children loved the giant and stuck by his side until their parents ordered otherwise.

That night, when they came, Zorian was with ten of the smallest children telling tales of the giants. How the children loved stories about giants, especially the dwarf giants.

"And then," said Zorian with his eyes as wide as they could go, "an Abaddon—the name of the dwarf giants—went all the way under the water and held his breath like this…"

Zorian loudly filled his lungs with air and held for a moment before continuing. "Now, giants have big lungs and they can hold their breath for a very long time, but he was down for way too long, even for a giant."

"What happened to him?" shouted Audrey, holding her blanket so tight that her knuckles had turned white.

"No one knows. His body was never found. But on the nights when the first moon is but a crescent, rumors tell of a ghostly white figure that comes and steals the shoes of little boys and girls who don't eat all of their greenies."

Ticor, the oldest of the children, frowned and shook his head. "That's not a true story! Dwarf giants don't even wear shoes."

"Well, your memory is strong, Ticor. But that doesn't mean they don't like shoes," said Zorian.

"That's not a very scary story," said Audrey, crossing her arms.

There was suddenly a loud scream coming from the far edge of the village. All of the children stiffened and craned their necks toward the frightening sound. Before Zorian had even a moment to assess the situation, Rosie came running out of the darkness.

The last flame of the fire had faded, but there was just enough light to see the urgency in Rosie's eyes. She had a bow in hand with an arrow already nocked. She spoke quickly as she caught her breath. "Children, the enemy has come into our village. You must stay with Zorian, he will protect you. Do everything he says and he will keep you safe."

Audrey, gripping her blanket even tighter, ran to Rosie. "I want my daddy. Where is my daddy?"

"Ticor, come get your sister. Both your mother and father

are positioned well, we will all be fine." It was a lie, but one that would calm the children long enough for her to speak to Zorian.

Ticor took his sister by the shoulder and looked up at Rosie with the meanest scowl he could muster. "I know how to bend a bow as well as anyone. I am not a child."

"I don't have time to argue, Ticor. It's true, you could fight, but your fight is here, to help Zorian protect these little ones." Rosie's face flinched as if in pain. As Rosie was pleading with Ticor, Zorian gently touched her leg and the unmistakable feel of blood warmed his finger.

"I must go with you," pleaded Zorian. "I could wipe out many of them before they take me down."

"No!" demanded Rosie. She reached for his hand. Zorian ever so gently lifted her up so she could whisper into his ear.

"Our only chance for survival is these children. I have never seen such warriors. There is no defeating them on this night. I pray for a miracle to slow them long enough for your escape. Now set me down and say not another word."

Just as he set her on the ground and before she turned to join the battle, she looked up at Zorian and loudly proclaimed, "I know you were right, giant. They would have come sooner or later, it is not your fault nor the fault of the Twelve. Your faith and your kindness here today have given me hope that there is indeed a God!"

Rosie, even with her wound, was fast and furious. She disappeared into the darkness leaving Zorian in need of the most profound miracle he could hope for.

The large moon had set, and the only light was from the smaller moon's fading reflection off the canyon wall. The dark night, the surprise attack, and the chaos all worked in the favor of the wicked. Unlike the Shirks, Zorian could have survived to live another day. They were not looking for giants, and he was fast enough and strong enough to escape, perhaps even holding as many as five children.

Yet ten children—that was not the miracle he had in mind.

The thought came to him immediately: the Fiery Furnace. It was a story his mother had retold countless times from the Old Testament about three men who refused to worship a false god and in turn were thrown into a furnace to die, only to be saved by the Lord God Himself.

He heard Shirk arrows spinning in the air and the occasional thump when one hit its fleshly target, but very few invaders fell. The children were all huddled around him, grabbing hold of whatever part of him they could. Piercing cries echoed throughout the darkened village, just after the sounds of swords leaving their sheaths. He knew he could not shield the youngest Shirks from the Mastadonians. He had to hide them, and quickly. Even if he were somehow able to carry ten children, they would never make it out of the woods alive.

The revelation of why his mother repeated the Biblical story of the Fiery Furnace so many times hit him like a sledgehammer. God was preparing Zorian for this moment all those turnings ago.

The smallest of the children clung to his ankles. Zorian could feel their tiny hands desperately pulling at his clothing. He whispered but was loud enough to be heard over the torturous sounds coming from all around them. "Do you believe what your parents taught you about our God? Do you have faith that God will protect you?"

The children futilely stared into the darkness all around them, confused by the unmistakable sounds of arrows flying through the air and the foreign sounds they had never heard before, the sounds of death. The answer to Zorian's questions eventually came through sobs and sniffles. Audrey, the last to answer, wiped her nose with the back of her hand before whispering, "You will protect us, Zorian."

His heart sank. In only a few days he had already fallen in love with these children. "Yes, we will be saved, but not by my hand, by His." Zorian pointed to the heavens with his giant hand. "I have faith He will see us through."

Zorian said a prayer so fast that the children only understood a few words, but God understood them all.

"Dear Lord, if it is your will, I pray that you save these children. I pray that the coals of these last burning embers would do nothing but keep your children warm until daybreak. I pray that Your Spirit will stay with them, as you did with your servants Shadrach, Meshach, and Abednego. Your will and your way, our Lord."

After he finished his prayer, he took a large, thick blanket and placed it over the hot coals. Without a miracle, he knew the blanket would burn along with all the children, but he believed God would honor his prayer.

He tore the smallest child from his leg as she desperately wailed, and placed her on the blanket in the center of the pit. The rest followed until the pit was full. Ticor hesitated for a moment, until Zorian's large, tear-filled eyes caught his, and Ticor knew, there was no other way.

He took hold of two children who were weeping and embraced them tightly as he motioned for the others to lay down as flat as possible. Zorian then laid over the top of them all as a hen would cover her brood. The deep pit with the surrounding clay rim was completely covered. Zorian spoke to the children one last time, giving them instructions to stay quiet, to pray, and what to do when it was all over.

Then he prayed again.

The Mastadonians thought it strange to find a giant among the Shirks, but their pleasure in killing him was no more or less gratifying. The gentle giant never raised an arm against the many swords that ripped through his flesh, and it took many swords to stop his breath.

The pit had to remain completely covered no matter the pain that was inflicted upon its guardian. He never cursed his enemies, but rather prayed for them until his lungs filled with blood. It was the prayers that distracted the murdering horde. They could not understand how the giant would pray for them while they inflicted such pain. It never occurred to them to look under his lifeless body.

The children remained quiet and motionless until the warmth of the coals had dissipated. Zorian told them that once the coals turned cold to join together and push through his legs. He instructed them to find their way to the Never Ending over the hill and to stay there until help arrived.

The miracle of the children who survived the Fiery Pit and the giant who prayed for those that killed him, would be remembered for eternity. No one, without the blessing of God, could have survived sitting on burning coals through an entire night. The miracle sparked a newfound hope for those remaining in the Five Realms of Here and the spark turned into a flame that would never burn out. It was the miracle that united all those battling against Mastad to never give up.

Chapter 18

REUNITED

Maximilian walked through the door as if he had been there a hundred times before. He slowly scanned the room until his eyes stopped at Duly. "Where is she?" Maximilian eased his pack to the ground and waited for an answer. Thai, still tucked away in Max's pack, peeked out through the loose flap. Saint Elmo and Francis brushed past Max. They had never before been behind the shadow to the secret hiding place.

"It's nice to see you too," barked Duly. "How in the realms did you find us?" He did not bother to lift his head. He remained focused on the puzzle piece between his small, gnarly fingers. "She won't come out. She's been back there for two days." He nodded in the general direction. "She hasn't eaten;

she's talked to no one. Of course, there has been no one else to talk to but me."

"We have a lot of news, most of it not good," said Max.

Duly finally looked up, taking a moment to assess everyone and everything. He looked at Max, then at Francis with her multiple packs, and finally at Saint Elmo. He shrugged and went back to his puzzle. "Your news couldn't be any worse than ours. You didn't answer my question: how did you find us?"

"Thai, of course." Max set his satchel on a nearby chair and inhaled deeply. It had been a very long day on his ray. "Empachics! They never cease to amaze me." He gave Thai a gentle scratch behind his ears. "Thai found the cliff. Beely gave me very detailed instructions on the shadow quite some time ago. I never thought I would actually see the place, though."

The beavers looked around, admiring the better-than-expected accommodations. It was much larger and well-appointed than one would have guessed by looking at the plain entry door and the fact that it was located on a cliffside in the middle of nowhere.

"Well, I am famished!" exclaimed Francis. "I'm sure you boys are hungry as well. I see there's some wood by the cooking stove, and the pantry can't be too far off." She headed toward the stove, and when Saint Elmo did not follow, she turned and gave him a stern look. He gave his wife a knowing glance, then looked at Max and Duly before resigning to Francis's nonverbal command to follow.

Max sat in the chair next to Duly. He picked up a puzzle piece, one that Duly had been trying to place for quite some time, and immediately snapped it into place. "What is she doing?"

"As best as I can tell, she's been praying. For days, she's

done nothing but pray," answered Duly.

"I thought you said she wasn't talking to anyone?"

Ignoring Max's comment, Duly picked up a cup from the table and walked toward the back cave wall where a spring trickled into a small basin. "Was the giant too big to pass over the shadow?" He dipped his cup into the basin and took a drink before returning to his chair.

The beavers, upon hearing the reference to Zorian, suddenly halted their activities in the kitchen. Before Max had time to answer Duly, everyone turned to look at Beely, who had just entered the main cavern. She was dressed comfortably and had her hair down, without its characteristic braiding. To Max's surprise, she appeared refreshed and relaxed. No one said a word; they just stared at Beely. "Well, what is everyone looking at?" she asked with little feeling.

The beavers immediately looked down and resumed their busy work, or at the very least acted as if they were busy doing something other than looking back and forth between Max and Beely with an occasional glance at Duly, who was still piecing together his puzzle.

"Zorian has been killed." Max swallowed hard before continuing. "A Roofah brought us the news. Not just Zorian. Almost the entire population of the Woodland Shirks has been murdered."

Duly finally stopped with his puzzle long enough to sneak a glance at Beely, who hid her expression well. He could read nothing on her face.

Max continued, "It wasn't enough that Mastad has destroyed the entire Five Realms of Here, but he wouldn't stop there. He's still killing. He attempted to wipe out an entire race of innocents. He will never stop until everyone is dead! There is no time to waste."

Max pounded his fist on the wooden table so hard that Duly's puzzle pieces flew in every direction. This made an already uptight Duly take hold of the arms of his chair, bracing himself for the second hit, which he knew was coming. The second table-breaking blow came with a gut-wrenching cry. Duly's hands sprang up, covering his face. Thai, whose head had been poking out of Max's satchel, quickly buried himself.

The momentary silence was far louder than Max's outburst. Beely eventually looked up with a sigh and broke the silence with very little emotion. "Don't worry about the table. We can use the wood to make a boat."

Beely walked over to Francis and greeted her with a traditional beaver nose rub. Francis glanced over at Max before giving Beely an awkward hug. "I didn't think beavers hugged," said Beely.

Saint Elmo grinned from ear to ear and nodded. "I always thought the Missus was allergic to hugs."

"You are a sight for sore eyes," said Francis as she took a step back to look Beely over.

Beely walked toward her husband, whom she had not seen for many moons. "You are correct. We have no time to waste. I miscalculated how insanely evil and destructive our demonic nemesis has become."

She stood in front of Maximilian, and he slowly took her face into his hands. She wrapped her arms around him until she clung fiercely, as though letting go would undo everything. Duly and Saint Elmo looked down, feeling somewhat uncomfortable with the affectionate display. Francis, on the other hand, looked upon the couple's reunion fondly.

Max whispered in his wife's ear. "I've missed you."

Beely gently slid her fingers under his long, thick hair and rubbed the back of his neck in the secret spot only she knew. She held onto him tightly, pushing her face into his broad chest. She did not want the others to see the tears falling from her eyes. The attempt was unsuccessful as well as unnecessary.

Francis was the first to offer an encouraging word. "No one could have foreseen the massacre of our dear friend Zorian or Woodland Shirks. One would need to imagine an evil far beyond the imaginable. I, for one, find solace that we cannot see such demons and the work they conjure."

Duly, halfheartedly preparing to shield his face once again, if necessary, spoke with reservation. "I suppose the Roofah also informed you of Cloy and Eudox."

It was obvious to both Duly and Beely by their reactions that they had indeed heard the solemn news. Francis bowed her head and placed her hand on Saint Elmo's chest. Max had no words, but his eyes spoke volumes. They all moved around the now-broken table. One by one, they sank into their seats, the silence heavier than words could bear.

Reverie, having sensed the mood in the room from afar, bounded out of the hallway that led to the pantry. She quickly found her way to Beely. Thai slowly wandered over to Max, but not before weaving around several ankles and jumping up and down with Reverie, unable to contain his squeaks.

Max, not one to beat around the bush, brought up what was on everyone's minds. "Both Cloy and Eudox knew the dangers of our mission, and Zorian even more so. The only safe thing to do would be to remain hidden, but even that is only temporary. There was, and there is, no other choice; we must continue doing whatever we can to regain our freedom, no matter the consequences."

When no one else had anything to add, Max leaned over and ruffled Reverie's fur. "She sure is looking better."

"We met an angel of the Lord," answered Beely. She took a deep breath and brushed a loose strand of hair from her face.

"What? When?" Saint Elmo and Francis asked, almost in unison.

"It was larger than a ray, pure white, some type of bird," answered Beely.

Duly was immediately taken aback. "Why didn't you tell me this?"

Max interrupted, "How did you know it was an angel?"

"Because he told me as much," she answered.

The beavers and Duly exchanged glances, but Max remained focused on Beely. "Why would an angel of the Lord come to you now?"

"Why not now?" said Duly. "We are losing; if not now, when?"

"Fair enough, Duly," said Max. "What did this angel say?"

"For starters, I know he was an angel, not just because of what he said, but because he also healed Reverie. There was a glow when he touched her. It was beautiful," said Beely.

"She does look amazing," said Max.

"The way she came bouncing into the room, yes, I would say she is in tip-top health," added Saint Elmo, who had already begun examining the broken table for the purposes of transforming it into a vessel capable of floating.

"Adriel, that was his name. He knew about the two of you," she said, looking at the beavers.

"Us?" asked Francis. Her voice went higher than usual; a sure sign she was delighted.

"He wanted me to tell you to build a small boat. Don't ask

me why," said Beely.

This made Saint Elmo smile. "Say no more." As the others continued quietly processing their losses and contemplating the future, Saint Elmo retrieved the gifts that the Woodland Shirks had collected for them. He rifled noisily through the rucksack until Francis shot him a look. Fortunately, he quickly found what he was looking for and held it up for everyone to see. "Shirk resin!" he proclaimed. "It'll go a long way in making our boat waterproof."

The reaction was not the joyous one he had expected. It did nothing but remind everyone of the dear Woodland Shirks. Francis shook her head and rolled her eyes as her husband subtly returned the resin to the rucksack. Duly paid them no attention. He began tapping his fingers nervously on his knee. The loss of Zorian, along with Eudox and Cloy, created more urgency. He thought of the vision he had of the Earthly Realm and the key that the young ones found. He felt that time was running out, and he had to finish what he started. "I need to get back to the Library of Truth."

"When we get the Bible, we'll all take it back there with you," said Max.

"No, I will go there first and you all will bring me the Book. I know the last bit of work that needs to be done to the hidden room. I need to make it so only one special key can open the door."

"What key?" asked Beely.

"A key that the Messengers will bring with them when they come here. The Messengers that will reveal the Words that will save both our realms and theirs."

"I thought you didn't believe in the Word or prophecy," said Beely.

"Willow showed me something. A glimpse into the other world. I believe what I saw was real. The Messengers will come, and we must be ready for them." Without another word, Duly got on his hands and knees and began picking up the pieces of the puzzle that had fallen from the table.

"That's it? That's all you have to say?" Max only half expected an answer, and when none came, he joined Duly on the floor to help him pick up the other pieces. Thai and Reverie seemed to want to help, but they only frustrated Duly by inadvertently scattering the pieces further.

Beely noticed Duly's growing frustration and picked up the empachics, holding them in her arms. "That's fine, Duly. It sounds as though you have determined your course. We will drop you off on our way to meet the others."

Francis, who had already begun lighting the stove to prepare dinner, stopped to ask, "Others?"

Beely nodded. "Propo, Lira, Leopold, and Malora."

"Do we know where they are?" asked Saint Elmo.

"No, but I know where they will be, and we need to make sure we don't miss them when they get there," she said.

"And how do you know where they will be? We haven't had word from them since we separated," said Max as he handed over a handful of his collection to Duly.

Duly spotted another puzzle piece under a chair. He made his way over to it, carefully crawling to avoid dropping the ones in his hand. Just as he picked it up, Thai jumped from Beely's arms and bumped into Duly, sending pieces everywhere. Beely's shoulders tensed, Max raised his eyebrows, Francis lifted her hands to cover her mouth, and Saint Elmo tried in vain to keep from chuckling. Duly simply sat up and stared at the cave wall, with his back to the others.

It was not until the following morning that they would learn that one piece remained lost. Duly spent the entire night looking for it, but he never spoke another word about the puzzle.

He simply let it remain incomplete on the floor with a part of some type of animal missing. There was an ear and a body with a long tail attached, but no head to reveal the completed creature. It was a fantastical image of creatures and fauna that did not exist in the Five Realms, only in someone's imagination.

In Mastad's realms, such art was forbidden. But behind the shadow, in the hidden cave, no unrighteous laws could silence words or imagination.

It was the next morning that Francis and Saint Elmo noticed that there was a change in Max and Beely. Over morning tea, Francis discussed how the unfinished puzzle perfectly illuminated their current circumstances.

Francis spoke at length, while the others listened in thoughtful silence. She spoke of how the love between Maximilian and Beely had grown since she and Saint Elmo first met them. Only the challenges they faced together could have brought them so close.

Beavers mate for life, she explained. No matter the challenges or lack thereof, there is no divorce among beavers as they have an instinct that often supersedes the sometimes-ill-fated choices of free will. God, Francis waxed, allows the challenges of the missing pieces to make His children stronger and more faithful.

Duly, who had remained respectfully quiet up to that point, scoffed.

Beely was appreciative of what Francis had to say, but there was little time for philosophical whimsy. Since Duly was still not speaking, she told the others of how he learned of the whereabouts of their friends when he visited Willow a few moons ago. Willow continued to receive news from all over the Realms from her winged visitors.

Max asked, in the most unassuming way possible, "Why didn't Adriel the Angel just tell you what we need to know? Why must we rely on rumors floating in the air?"

Beely flashed the one-sided smile that she often gave when stating something she felt was obvious. "Sometimes it seems not to matter what we know, as much as it matters to have faith in moving forward."

Max furrowed his brow. "What is that supposed to mean?"

Francis interrupted, pouring more Ognatia into Max's cup. "If one has enough faith, Maximilian, it has been told that they can move mountains."

"That's fine," said Max, stopping to take a sip of his hot tea. "I just want to know where the mountain is."

Saint Elmo playfully slapped Max on the back with his large, oval tail, causing a bit of tea to splash from his cup. "Wait 'til you've been married as long as I have, you won't ask where the mountain is. You'll ask how high you'll need to climb to make it to the top," said Saint Elmo with a chuckle.

Francis looked at Saint Elmo with her hand on her hip. "What is that supposed to mean—"

"Found it!" exclaimed a muffled Duly. They all turned to see nothing but the feet of Duly sticking out of a large ceramic vase next to the basin. It did not matter to Duly that he was stuck. "For Duly, nothing else mattered—he had finally found the missing piece."

Chapter 19

THE SALT VILLAGE

"Have you ever felt this free?" yelled Beely as she joyfully lifted her hands into the air. She and Joshua were flying beside Francis, who was on her own ray and was anything but joyful.

Francis maintained a death grip on the horn of her ray. She could barely muster the courage to turn her head and look at Beely. Her stomach was churning, and she could feel the nausea creeping upward. Beavers were not supposed to fly, and her body knew it.

Maximilian and his ray, Searing, were in front, leading the others. Max turned his head and instantly smiled when he saw the joy in his wife's carefree riding. She was a natural. It had been a long time since he had seen her have fun.

The beavers, on the other hand, were the most awkward students he had ever trained. Of course, considering that they were the first beavers ever to set foot on a ray, he thought they were managing well.

The four great flying beasts, with their riders on their backs, soared through the air. Two riderless rays followed closely behind to help carry the others when needed. Although rays could carry up to two riders over short distances, Max did not want to cause them stress if the journey turned out to be long. They would spread the load around as needed. Max and present company were currently unaware that Malora was missing.

Six rays traveling together between realms before the Dry Death would have been a majestic sight, but after the Dry Death, it was nothing short of miraculous. The lands below were desolate. The inhabitants were either long dead and buried or in hiding.

Although there were very few creatures to appreciate what was happening in the skies, there was no denying the momentous occasion. The rays flew in harmony, always aware of one another. They appeared to be riding the currents of a winding river. They traded positions like acrobats in the air, using one another's uplift to conserve energy. When their wings were completely open, they resembled sleek, gleaming discs, but when their wings were positioned upward, they appeared to be praising their Creator.

There was something about flying that brought peace and tranquility to those not fearful of falling to their deaths. This is why Max loved flying. He had no fear. Even as a small child, he had never been more at home than when he was in the clouds.

Overcoming their own fears took a while, but Saint Elmo

and Francis eventually became more comfortable on their rays. Because of their sheer size, long floppy ears, and fat, oblong tails, they would always look awkward as ray riders, but they were in little danger of slipping, thanks in large part to the riding gear that Max had specially assembled just for them.

It was their large, flabby tails that were the most difficult to contend with. Not only did their rear appendages cause unnecessary drag when they flapped wildly in the wind, but the rays did not take kindly to their backs being beaten with beaver tails, especially when flying in a tailwind.

Beely eventually thought of a way to stop the beavers' problematic involuntary tail-flapping. She fashioned overcoats with enough room to tuck in their tails. The outfits were not becoming on the already large and colorful beavers, but other than an initial roasting from Max, there was no one else to see or mock them.

No one, not even Max, had traveled so far and so long through the skies of the Realms. He no longer knew exactly where he was. Once they had passed over the last part of the great canyons, the terrain below looked mostly the same: dry, brown, and lonely.

Thai, who had become so accustomed to flying with Max that he now felt secure enough to ride on his broad shoulders, knew exactly where they were. Reverie, snuggled comfortably in Beely's pack, was also constantly aware of their current location and, more importantly, their future destination.

No creature had better tracking and positional skills than an empachic. They were born connected to the Realm's magnetic field. Although neither empachics nor rays spoke with other species verbally, they could understand many forms of communication. Duly had repeated to the empachics, just as

Willow had told him, where Propo and the others would be by nightfall. The empachics seemed to understand, and they, in turn, guided their flying companions each step of the way.

"You can see his eyes and nose so clearly," Beely shouted to Max from her ray.

"He's quite the handsome fellow, is he not?" replied Max.

Empachics usually looked like large balls of fur with only an occasional foot or ear visible. With the wind aggressively pushing back Thai's fur, his usually hidden features were now on full display. His tiny nose was just a bump of pink. His eyes were also tiny, but the lashes surrounding them were strikingly thick, dark, and resilient.

Empachics had laser vision but very little peripheral acuity. They seemed like such simple creatures at first glance, but the more one understood them, the more fascinatingly complex they became in both physicality and personality.

"The first moon doesn't have long before it sets; the second won't be far behind," shouted Beely.

Thai extended a long, sinewy appendage out of the top of his head, attaching it just below Searing's horn. It was the beavers' first time seeing the phenomenon. Rarely did empachics use these appendages, something Beely's father called periscopes. Hardly anyone knew they had such an odd attachment, and even fewer had any idea what the long, rubbery things could do. Once his periscope was fully retracted, Searing made a slight turn to the east; the rest followed in order. Thai had once again successfully communicated the coordinates to where they needed to go.

They had been flying nearly all day with no stops. Everyone, particularly Saint Elmo, was weary. They carried as much water and food as their packs could hold, but Saint Elmo could neither eat nor drink while in the air.

He perked up a bit when the rays soared closer to the ground. He was hopeful they were near their destination. Francis could not help but chuckle when she saw her mate's chompers involuntarily chatter. She too was hungry, but she was much too vain to show it. She did her best to keep Saint Elmo distracted.

"My darling feller, look below at the empty creek bed," shouted Francis. Saint Elmo complied, albeit cautiously. It took all of his will to look down. She continued, "Look to your right. There is an old beaver dam, still fully intact. Very large and quite well-made, it appears."

Francis was still somewhat queasy looking down herself, but she thought if this was the new fashion of travel, she must force herself to adapt.

"I can't see it well enough to denote the mark of its crafters," he shouted to his wife.

Francis sighed, and her pleasant smile slowly faded. "I wonder if they made it out alive."

She did not intend to say this out loud, and she hoped no one heard. Francis was naturally optimistic, but felt, in these dark times, it was her duty to keep everyone focused on only the good that remained, as little of it as there may have been.

On their way to find the others, after dropping Duly off at the Library of Truth, they flew over the realm of Pixanese. Beely knew home would always be beautiful, no matter the Dry Death. Her memories held Pixanese in the highest esteem; it would always be home.

Although the waterfalls had stopped falling, the framework and bones still stood, vibrant and unyielding. The carrier vines, having long lost their leaves and flowers, still held tightly to the canyon walls. Their age and their hold on the land had never before been so evident as it was now.

She could see the roots of the vines clinging to the land, and every curve and crevice of the woody vines was nakedly bare for all to see. The canyon walls themselves revealed colors she had never before noticed. Hues of purple, orange, and yellow burned through the mostly grey and brown stone.

At one point, as they flew over her home realm, she cried, not at the loss, but at her failure to have ever appreciated the unpretentious beauty resting quietly underneath its showy covering.

Beavers were few in number across the Realms, but unlike most other species, they were scattered across them all. Still, they rarely—if ever—ventured far from home. Beavers helped regulate the flow of water in a world where it did not fall freely from the sky.

Francis and Saint Elmo were born and raised in the realm of Okrad. This was why Mastad employed them to do his dirty work by damming the Lake of Prosperity, later known as the Lake of Entitlement. It was the beavers who suggested the flight path to avoid the Mastadonians in Okrad. They knew every tributary and woodland trail in the realm.

Unlike Beely, they did not look back fondly on their homeland. They felt betrayed and also guilty for what had become of it. There were a few areas in Okrad that still had access to water, but those places were occupied by the enemy and avoided by all who revered freedom. Instead, they flew over the barren Salt Lands, which had been covered in salt even before the Dry Death.

The Realm of Many was the largest of all the Realms, but thankfully they only needed to fly over a small corner of it. The realm of Many was where the Mara people gathered. There was no one single people group known as the Mara People. Rather, it was a group of refugees that had survived the Dry Death long enough to make it to the deep canyon floor.

They called themselves the Mara People because they were bitter about their struggle for the only large, open water source that Mastad had allowed to keep flowing. It was here, in the deepest part of the canyon, that Mastad and his Mastadonians could keep tabs on them. Here, it was thought, Mastad could kill them all quickly if the need arose. For now, Mastad allowed them to live, just in case he needed them. There were giants, both dwarf and tall, Oakridians, and even a few Necatarions, as well as many other creatures from all over. This was where Lira and her only child, Benjamin, had lived for many cycles.

In between the Realms lay deep channels of moving sand, which once had a shallow covering of water before Mastad's reign. The sands sometimes moved quickly, sometimes slowly, and sometimes not at all. The Realms changed positions as the sands undulated underneath them.

This was the primary reason each Realm had remained independent and distinct. It was very hard to travel and avoid becoming lost. Settlements were few amid the vast and open spaces. To get lost was not only easy but also deadly. Travelers either had to have the best of guides or a deep, abiding knowledge of exactly where they were going and when to get there.

There were tunnel guides and the mysterious oarsmen of the waterways, but both were reluctant to help travelers between realms. The only other way to travel was by air—the most efficient and safest route between realms, but unless one had wings, flying was not readily accessible. The only creatures able to transport passengers in the air were the rays, but they were few and highly selective in their exploits.

Eventually, they would meet Propo and the others in the Realm of Restoration. It was a realm few knew much about. It was perhaps the most ancient and rugged of them all. However, before seeing the Realm of Restoration for the very first time, they planned to make a quick stop on the outskirts of Okrad in the Salt Lands.

Max could see that Saint Elmo needed a break, and it would do them all good to stretch their legs. He gave Searing the signal by tapping just below her horn. They slowly descended to the first settlement Max had seen in quite some time. The chances of anyone still living there were minuscule, but Max wanted Beely to see how the people of the Salt Lands once lived.

It was like no other place, but like the village of Pixanese, the Salt Village had a beauty all its own. He also wanted to remind everyone of the urgency of their mission. Every realm had been destroyed by Mastad, and unless they did God's will, they would never recover.

Searing slowly glided down and hovered just above the hard, dry salt. Each of the other rays followed closely behind her. They were several paces shy of the Salt Village. There were houses and structures made entirely of hardened blocks of salt. So much light reflected off the buildings and the ground from the last remaining rays of sunlight that everyone, including the rays, squinted for several moments after landing.

Beely placed her hand in front of her face to shield her eyes as she looked around at the foreign landscape. It was like nothing she had ever seen. She felt the ground beneath her feet crunch as she stepped off Joshua. She stared straight ahead of her at what resembled a beautiful fairy tale.

The buildings looked as though they had been carved by hand. There were structures with curved domes, some had pointed tops, others were flat, and still others looked like waves of water, but the one thing they all had in common was their color, or lack thereof—pure white. There were minimal colors in the trim of the windows; the doors were mostly blue, with the occasional brown or red.

With Reverie in her shoulder bag, Beely absentmindedly walked toward the village, wondering if she would find anything similar to her own home in Pixanese. Max, helping the others off their rays, shouted, "Stay close, sweetheart. We won't be staying long."

He knew Beely would fall in love with the place. His wife, like himself, was fascinated by how others lived and how others utilized their God-given resources. Beely was too fascinated with what lay before her to completely acknowledge Max. She did hear him, though she was not at all sure what he said.

"Just going to…"

Before she finished her sentence, her foot encountered something soft and squishy. She looked down. It was a child's doll, a familiar sight that could have belonged to any child— even one from Pixanese. Unlike almost everything else here, it was neither white nor made of salt.

A sudden feeling of loneliness enveloped Beely as she looked at the doll's painted-on smile. It stared back at her with eyes that seemed to plead, helpless and still. There were no voices, no townsfolk, and no children playing on the abandoned streets.

She looked back at the others and shouted, "I'm going to go a little further. I won't be long."

Max was still preoccupied, carefully helping a reluctant Francis dismount her ray. He did not immediately notice Beely.

As he loosened the stirrups around her feet, Francis gazed in Beely's direction and sighed. "You can undo those straps, but I'm not setting foot on that stuff." She looked down at the crusty salt. "I don't walk where trees don't grow."

"It's just salt. We need salt to live," said Max.

"That much salt will kill you!" she exclaimed while pointing at the ground. So much for being positive, she thought. Max pursed his lips to one side and raised his brows before moving over to Saint Elmo.

"What about you?" asked Max.

Saint Elmo waved his hand in an attempt to ward off something buzzing around his face. "Let me off this thing. A beaver standing on salt makes a lot more sense than a beaver in the air."

Max finished loosening his stirrups, and Saint Elmo immediately, albeit awkwardly, slid off his ray. He ended up on all fours. He furrowed his brow and then gave the ground a quick lick with his tongue. "Hmm." He sat up with a quizzical look on his face.

"What is it?" asked Francis.

"Salt—tastes just like salt," he answered.

"My realms! That is disgusting. Who knows what's been on there?" She shook her head disapprovingly.

Saint Elmo stood up quickly and positioned his back in front of Max. "Now help me out of this ridiculous coat!" They spent the next several minutes struggling to free Saint Elmo's tail.

Francis looked on with amusement until her husband was free from his impediment, and then she appeared a bit envious. She was not only stuck sitting on her now-hot and odorous beast, but she could not move her tail to fan the blidgets away.

Blidgets were tiny, opportunistic bugs that lived off the

resources of others—in this case, the sweat of the ray. Suddenly, Francis realized, "Say, Max, when was the last time you encountered a blidget?"

Saint Elmo interjected, "A blidget? Did you say blidget?"

"Yes, dear, a blidget. There are several buzzing around," she answered. Beavers despised blidgets because the highly annoying pests were very good at burrowing through fur. A beaver had to be extra fastidious when blidgets were around.

"Wherever there are resources, there will be blidgets. I haven't seen any since we left Pixanese. There were none in the shadow cave," said Max.

Saint Elmo's eyes widened. "Isn't this village abandoned? If there are blidgets here—"

"You're right. There must be survivors here as well," said Max.

A sudden sense of concern overcame him, and he immediately turned in the direction that Beely had gone, but she was nowhere to be seen. She had already disappeared behind the many crystal-esque buildings.

****

Beely took a deep breath, relaxing as she exhaled. She had just become aware of the tension in her body and the feeling that she had been forgetting to breathe. She shook her arms and rolled her shoulders in an attempt to approach her new surroundings confidently, with an open mind.

She took a few steps forward before turning to the right. She ran her hand along the wall of what was once a flower shop. The salt wall was silky smooth to the touch, either sanded down by hand or by time. There were a few empty baskets strewn about on the sidewalk, and although she could not understand the language on the sign in the window, the pictures of the merchandise made it obvious that the baskets had once held flowers.

She wondered where the townspeople had gotten their produce and other essentials. Nothing could be grown in salt. The answers came after a few more curious steps along the lonely sidewalk. She paused to peer into an abandoned courtyard with raised beds of dirt. Nothing was growing, but if there had been water, the plentiful light would have supported the growth of abundant crops of nearly anything.

Although the village seemed completely deserted, the streets were mostly clean, and the buildings appeared to have escaped vandalism. This was unlike Pixanese, where pandemonium and destruction had been plentiful during the early stages of the Dry Death. There was something about this place that gave Beely a peaceful feeling. It was so clean, pure, and free of distractions. She walked, aimlessly at first, and then let the architecture guide her.

The more she walked, the more appreciation she had for the artistry and talent of those who built this village. Her entire life had been spent in lush, green, overgrown gardens teeming with life. This was different. There were no trees, canyons, or hills obstructing views, and it was serenely quiet. She walked deeper into the village, oblivious to where she was or how far she had gone.

Just before she was about to turn around and head back, Beely reached into her bag for her waterskin. Her first sip since they had landed was more refreshing than she expected. Reverie took the opportunity to peek out of the rucksack over Beely's shoulder. She looked straight ahead at where they stood and gave a high-pitched trill. It was a sound she rarely made, and only when she was highly curious about something.

Beely would not have noticed had it not been for Reverie's vocalization, but across the street, slightly to the right, at the beginning of a small alley, sat the most breathtaking sight yet. The single-story complex had five large, curved domes with meticulously designed geometric patterns carved into the salt. The patterns flowed harmoniously, creating shadows and highlights that made the whole building look like a beautiful sculpture.

There were chandeliers with dainty red flowers hanging in each archway. The red flowers complemented the bright green carpet of moss directly in front of the entrance of the middle arch. These plants were the first and only living things she had seen since entering the village.

She froze in position to contemplate what to do next. A chilling awareness of vulnerability swept over her. She brought no weapons, and she was very much on her own. She mumbled quietly to Reverie as she stared ahead. "Why didn't I wait for Max to come with us?"

She assumed whoever lived in the otherworldly structure must have already seen her. Were they wary of strangers and hiding, or were they preparing to mount an attack? How many lived there? She looked behind her but was unsure which way led back to Max and the others. As unique as every structure was, together they all looked alike. She was lost.

Reverie was in no mood to help. She had tucked herself so far down in Beely's bag that not even a hair was sticking out— very uncharacteristic behavior for the usually curious and extroverted empachic. Beely, unlike Reverie, could not smell the faint but strange chemical odors emanating from the building.

She could have turned around and eventually found her way back to the others if Reverie had been inclined to help, but there she was, walking step by step toward the unknown. Beely clenched her fists tightly and then released the tension before facing the door of the ominously manicured structure. She could not let fear keep her from discovering more about this place and the people who once lived there. There might be a clue or a bit of information she could use to locate the painting.

Still, doubts flooded her mind. They were not even supposed to be there. They had somewhere very important to be and not much time left to get there. She shook her head, ignoring the doubts, and raised her hand to the lavender-colored door. She could have chosen the shiny metal knocker, but it felt better to use her bare fist. It felt good to hit something. She refused to appear the slightest bit timid to whoever or whatever was on the other side.

The beautiful, red-haired woman with emerald-green eyes slowly opened the door and looked at the stranger before her as if it were just another ordinary day. That alone was enough to startle Beely. Nothing had been ordinary in the Five Realms of Here for quite some time.

Before either of them had time to speak, a small, white, four-legged animal darted between them and ran out into the street. Reverie wasted no time overcoming the shyness that had overtaken her only moments before. The empachic pushed her way out of the bag, jumped to the ground, and quickly chased the other creature. Beely called out, but it was too late; Reverie was gone.

"Don't worry, friend, no harm will come to your empachic. My sweet cat is perfectly harmless. My name is Harmony." The woman's voice was even more enchanting than her appearance.

Her cadence was so eloquent that it seemed as if she were singing. Her hair was red, but not like the red of the Mindalites. Harmony's hair sparkled as if tiny stars were woven throughout, and her eyes were a deep emerald green that Beely would not soon forget.

"I'm not worried about Reverie. She knows how to find her way around. What was that other creature?"

"It's called a cat, the only one of its kind in these realms, so I have been told. It was a gift from a friend. Won't you come in?"

Beely looked behind her, more out of habit than concern. "Maybe just for a moment. My friends are not far, and I need to get back to them, but I couldn't leave without Reverie, now could I?"

She should have been apprehensive, yet her intuition told her to go inside with Harmony. She was not sure if she felt compassion for, camaraderie with, or simple curiosity about the emerald-eyed stranger. Harmony smiled as she opened the door fully for Beely to follow her inside. "We so seldom get visitors these days. This is a most welcome treat."

"Are there others here too?" Beely looked around and saw no one other than the many reflections of herself and Harmony. There was an unusually large number of mirrors in what seemed to be the main living area. Mirrors adorned every wall and every table. They came in an odd assortment of shapes and sizes.

"Other than myself and my cat, I have a few servants. Unfortunately, I never had much family, certainly no children, and the family I did have has long since departed."

"I see." So many thoughts bombarded Beely all at once: How long had this woman been here? How was she surviving? What had happened to the rest of the village? Why so many mirrors? Fortunately, Harmony interrupted Beely's chaotic musings.

"You must have so many questions, but first, let's have some refreshments."

No sooner had she finished speaking than two women, her servants, entered with trays of food and drink. They set the trays down on a long, black table with unusually short legs. There were hot, steaming teas, cold juices, and all sorts of colorful and intricately crafted edibles.

Beely sat down across from Harmony as one of the helpers gave Beely a warm cloth to wipe her hands and another to refresh her face. The other helper poured them both a cup of hot tea in what Beely believed to be solid gold cups before taking the soiled cloths away.

The servant seemed to stare at Beely for an awkwardly long time before Harmony snapped her fingers, abruptly breaking her gaze. The woman seemed embarrassed but still managed to reach out and almost touch Beely's braid, probably curious about the silver strand woven throughout.

"Most of the women and men from my realm weave silver or copper wires through their hair. It's an age-old custom," said Beely directly to the servant, who quickly cast her eyes down to the floor.

Harmony nodded to the servant disapprovingly before looking back at Beely. "How interesting. What does it signify, the metal strands in your hair?"

Beely smiled, eager to answer. "The metal is quite malleable, yet it adds strength to something that would otherwise be considered weak or frail."

"I can see that you are neither of those, with or without the silver braids," mused Harmony. "Please, have some tea while it is still warm."

Beely did not know the type of tea, but it smelled delightful.

She took a small sip, and her eyes opened wide. This pleased Harmony. "Most assume the Salt Lands have no specialties of their own." She frowned disapprovingly before continuing. "Nothing could be farther from the truth. This tea can only be grown here. It requires a much higher salinity than other teas, they say. We pride ourselves in curating the finer things that life has to offer—at least, we once did."

"If you are able to survive here, where are the other villagers?"

"The Dry Death—that's what they call it, right?" Beely nodded. "Yes, well, it affected us too, but my house alone was able to remain, thanks to the help of a generous benefactor."

Beely paused for a moment before slowly setting her cup down on the table. "You mean Mastad?"

"I'm sorry, but I don't know anyone by that name. I've actually never even seen the one who provides for us."

"I don't understand. You do realize that ninety percent or more of the entire population has either died, been murdered, or been displaced by Mastad. No one survives untouched unless Mastad alone approves."

For a moment, Harmony seemed taken aback by Beely's accusatory tone, but she quickly regained her composure. "Well, I'm sure what you say is true. But as for me and my house, we shall serve the Lord."

At her final words, one of the servants, startled, dropped a plate. Harmony, though clearly annoyed, maintained her composure once more. But Beely was no fool—she saw the nervous glances of the servants and the fire smoldering just beneath Harmony's cool façade.

"What lord would that be?" asked Beely.

No sooner had Beely asked the question than Reverie came

bouncing back into the room and into Beely's lap. "Reverie, there you are, my sweet girl." Beely gave the empachic a gentle hug and then made an opening in her bag into which Reverie wasted no time burrowing deep inside.

"You're looking for something," said Harmony.

"What makes you say that?" Beely asked, noticing that Harmony was becoming increasingly distracted by the mirrors. Though she tried to be discreet, Harmony kept stealing glances at her reflection whenever she thought Beely was not looking.

"No stranger has been through this village in many, many moons." Harmony paused as she looked at Beely in an almost accusatory way. "You are quite young. Even beautiful, I might add, but definitely young. One must never take one's youth for granted. It's not hard to be beautiful when you are young."

Beely tried to appear as cool and collected as her host, but she was finding it increasingly difficult. "I really must get back to my friends. Thank you so much for the hospitality."

Beely placed the strap of her bag over her shoulder with Reverie once again tucked inside. Thoughts raced through Beely's mind yet again: Could Harmony know that she was looking for the most powerful object in all of the Realms? Could this woman in the middle of nowhere know about the painting? Beely could not help but consider the odds of meeting the only survivor of an entire village in a realm she had never been to and knew nothing about. The odds were not good.

"Really, must you leave so soon? I'm sure your husband won't leave without you. I'm enjoying the conversation. It's been so long—"

Beely was very much aware of Harmony's slip. Beely had never mentioned her husband. "May I ask you just one more question before I leave?"

"Of course, I'm all ears." Harmony once again glanced in a mirror, adjusting her hair ever so slightly.

"Why do you serve your lord?"

"He has allowed me to live abundantly. You've just tasted of his delights. He gives us everything you see here. All the gold you can see in this room was gifted by him. Every mirror is trimmed in gold. All of the cutlery and ornaments—all solid gold. He also helps me maintain my vigor and, dare I say, my beauty with vials containing the secrets of youth. I am quite old, much older than you would guess, surely. What did you say your name was?"

"You know, I don't think I did."

There was an awkward moment as Harmony waited for Beely to give her name, and when she did not, Harmony managed a smile that resembled more of a grimace as she continued. "Vanity is highly underrated." She laughed, but Beely did not join her. "All that I have, he has given me."

"That's not true. He may give you things that last for a time, but the Lord I serve gives that which will last for eternity. And although you are very beautiful, there is no number of vials that will sustain you forever; only the Lord and His promises will last forever."

"I am no fool. Nothing lasts forever, friend. Not even my beauty will last forever." She looked into a small mirror on the table and ran a finger along her brow.

Beely inhaled deeply and pressed Harmony further. "Did your lord make the very salt beneath our feet? The One who created something from nothing promises eternal life for all who believe in Him. It's ironic, you know?"

"I'm not sure what you mean."

"We are called to be salt and light. Few know more about

how special salt can be, and what it can do, than you. Yet you have chosen to serve a false lord. Are you one who thinks the Realms are all imaginary, just a figment of someone's imagination?"

"Of course I believe this is all a figment. That is why I do not follow the God of your book. We are not real," answered Harmony with as much bravado as she could muster. She was no longer covert in glancing into the mirrors. The longer Beely was there, the harder it was for Harmony to refrain from her compulsion.

"Then what are we?" Beely looked directly and confidently into her eyes. She wanted to make Harmony as uncomfortable as she herself had become sitting in Harmony's salt demesne, surrounded by smoke and mirrors.

"We are merely here to serve those in the realm of reality. No one cares about us. We can do as we please. We can bring down any realm because no one believes we are real, because we aren't, really, are we? It's an amazing realization." Again, Harmony gave the faintest of laughs, but Beely remained steely. "You are a dry one, aren't you? No fun at all. You really should join us. I promise it's a lot more fun to do as you will than to do His will."

"We all do someone's will. You have chosen to do the will of the one whom you don't even have a name for. Whom we serve matters, not only in our realm but in all realms. The Word from the Book says to take every thought captive and make it obedient to Christ. Even if we were figments—and I'm not saying we are—we have a choice to do good or to do evil. Even if our sole purpose was to serve those where the Christ will one day walk, I will do it with all of my heart, soul, strength, and mind. The One I serve is good, and all good things come from

Him, unlike your god, who brings destruction, death, and lies."

"It really is a choice, and it seems we have both chosen. I may be a mere figment, but I refuse to act like one. I will never be second to anyone or anything, as if I were a mere tool."

"You knew I would come here, didn't you? I never told you my husband was waiting for me. But if you knew who I was, why spend all this time discussing things you think are of little consequence?"

Harmony walked over to the largest mirror in the room as she answered Beely. It was directly to the right of the only exit that Beely was aware of. Harmony stepped onto a purple rug in front of the gold-framed mirror and spoke to Beely as she stared at her own reflection. "It has always been about prophecy, my friend. If one can untangle the words to the point where they mean something, one's destiny is clear. My lord simply wants you to join us, and he's giving you one more opportunity."

Beely was keenly aware of Harmony's positioning between her and the only exit. She should have been worried, but Harmony's mention of prophecy put her at ease. Beely's unease subsided because she knew that God was in charge of all things and that neither Harmony nor her evil lord could do anything that the One True God did not allow.

"That's nonsense. Mastad, the one you serve—whether you have seen his face or know his name matters not—has fooled you or perhaps merely reinforced your own foolery. He knows I would never choose him or his ways. So, what is it you want with me, really?"

"It's not you we want, silly girl. He knows he can't touch you," said Harmony with an insidious smile. The laughter and frivolity disappeared, and only a seething undertone of hate remained.

Beely shuddered at the sheer tone of her voice, which had changed from melodious to shrill in the span of a heartbeat. Beely suddenly realized that this visit was not about her but about the others. They were in danger. Why had she left them?

They were not safe without her because prophecy had foretold that it would be Beely who would find the painting. Yes, God was in control, but Beely's instincts to intercede kicked in. She silently begged God for favor and to protect her husband and her friends. She simultaneously contemplated how to get out of this house of horrors.

Yet it was unnecessary once Harmony saw the expression on Beely's face. It was an expression of recognition and understanding. Harmony simply stepped aside and waved her hand toward the door. "You look a bit panicked. I would never keep you here against your will. You are the chosen one, after all. Yet there is no need to rush; you will never make it back to your companions in time."

It did not matter what Harmony said. Beely rushed toward the door, which was already partially open, and ran as fast as she could out into the street with no name. She looked up and around, overwhelmed. Harmony was correct about one thing: Beely would not make it back in time. Without a miracle, Harmony's servants or Mastad's minions were well on their way to Max and the others. She prayed as she chose a direction and rushed toward what she hoped was the way to her beloved.

She turned the second corner, and again, everything looked the same. There were no distinguishing landmarks to indicate the way from which she had come. She ran further, never bothering to look back to see if she was being followed. She ran down main streets and what appeared to be back alleys, desperately scanning every building for anything that looked familiar.

She could not keep the negative thoughts from slowing her down. Why had she not paid more attention? Why had she been so naïve? If she made it back in time, she would never take her journey or her mission for granted again.

She ran until she was breathless, having no idea where she was. She had to stop and think. As she wiped the perspiration from her forehead, she saw a shadow move behind the corner from where she had just come. "Probably just the light playing tricks on me," she thought.

Her only hope in finding the way back lay with Reverie. Beely leaned against a wall and slid down to the ground, inhaling deeply. She gently but quickly pulled Reverie out of the bag and brought her close to her chest. She squeezed and felt the reassuring and calming purr of the empachic. "Reverie, I know you haven't been well enough to track on foot for many moons, but I need you to lead us back to Max and the others. Do you think you can do that?" Reverie chirped and trilled confidently.

Before Reverie set a paw on the salty ground, Beely heard footsteps. She was still seated when a woman, one of the servants from the house of mirrors, appeared. Beely recognized her as the one who had poured the tea. She was dressed in all white, and even her hair was wrapped in a white turban, which magnified her already exceedingly pale complexion even more.

The servant was breathing as if she had been running behind Beely the entire way, trying to catch up with her. "Please..." The servant paused to catch her breath before continuing. "Please, don't be alarmed. I have only come to warn you." She stopped, still breathing heavily.

Beely held tightly onto Reverie as she rose to her feet. "About what?"

"My lady has not sent anyone after your friends. She does not need to. She was simply stalling your departure. There is a salt storm brewing between us and them."

"What exactly is a salt storm, and why should I trust anything you say?"

"Many moons ago, I met someone who wore similar clothes to you."

Beely responded skeptically. "There are many others who dress in tunics and cloaks like the Necatarions."

"He had thin metal woven through his hair, very similar to yours."

"What of this? You met someone from my realm, and this is supposed to make me trust you?"

The servant was now breathing easier. "For me, it is more than a coincidence. I have never before, nor since, met anyone like him until you. He was not alone. The man you spoke of, Mastad—he was then known as Ankur—was with the man. I did not care for him much."

"So Harmony lied to me; she knows Mastad."

"No, neither man came for her; they came for me. I have no idea if she spoke to either of them."

"Even if someone from Pixanese came here, what does that mean? Do you even remember his name or what he looked like? And why would Mastad be interested in a servant?"

"He never told me his name. He was tall, very handsome, and had dark hair with thin copper strands. He knew much about me, however—my name, where I came from, and he knew prophecy."

"Why did he come here?"

"He came for an object in my possession."

Beely looked around pensively. She was rested enough to continue on but felt torn about finishing listening to what the pale woman had to say. "What was this object?"

The servant's eyes softened, as if recalling a hidden hope from her past. "They were seeking a relic tied to the prophecy, though they were not sure it was genuine. I cannot tell you more than that. I swore an oath of secrecy to him and to my people. Yet my intuition tells me that you have something to do with all of this that happened so many moons ago."

Beely shook her head in frustration. The mention of Mastad changed everything. It only brought more confusion. "Tell me about the salt storm. How do we get through it?"

"The air becomes rich in salt and then hovers until a cleansing wind passes. It is unbreathable even for those who live here, but for blanders—those like you and your friends who are not from the Salt Lands—you would not survive for more than a few breaths."

"My friends have a way to rise above the storm. We do not have to stay where it is hovering."

"She knows this. It's not the storm that will kill them. It is the way they will go to escape the storm. They will not rise above it but most likely go in the opposite direction of the storm toward the burning sulfur."

"I don't know what that means." Beely's hands flailed, and her voice rose in frustration. Torn between fleeing with Reverie as her guide or lingering to hear out a stranger she barely trusted, she hesitated, heart pounding.

Zara's voice dropped. "The storm will push them toward the sulfur pits, where ancient traps ignite the air, burning all who venture too close." A look of desperation overcame Beely. The pale woman placed her hand on Beely's arm. "There is no way for you to get to them in time to warn them. They will surely die."

"Then I will die too. I will not remain here on the words of a stranger." It was obvious that Beely was unbending. Her resolve was only getting stronger, and the servant could see this.

"I will go. I will tell them. I will send them here to get you. It is the only way," said the servant.

"Why would you do this—risk your own life for strangers?"

"It is true that I am a servant to an evil woman. We, her servants, are not pale by birth. We are bleached and marked as her property. This whole place gives off an odor of burning skin. The animals can smell it. The process is painful and never ceases until we die. I have spent a lifetime praying for answers as to why me, which remained a mystery until now. I have always believed in the God of the Book. I have been to the Library of Truth. I now know that I was chosen to be here for you. I have been good and kind to my mistress, even though she has not been so in return. I found comfort in the Book, which always said to do our work as if unto the Lord, and that is whom I have been working for all this time."

"I believe you—" Beely was moved beyond words. With tears welling up in her eyes, she wrapped both of her arms around the thin, pale stranger and held her tightly.

"I am not of this realm; this is not my home—the Salt Lands—but my exile. If you are truly who I think you are, you will be visiting my homeland before this is all over. It is a beautiful place, a safe place with neither day nor night."

"Why are you telling me this?" Beely asked.

"There is no time. I only ask that if you find yourself among my people, please tell them that I love them. My name is Zara.

Please also tell them that I am sorry." She untied the turban from around her waist and pulled a small mirror from one of her pockets. "I must be on my way. Wait here until your friends come. Point this mirror, reflecting the sun's light, in that direction." She pointed where she wanted Beely to signal. "You will be safe."

She turned to go, but Beely grabbed her arm. "If my husband doubts your loyalty or whom you really serve, tell him…" Beely looked around, just in case someone else had followed her, and whispered the rest into Zara's ear. One could never be too safe.

Zara straightened the turban before pausing a moment longer. "You will bring back the Word. You are real because you do the Will of your Father. You share His Word, and you will bring His Word to many. The Messengers will come, and you will know. They will continue to spread the Good News to all who will listen. It is the Messengers' lesson to learn and your work to do unto the Lord, as it has been mine."

She then quickly wrapped the turban that had been fastened to her waist around her face and nose, leaving only veiled slits over her eyes. She raised her hands to the sky and then turned to Beely and gave a slight bow before heading off into the storm.

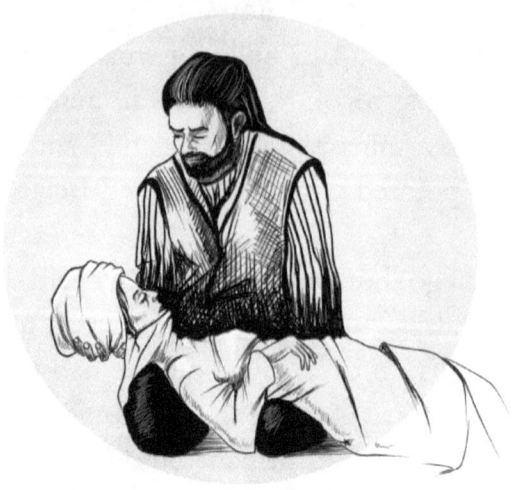

Chapter 20

THE COMING STORM

At least an hour had passed since Beely left on her own to explore the abandoned Salt Village. Francis, still sitting atop her ray, watched her husband, recently refreshed from food and drink, grind his four incisors—a sure sign that he was nervous.

Max had set his eyes on the looming storm, trying to gauge its direction, velocity, and composition. The rays, highly sensitive to potential danger, had not yet shown any signs of impending trouble, but they were perhaps as unfamiliar with the area as their riders were. After finishing the small bit of rations Max had brought for them, the rays appeared content to simply rest their wings.

"Do they have teeth?" asked Francis to no one in particular.

"Do who have teeth?" responded Saint Elmo.

"Did you notice any teeth when the rays were eating? The strangest creatures, if you ask me," said Francis.

Saint Elmo bent his knees and tilted his head in a futile attempt to get a better view underneath the rays. "Honestly, my talented whittler, even from down here you can't see their mouths, or their faces for that matter." Her question was enough to distract him from grinding his teeth and wearing out the webs between his toes from all of his pacing back and forth.

He was now on all fours, trying his best to see underneath Ausalia, his ray. When he got too close, he inadvertently tickled the fine cilia under her wing, and she let out a huge snort while simultaneously flapping her large wings, causing a cloud of salt dust to rise up from the ground. As soon as Saint Elmo inhaled, he began to cough and gag uncontrollably. He grabbed at his throat and kept repeating "Bruahn!" Francis could not make out what he was saying, nor was she in a position to help him regardless.

Max sprinted to Saint Elmo's side and helped him up off the ground. "He's saying it burns. The salt dust must be burning his throat. He probably won't be able to speak until his lungs clear…" He stopped mid-sentence and looked back at the approaching storm, which seemed closer than it had been only moments earlier.

"What is it?" asked Francis.

"We have to get out of here. We won't be able to breathe if we get caught in the middle of that oncoming storm. I think it's a salt storm."

"Wouldn't the rays warn us if the air was getting bad?" asked Francis.

"Not necessarily. They don't have the same type of lungs as we do. They can filter the air. They can even breathe underwater for short periods of time," said Max.

"What'll we do?" asked Francis. "Beely isn't back yet. We can't leave her here."

"She must be between us and that storm. We can only pray that she is safe. But if we stay here, we will not live to know her fate," said Max. He quickly prepared the rays for flight and motioned for Saint Elmo to saddle up.

Saint Elmo was finally able to cough up a few articulate words, "Where will we go?"

"The prevailing winds are blowing southwestward. I think our best bet is to go to the southeast and hope the winds do not change course and follow. God willing, we will wait the storm out and come back for Beely when it's safe."

"Why not ask Thai? Won't he know the safest route to avoid the danger?" asked Francis, who had begun to grind her own incisors.

"Empachics know direction, but they don't factor in dangers like salt," answered Max. He finished helping Saint Elmo back into his rider's coat and onto Ausalia. After securing the remaining rations onto Joshua and tying up his loose reins, Max then moved over to Searing and was just about to secure her reins before seeing a ghostly figure coming toward them. "Do you two see that?"

"It's an apparition," whispered Saint Elmo.

"No, it's a woman," declared Francis. She knew the slight figure coming toward them was someone who had worked themselves near death. She knew the walk. Her own parents, particularly her mother, had the same gait during the middle of the Dry Death, when the water was drying up and her family could not make dams quickly enough to hold the little water that remained. Her mother and father had refused to move from their home, and they sadly wasted away. Francis would never forget what the walking death looked like.

When Max met the woman walking toward them, she collapsed in his arms. She motioned for him to remove what remained of the tattered and beaten covering from her face. What he thought was a pink veil turned out to have originally been white, colored by the blood of its wearer. Underneath the wrapping lay the raw, salt beaten skin of a woman who did not have long to live. It was amazing she had made it this far, thought Max.

"Where did you come from?" he asked.

She struggled at first to speak, still lying in Max's arms, but she eventually managed to utter one word. "Water."

"Of course." Max reached into his satchel and pulled out his waterskin. He held it to the woman's lips, but she was unable to drink. He squeezed a small amount, but it only trickled down her salt- and wind-beaten face. She winced in pain, but the moisture on her lips was enough to aid her voice.

"You can see that I do not have long. You must listen well. Are you Maximilian, the beast tamer?" Max nodded, and she continued as she labored to breathe. "Where are you from?"

"I am from Pixanese. I am a Nectarion."

She tried to laugh but only managed to cough up a small amount of blood. "We know you as Pixanoans."

Max managed a smile, not wanting her to see how pained he was to see someone in such a frightening state. "Yes, I have heard some call us that."

She lifted her thin, frail, trembling hand to Thai, who had already taken up a healing position on the woman's abdomen,

227

but they all knew not even an empachic could save someone so far gone. The healing vibrations, though not strong enough to cure, did offer a momentary reprieve. She looked up at Max with her gentle eyes and spoke softly. "We once had men like you—men willing to die for what is good. They were the first to be slaughtered when they fell for the lies of the evil one." She managed a deep breath before continuing. "The evil one wishes to separate you and your wife. The two of you have borne much fruit, and he will never stop trying to tear you apart. If you must part, let it be death and death alone that accomplishes the dreadful deed."

"Where did you come from? Have you seen my wife? Is she alright?"

"Yes, she is safe. She is waiting for you." She coughed and closed her eyes momentarily before resuming. "You must not fly where the storm is not, or you will burn and turn into a pillar of salt. There are statues standing as witness to the many who have been fooled into fleeing from the sandstorms only to burn in the sulfur pits."

"What other way is there, other than into the storm itself?"

"Salt storms are heavy; they spread more than they lift. You must fly over the storm. The air will be thick from dust," she coughed and spoke so softly that Max had to lean over, his ear almost touching her lips. "Above the salt, higher, is just dust...not salt. It is breathable."

"How will I know where to find my wife?"

"After you pass over the storm...look for the reflecting mirror. It will be shining this way," she pointed to the northeast with a trembling finger. "After the sun sets, there will be no more signal. You must go now." She was getting weaker; with every word, she struggled to speak. "If you are doubting my allegiances—"

He interrupted, "No, not at all."

She wheezed as if her breath was escaping before it ever made it to her lungs. "Of course you are, and you should," she paused to absorb what little oxygen was available, and then she managed a sincere but weak smile. "The way your wife looked when she spoke of you… She clasps the cloth resting over her heart gently, and her eyes blink twice as fast." She wheezed again, this time taking longer to recover. "She told me to tell you that she had been sneaking her prized rubio flowers to Joshua since he was a small pup."

Max looked down, shook his head, and then smiled. "I never knew, but that explains so much." He smiled again before noticing that the young woman in his arms had closed her eyes for the last time. He leaned his head closer to hers but could not detect any life. She was gone.

The storm was fast approaching, and the sun was setting. There was no time for a burial or to take her with them. She was from the Salt Lands, and he felt that she would not have minded being left to the salt winds and time. He gently laid her down and crossed her arms.

As he stood over her, he said a quick prayer and regretted that he did not have time to share the story of his Lord with her. He could only hope she knew of the redeeming Christ, and if so, they would meet again someday.

Chapter 21

THE SEYFRETS

The rays, with their passengers in tow, flew back and forth along the jagged cliffs over the shifting sands separating the Realm of Restoration and the Realm of Okrad. The largest chasm between any of the Realms yawned wide below them— once a body of water, now nothing but arid dunes.

The empachics and the rays had brought Max, Beely, and the beavers this far, and now the next crucial step was theirs: to find the secret entrance to the caves of the Seyfret people. The servant who had given her life to save Beely whispered that the Seyfrets knew where the painting was.

Zara told her about a hidden opening on a cliff with horizontal striations underneath and vertical striations above it. The opening would only be visible with the setting sun, when the colors on the cliff wall would change from hues of orange to shades of violet. Zara did not have time to give any more details or to mention that only those with faith would be able to enter.

Saint Elmo and Francis held tightly to their rays, focusing all their remaining energy on the expansive cliffside as they glided across the darkening sky. A beaver's vision was not made for such a task, and it was unlikely that they would be the ones to find the opening. Yet, Max was impressed with their passion and dedication to the task. Max was the first to break ranks from their systematic pattern when he signaled for Searing to move closer to the side of the cliff.

The wall cast many shadows, making the task of finding an opening all the more difficult. He signaled for Searing to turn her belly inward as he lay flat on her back. He moved his head just in front of her horn in order to get a better view. She skimmed so close to the jagged edge that Max could have reached out and grazed it with his fingertips. "Beautiful job, Searing. You fly like the very wind itself."

The others watched in amazement at how well Max and Searing moved together. Max was truly the most skilled ray rider who had ever lived. When he rejoined the formation, a little farther out from the cliff wall, Beely shouted out a reminder. "It will be the only area where the orange sandstone will appear to have turned violet."

"Up close, it all looked purple to me," he shouted back.

"Clearly still orange, fearless rider," Beely exclaimed. The beavers looked at one another and shook their heads; to them, the entire cliff looked like plain old dirt—just brown.

Everyone was starting to worry, as the sun was almost completely down. It was unlikely that they would find anything in the dark. Their rations were almost gone, and there was no cover in which to wait and try again the next day. They needed to find the entrance that led to the Seyfret people before the sun completely disappeared below the horizon.

No one felt the pressure more than Max. "Lord, I know another day is nothing to You, and Your will may be for another day to pass before we find our way, but if it is possible, I pray that you would reveal to me where we need to go next."

A mere moment passed before Max thought he saw a dark spot that seemed more than a shadow. Beely was too far back to hear him, so he shouted to Saint Elmo as he pointed. "Does that look purple to you?"

Saint Elmo squinted. "It looks purple to me." He immediately grimaced at his own response. The entire cliffside looked the same to him—the color of ordinary sandstone. Yet, before he could stop himself, and for reasons he would never understand, he answered as confidently and incorrectly as he ever had. Before he could take his less than shrewd answer back, Max and Searing were speeding directly into the side of an unforgiving cliff. If there was no opening, they would surely be killed. Saint Elmo closed his eyes and ground his teeth so hard it hurt.

Farther away, Beely was shocked to see her husband's speedy trajectory toward the cliff face. "Why in the realms is he going so fast?" she whispered to Reverie. She shrugged her shoulders just before tapping Joshua's horn, signaling him to follow Searing.

From her angle, there was no purple on the cliff—only orange. Her heart rate increased, and she covered her mouth with her hand. Reverie, aware of Beely's fear, stuck her head out of the shoulder bag and nudged her arm reassuringly.

The others hovered in place, watching with growing tension—except Francis, who had accidentally directed her ray to face the wrong way. By the time she got turned around, it was all over. As quickly as that, the suspense had ended. Everyone was silent for a moment before Beely screamed—in relief. Saint Elmo prayed for the Lord to forgive him and slowly opened his eyes.

"What happened?" yelled Francis, who slowly eased alongside Beely and Joshua, finally facing the cliff once again.

"He found it! He's inside!" Beely exclaimed. Without saying another word, she followed her husband into the opening of the cliff wall.

Francis turned toward her own husband, who had slowly crept up beside her, and asked, "What's wrong with you?" She crinkled up her nose as she took a closer look at him. "Are you crying?"

"Of course not!" he shouted after sniffling. He rubbed his eyes. "I'm just happy that we found the opening, that's all."

"Well, come on then." She gave the command for her ray to follow Beely. The other two riderless rays followed Francis and Saint Elmo, and one by one, they disappeared into the opening. Behind them, the last bit of light faded, and the entrance vanished from view.

The darkness behind the wall was deafening. Upon entering, nothing could be seen, not even one's own hand. The air was cool and surprisingly fresh. In the Five Realms, there was no rain, but there was a cleansing dew that permeated the air during certain seasons. The smell after the dew was familiar to everyone. It was the sweetest, freshest, and most awakening aroma, and it was cherished by all living creatures.

The familiar smell of the dark place eased their

apprehensions about flying into the unknown. It smelled of home. The rays, although naturally equipped to see well in the dark, only flew as fast as necessary to maintain altitude.

Slowly, one by one, they appeared: points of light, twinkling orbs, stars in the night sky. There were more of them than could be counted. The Five Realms of Here had stars, but not like this. There were thousands, millions, an incalculable number of lights above them. Slowly, the darkness was not so dark, and all who had entered into the realm behind the wall could begin to make out forms.

Maximilian and Searing hovered on some sort of pedestal. It resembled a pad in the waters that animals and insects would rest on. There were many of these pedestals floating in the air. They resembled very large tree leaves, yet were something entirely all their own. These small floating islets had veins stretching out from a main stem. Some were green, some yellow, a few red and orange, and others brown. Searing, with her wings fully extended, coasted down until making a perfect landing on a beautiful, bright green pad. It was not long until all of the rays had found individual islets near each other where they could rest after their long flight.

No one said a word; this place was speaking and being heard all on its own. Had the birds been singing when they first entered? The songs and the chirping filled the air in blissful splendor. The songs the birds sang were new to everyone, but they were familiar all the same.

In the far distance, there were what could only be described as mountains. The nearest one had stairs weaving around it: up and down, in and out. The stairs were trimmed in gold and reflected the sparkling stars above them. Balconies populated the hillside in great numbers. They were covered in voluminous, airy fabrics that moved ever so slightly in what was barely a whispering breeze. There was so much to take in. The beauty, the serenity, and the sheer scale and depth of this place were overwhelming for the newcomers. They remained speechless, taking it all in.

"I see you like our home," said the salafus. "We are rather fond of it as well." The plump creature, with wings seemingly far too tiny to carry its weight, speedily flapped the tiny appendages as it flew around, inspecting each one of his guests. Assiduously following the salafus were tiny, flower-like bugs. With keen ears, one could hear them buzzing, and if the breeze flowed favorably, their scent could be savored as if a fine perfume.

When the salafus made it over to Beely, her eyes grew wide, and she pointed at the odd creature. "It's you! Is it you?" Reverie, already poking her head out of Beely's bag, took the opportunity to crawl into Beely's free arm. "We've met before."

How could Beely ever forget such awkward, stubby legs and a long, wrinkly snout that acted more as a hand than a nose? The salafus paused in front of Beely, inspecting her thoroughly with his tired but wisdom-filled eyes, while the little flower bugs decided to inspect Reverie. They had never before seen an empachic. Reverie sneezed but seemed otherwise unperturbed by the intrusion. Beely remembered the bugs and their exotic smells well.

The salafus answered with his deep, baritone voice. "Yes, you and I have met. How could I ever forget such a lovely lady with dark braids woven with strands of silver?"

"If I recall, you never told me your name," said Beely.

"Yes, yes, you must forgive me, I was not sure it was necessary, as this meeting here now was uncertain. If we had

never met again, what would have been the point?" The little
flower bugs, having approved of the empachic, rejoined their
favorite salafus.

"Are you going to tell me now?" she asked.

"I don't see why not. My name is Sir Monchum. These little
ones are Midie, Lots, Such, Fuss, and the tiniest one right
there," he said, using his long snout, as he pointed at the
smallest flower bug. "That one is Misty." Misty took the
opportunity to land on Sir Monchum's nose, only to be
immediately shaken off. "Beware of Misty; she often goes where
the others wouldn't." Francis was caught off guard by this last
comment and cleared her throat. She certainly did not want
bugs invading her personal space. Sir Monchum took notice of
Francis' discomfort and quickly darted over her way, followed
by the dutiful flower bugs, of course.

Francis stared at the chubby, long-nosed salafus directly in
front of her, looking him over as nonjudgmentally as possible.
"I'm Francis and quite pleased to make your acquaintance, Sir
Monchum."

"A beaver? I really can't blame you for hiding that tail of
yours. The first time I witnessed a genuine beaver in action, I
couldn't stop laughing. A tail to remember. The tail of all tales."
The little buzzing flowers buzzed a little more vibrantly than
before. They were giggling, but no one would have known this
other than the salafus.

"I beg your pardon? My tail serves many wonderful
purposes. If it were free from this coat, I'd be happy to show
you one right now, Sir Monchum," Francis said, lifting her chin
high.

Saint Elmo quickly interrupted, "Now, Francis, I don't think
the..." He scrunched his nose and twisted his head before

continuing. "What exactly are you? I can't say that I have ever seen one of your kind. At least not in the lakes and rivers we're accustomed to."

As the salafus moved over to greet Saint Elmo, with flowers in tow, Beely answered the question. "He's a salafus. My father knew of their existence, and they have been written about in books of old, but few believed they really existed, and even fewer have seen them. Consider yourselves among the privileged few."

Finally, the salafus made his way over to Max. "So, you're the one who found our door between here and there? You entered first, did you not?"

"Yes, why do you ask?" responded Max.

"All in good time," said Sir Monchum. He flew a little higher in order to better address them all. "Welcome to my home—our home. This is the dwelling place of the Seyfret people and their many friends, of whom I—and these"—he gestured toward the flower bugs with his snout—"are among."

Beely politely raised her hand to get Sir Monchum's attention. "Thank you so much for welcoming us. I have so many questions, as I'm sure we all do, but I was hoping you would know where our friends are."

Sir Monchum quickly darted back down in front of Beely. It was astonishing how such an awkward-looking creature could move so swiftly. "You'll be thrilled. We have so much to share with you. Rest assured that your three friends are safe and sound. They have been resting and enjoying the hospitality of the Seyfret people while waiting for your arrival."

"Three? There should be four," said Max worriedly.

"Yes, well, I'll let you and your friends sort that out. I really don't think it's anything to be concerned about. They'll join us soon. If you would kindly follow me, we have a beautiful grazing spot for the majestic creatures that carried you here. I've never seen so many rays in one place. It speaks volumes about those they have chosen to serve. Once we get them settled, we will introduce all of you to those who keep this place between here and there." After he said this, the salafus raised his snout into the air and blew like a trumpet, announcing guests. That was exactly what he was doing, though no announcement was necessary. All of the Seyfret people were very much aware of the new arrivals. They had been waiting for them for a very long time.

Chapter 22

THE SALAFUS

Max had purposefully chosen to walk next to Francis. Their journey thus far had not given him the chance to know her as well as he would have liked. Her usually calm and thoughtful demeanor reminded him a little of Beely.

"I thought you wouldn't walk on any ground where trees don't grow."

"I wanted to show off my tail to the pudgy little fairy," quipped Francis.

Max chuckled. "That's not like you—to be so easily offended."

"Secondly, I'm quite certain trees could grow here, if only they were allowed to."

"What are the two of you going on about?" asked Beely, who was a few steps ahead.

"Nothing important, I assure you," said Francis.

It was true that there were no trees where the Seyfrets lived, and Francis was correct—they could have grown there, but trees were needed elsewhere in the Five Realms. There were plenty of other things growing. They were familiar plants, but a little more vibrant, slightly fuller, perhaps taller, and definitely more colorful than those on the other side of the cliff wall.

The sky was still filled with stars, as they never disappeared. Most everything on the ground below the stars had a bit of a glow. As if illuminated from within, all life seemed to emit light where no sun shone. This was the Seyfrets' home, "between here"—behind the cliff—and "there"—the rest of the Realms.

Saint Elmo was following closely behind their leader, Sir Monchum, who was graciously flying as slowly as his wings would allow. Francis had known Saint Elmo nearly her entire life, and yet she had never seen him to be as inquisitive as he was the day he met Sir Monchum. She was certain they would have become the best of friends had they lived near one another.

"Why does everything glow here?" asked Saint Elmo.

"What do you mean?" replied Sir Monchum.

"What do you mean, what do I mean? Isn't it obvious? Why, even you yourself glow. And those buzzy little flowers about you, they glow as well. Like little lights…only not lights at all…"

Saint Elmo bent down along the trail and ran his fingers through a small shrub-like bush. "See? These plants, they glow. All around us. They all glow."

Sir Monchum, while enjoying the curiosity of the visitors, was primarily focused on getting them to the Seyfret Elders.

The Elders lived down in what was called Sweet Berry Hollow. There were no questions as to why the Hollow was named such. There were berries of every shape and size with colors so bright that it made finding them effortless. The smells made everyone hungry.

Saint Elmo had ceased asking questions only because he was dreaming of berry cobbler—Francis's specialty. Sir Monchum, knowing Max would be thinking about the rays, assured him that they were likely already enjoying the delicious native offerings. The empachics, both Reverie and Thai, had already had their fill of what seemed to be their favorite variety, something Sir Monchum called the everberry.

The Sweet Berry Trail, which led to Sweet Berry Hollow, was situated between three very tall peaks. The path, as well as most of the ground as far as the eye could see, was covered in a cushion of dark green moss that immediately sprang back after being stepped upon.

Beely noticed how everything appeared to grow wild near the trail and on the mountains, yet there was a certain harmony to it all. There were no weeds or tares of any sort. The landscape, both high and low, was perfectly pleasing to the senses. She wondered what a garden by her hands would look like in such a place.

Max looked up into the mountains and wondered how many people lived there. What did they eat? Did they hunt, gather, or both?

Francis strained to see the faraway hill dwellings as best she could. There were so many of them. Most of them appeared to be inside the mountains with verandahs and balconies protruding out. Some openings were covered in flowing fabrics, while others were adorned with walls of pure crystal. She

241

wondered if anything was made out of wood. There may not have been trees, but surely there was wood. Even so—wood or no—she found herself comfortable amidst the sweet smell of berries, the lush, green-carpeted walkway, and their charming guide.

Saint Elmo's daydreams of cobbler did not last as long as Sir Monchum might have hoped. Francis was beginning to think her husband was more interested in his new friendship than anything else. Whatever the case, Saint Elmo excitedly resumed his questioning.

"Are there more funny-looking things like you here?"

When the salafus did not respond, Saint Elmo continued. "It's true that our tails are mighty peculiar in comparison to other tails you may have seen."

He whipped his tail on the moss, and it bounced back a little more quickly than he had anticipated, momentarily affecting his balance. He took hold of a copper railing along the side of the trail to steady himself before continuing.

"But you…you are quite the fellow, if I may say so myself. Very interesting appendages. Those ears of yours, if those are indeed ears, look like someone coughed them up after a bad illness."

The flower bugs loved this and buzzed heartily with the tiniest bits of laughter. Sir Monchum waved them away before changing the subject.

"We are almost there. Nothing is far between here and there," announced Sir Monchum, loud enough for those in the back to hear.

As they got closer to where the Elders lived, they began to see more people. The beavers thought they looked similar to the Nectarions in shape and size. Max and Beely did not see the resemblance. The most intriguing quality was the exuberant glow all the living things radiated.

The glow, as it would later be called amongst the remaining Twelve, was hard to explain. Perhaps Beely put it best: "The glow reminds me of the feeling I get on a sunny day, lying on a warm boulder near the water's edge. A fleeting feeling in the Five Realms, but one that never seems to go away here."

They all knew they had arrived at the meeting place without having to be told. It was a most awe-inspiring—Francis called it enchanting—place. The feet of three towering mountains melted together, forming an ethereal, yet grounded, enclave.

Along the sides of each highland were giant smoky, rose, and milky-colored crystals that protruded upwards as if proclaiming good news, and of course, they too glowed. In the center, where the three mountains met, stood a spectacular rotunda carved and polished from crystal. Flowers and vines draped over trellises and walls.

The crystal pavers on the floor of this open-air courtyard were inlaid with pure silver. There were many places to sit on various levels around the veranda, and each of these were also carved out of huge crystal formations. There were bioluminescent lights hanging from pure silver lampstands trimmed in bronze and copper.

All of this was surrounded by the forest-green-colored moss, which filled all of the crevices and crannies, as the mountains crept upward. The occasional songbird sang, many stars could still be seen, and the smell of the fresh dew meandered through every once in a while in this, the deepest part of the Sweet Berry Hollow.

Sir Monchum and his flower bugs led their guests up a few steps onto the crystal- and silver-paved walkway until they arrived at the center of the courtyard. Waiting for them was a tall man dressed in a pale, sky-blue, sleeveless, knee-length tunic.

Beely was startled when the man turned around. Taking notice of his wife's reaction, Max asked, "Have you two met before?"

She whispered to Max. "No, but don't you think he looks like Zara?" She turned back to the man. "You look so much like someone we just met," said Beely.

He, like all the others, had the glow, only it was a deeper, richer glow, if that were possible. He looked to be young, yet he had a way about him that was far more mature than his appearance suggested. His eyes were light golden brown, matching his wavy, short hair.

The man answered Max directly. "I assure you we have never met." He waved toward Sir Monchum, who quickly flew to his side. "Sir Monchum, thank you so much for escorting our guests. Would you kindly let the others know of their arrival?"

"I would be delighted to do so," he said, and off he was, followed by his little entourage.

"Please, make yourselves comfortable. We have much to discuss, and I am sure you are exhausted from your travels. My name is Benjamin."

Each of them took a turn introducing themselves. Thai and Reverie even made a point to rub the ankles of their host before returning to the fountain of water flowing near the far end of the courtyard.

Saint Elmo and Francis were thrilled to find accommodations large enough to seat them both. They sat together, hand in hand, on the silky-smooth crystal bench with a back so high that it allowed them to recline in comfort. The struggle of riding on the rays had made them two very weary beavers.

Chapter 23

Unleashing Captive Thoughts

It had gotten darker in Mastad's house of horrors since her last visit—much darker, if that were possible. Mastad sat on his throne amidst an otherwise nearly empty room. Other than the two dead Mastadonians lying at his feet, there was a broken table, several overturned chairs, and dried blood spattered across the floor.

The unelected leader of the Five Realms was drowsily slumped over, with his long fingers resting under his chin, his glazed eyes fixed on nothing in particular. He was unaware of the gurgling noises he made as he inhaled or the hissing as he exhaled. Just as his eyes closed, and just before his chin slipped from his webbed hand, he was startled by someone daring to intrude upon his presence.

Athaliah had not seen her cousin in many cycles of the moons. His need for her lessened as he became better able to protect himself and kill at will without anyone else's assistance. She had learned to be more careful around him, choosing her actions as well as her words more carefully, but she was feeling unusually bold at the moment.

Mastad was once again stronger than his second-in-command, yet he remained aloof and seemingly unstable. Still, she would no longer allow herself to fear him—but she was not naïve enough to push him too far, or so she thought.

"I like what you have done to the place. The color red always looked good on you, Cousin."

Still seated, he opened his wings, acknowledging the bloodstained webbing before pausing to admire his finely sculpted body. His eyes followed the huge veins in the strong, rich, dark membrane of his skin before he wrapped both wings around his chiseled physique, caressing himself.

He finally looked down at Athaliah. "What brings you here? It's not a good day for visitors, as you can see."

"The woodland Shirks, I'm sure you have heard, have been taken care of," she said.

"Old news, yes…So few enemies left to conquer…"

They were both unaware—and would likely never know—that a few Shirks had survived their demonic massacre. The orphans of the Shirks would live to carry on the traditions of their people. Had Mastad known this, Athaliah would have been added to the new décor on the floor of Mastad's throne room.

There were many things he did not know about Athaliah, and his habit of underestimating her would not serve him well.

Athaliah was growing weary of serving the one she had long since grown to hate. She credited him with turning her into the miserable, unrecognizable woman full of regrets she had become. She had no home, no family that she could turn to, leaving her to roam in search of something she had lost. In search of a soul that no longer existed.

She had failed to take advantage of her master when he was weak and vulnerable, but she refused to be his subject for the rest of her life. The only thing she had left to salvage was her freedom, or so she thought. At least it gave her a goal, something to strive for in a world where all was lost.

She picked up one of the upended chairs that still had all four legs and placed it in front of Mastad. "I know what you want the painting for—what it can do."

"How could you possibly know that?" he said without looking up.

"This was never going to be enough, was it?"

Mastad's claws tightened against the arm of his throne. "What are you going on about?"

"Did you know before you started all of this that it wouldn't be enough to satisfy that dark, empty hole in your soul, or were you surprised by the never-ending gnawing to satisfy a bottomless craving?"

Finally looking up, he smiled a half smile and tilted his head as if searching for something profound to say. After a few moments, it was obvious he had no answer for Athaliah's question.

She continued, "What a mess you have gotten yourself into. You have nowhere to go but into a world where they don't even believe we exist. What then? What will you do after that? Where will you go then?"

"Do you think you are so different from me?"

She studied him for a long moment. "No, I don't." Her wings shifted slightly. "I'm just as lost as you are."

"I know exactly where I am, and I know exactly where I am going," he said with a growl.

"Maybe. But you and I are both pawns in a larger game. You played me, and I let you, but the one who played you, the one who is still pulling your strings, he has the same bottomless craving that will never be satisfied. What? Did you think you could beat him? Did you think he would ever set you free? Surely you are not that blind."

"I will go where he is not." Mastad rose slightly from his throne, his shadow stretching toward her.

"There is only one place he is not, and you will never be there," she said.

Growing impatient, but curious as to why she had come, he asked, "What is it you want, Athaliah?"

"I don't know anymore. I know what I once wanted. Do you know what that was?" He lifted his brows as if to say he could not have cared less. She answered her own question.

"Love…that's all I ever really wanted. I tried to get it from my beloved chiropters. I tried to get it from you. I tried to get it from Michael. I failed. So, I found myself here, with you, doing things I never thought any being could do. Yet, so many offered me love along the way, my parents, that tree in the orchard, even Michael, but it was never enough, and I don't know why. Maybe that's what I'm looking for now. The answer to why it was never enough."

It was then that Mastad said the first kind thing to her. "I

249

hope you find what you are looking for, Athaliah."

"Hope? That's an interesting word choice, Mastad. Hope is faith in what is unseen."

For the briefest instant, something unreadable passed across Mastad's face. "Do you think I have no faith?"

"If you had faith, you would not be so—"

Mastad's wings twitched, the membranes tightening with a low hiss.

She did not finish her thought; instead, she simply opened her wings, extending them toward the wretched creature before her. "Someone once told me that everything begins with a thought. She wisely instructed me to take every thought captive. I didn't listen. I didn't have the will or the discipline to do so. That is where you and I are the same, Cousin.

But you...You control most everyone, but the one thing you failed to take captive was your own thoughts. You have controlled everyone and everything, but not yourself, and you will forever pay the price."

Mastad finally stood up from his throne. Athaliah was taken aback at how tall and even more imposing he had become. He stretched his wings wide, almost touching both sides of the room at once.

He lifted off the ground, with no effort whatsoever, reminding her that he was indeed a creature to still be feared. One strike of his thick, long, powerful claws would end her before she had a chance to move. Yet, she had little fear. She had plans.

Mastad flew over to the only window in the room. He pulled the thick satin curtains back, allowing the light to penetrate the darkness. Athaliah followed him, and they both stared out into the deserted grounds of Mastad's palatial stronghold.

"I know where the painting is," she said. "Michael never had it in his possession. He may have thought he had the real thing, but it doesn't matter now. He would have never found it in a million lifetimes. The prophecy was right; she, Beely, led the way to it."

"Now that you know what the painting can do, what are your plans?" he asked.

"I plan to let her have the painting and to use the painting for her purposes."

"Which are?"

"The Word must be brought back to the Five Realms of Here," she answered.

Mastad hissed and raised his wings toward Athaliah in a striking position. Just the mere mention of the Word made him angry.

She smiled the same half smile as he had done earlier. "You kill me, and you will never get your hands on it. I promise you that. I am the only one who knows where it is, other than those who have been guarding it for all of this time. I have set things in motion for the painting to be kept for me after she gets what she is looking for."

"You will bring me the painting after she uses it?" He lowered his wings and relaxed.

"Of course, I'm a woman of my word."

Mastad was not convinced. "Why? Why bring back that Book?"

"Once you are gone from this realm, I will still be here. As wretched as I have become, I still need to know why. I'm afraid that Book is the only thing that can give me the answers I need.

Besides, these realms are unlivable as they are now. The creatures that remain here need hope. It benefits all, even those who don't believe. I don't understand everything, but I'm not stupid. I see the difference between then and now…with and without that Book."

Mastad laughed a laugh that sounded like someone gargling sand. He spit on the floor and looked back at Athaliah. He had her throat in his claws, before she had time for the slightest reaction. She dared not move.

"You think you are going to rule these realms?"

Realizing that she could not speak with his hand wrapped around her throat, he released her.

Rather than taking a step back, as anyone else would have, she took a step toward him. "Someone will need to fill the void."

"What makes you think I won't simply kill you after I get what I want?"

"While you have been holed up in this place, giving orders, I have been to the far reaches. Securing allies, strongholds, secret places of which you will never know. You will never find me. I'm only giving you the painting to be rid of you."

"You really are a stupid, silly girl. You have no idea what you are getting into. You will need me long after you bring me the painting. There is so much more happening here than your little mind can comprehend.

While you have been out frolicking about, I have spent my life studying the Word that you want to bring back. I have spent my life studying the prophecies. Things of which you have no understanding."

The words stung Athaliah more than she could keep from showing on her face. She never thought of her cousin as being a well-read man. Had he fooled her all this time? Was he more than just a shrewd, power-hungry madman?

She had not intended to speak of the other thing of which she knew, but the moment of weakness overtook her like an involuntary muscle. Her pride had been stricken, and doubt filled her mind. She blurted out what should have never been spoken.

"Did you know she was your daughter?"

A deadly silence filled the room. Not even a breath could be heard. There was no movement. It was as still as death.

Mastad looked at Athaliah, moving nothing but his cold, steel eyes. His lips turned downward just before his screeching, bloodcurdling roar pierced the air.

She had no time to react. He took her into his wings, squeezing the very breath from her lungs. He lifted her off the floor as he rose up, swirling like a tornado until he had enough momentum to release her body through the thick glass window, shattering it into a thousand pieces.

Her lungs were vacant. Her wings never opened. Her blood flowed freely as she spiraled high into the air, only to fall like a bag of rocks onto the hard ground.

Athaliah was correct; she had not the discipline to take her thoughts captive, and, like the one who ruled her, it would forever be her downfall.

Chapter 24

THE LADIES

Beely quietly watched Lira for a moment before suddenly startling her. "What're you doing?" Lira, seated in front of a small sink and mirror, gasped loudly.

"Don't sneak up on me like that! The tunnels didn't scare me that much." They both laughed, as Lira continued. "They call it 'betweening.' The Seyfrets have these fine threads that you use in between your teeth and it cleans them."

"How odd," replied Beely.

Lira shrugged, "I guess they don't have polishing slugs here." She missed the miniature slugs, which had earned their name for their remarkable ability to clean teeth.

"Betweening—seems very unsanitary for such an enlightened people," Beely whispered, not wanting their host to overhear.

"Indeed, but listen." Lira leaned closer, lowering her voice, "When you have been away from home as long as I have, and you have no polishing slug, you do what you have to."

Beely reached over and took a thread from the counter, "Let me try."

Francis was standing just outside the cleansing chamber, leaning in the open doorway. There were not too many small rooms that could accommodate an eight-foot, three-hundred-pound beaver with two other adults. Francis and Saint Elmo preferred open floor plans for this reason.

Beely and Lira insisted Francis come with them on their quick tour of the Valley while Saint Elmo stayed with the other men. Francis could not have been happier to be with the ladies. She very seldom had a reprieve from her boorish husband.

"If you two used your teeth on more productive projects, you would never need to clean them." Her smile widened farther than anyone knew it could, exposing her four very large incisors. The two ladies giggled as sweetly as they could. Francis was not sure why they were laughing, but she could not help joining in.

The seven-member reunion of the remaining Twelve had been bittersweet. The Seyfret people were nothing but kind, and their hospitality unmatched, but no amount of creature comforts could make up for the loss of their friends. Cloy, Eudox, and Zorian had been killed, and now Malora was missing. It weighed most heavily on Beely as she was the one who had recruited them.

As the other two compared beauty tips, Beely stared deeply into the mirror. She did not recognize herself. She traced a new wrinkle along her forehead and tried to convince herself it was just from lack of rest. Beyond the superficial, even she could see the sadness in her eyes. She was a different woman than the one with so many hopes and dreams of just a few moons ago. She thought of her father and prayed his theories and his understanding of prophecy were accurate. She prayed that she was not leading everyone to their doom.

Lira tapped Beely gently on the shoulder. "Are you still with us?"

Beely's eyes widened, and she managed a smile, "You bet. Just reflecting a bit."

They were resting in the home of one of the Elders while waiting to discuss their next move, the painting, and anything else the four Elders might be able to help the remaining Twelve with. The home, they had been told, was much like the others in Sweet Berry Hollow. Minimalistic furnishings crafted from natural crystals and metals were accentuated with elegant, softly colored fabrics. Pillows, wildflowers, and curvy glass sculptures decorated the spacious cliffside dwelling.

Beely stepped out onto the balcony overlooking the great valley and hills around them. Lira followed and sat down on a large feathery pillow.

They were both silent for a few moments. "You must miss your son so very much, Lira."

"I find comfort in knowing that I raised him well. He is strong and independent and will thrive…if we can ever get life back to the way it was. I'm ashamed to say—I only do this for him."

"Ashamed?" inquired Beely as she sat next to her.

"I would like to say that I would have done all of this just because it was the right thing to do. But I wouldn't have. I saw Ankur—Mastad—from the very beginning. I saw my people nurture the monster. I was foolish to think he would eventually just fall out of favor…I want my son to have a future where he can worship and learn about his Creator, where he can live free and become the man of his choosing."

They looked out over the beautiful surroundings, both in deep thought.

"What about you, Beely? Why go through all of this? You have been enemy number one to Mastad since the beginning, so I hear. Why put yourself through all of this when you have no children and very little family to inherit the mess left behind?"

"Maybe having no family means everyone is my family. I'm not sure. My father ignited a passion in me to do the right thing, to always fight for good, but I don't know exactly why I do all the things I do. I just kept moving my feet, and before I knew it, here I was."

Lira pushed the curtain aside and peeked back into the main living area toward Francis. "What about you, Francis? Why did you and Saint Elmo agree to join with us?"

Francis, nibbling on a starfruit she had found, walked to the balcony. "You two may as well be the first to know, other than my husband, of course. I—" She stopped mid-sentence and just stood in front of them rubbing her furry belly.

Lira glanced at Beely before looking back at Francis. "You don't like the food here? What? I'm sure we can find something else for you to eat."

Beely nodded. "What would beavers prefer, if they had a choice?"

Francis moved her hand from her belly and began to fan her face. She looked as though she were about to cry. Both Lira and Beely immediately went to console her, but she waved them off.

"These are happy tears—I am with child!"

Beely and Lira looked at each other and then quickly back to

Francis before jumping into the air with loud cheers. After the initial exuberance waned, the two women wrapped their arms around Francis, and there was plenty to wrap their arms around. Her thick fur was surprisingly soft and silky.

"When did you find out?" asked Beely.

"Several moons before Duly contacted us about the Twelve. It was because of the baby that we had to join the fight. Our species gestates for a very long time, so there is no fear that my pregnancy will become a problem any time soon. Besides, I know God has plans for our little one." Francis was beaming, and her smile, teeth and all, was infectious.

"I'm so happy for you, Francis," said Lira.

"If it's a girl, we have decided to name her after Beely."

"Beely the beaver—very cute, I think," said Beely. "I am very honored and surprised."

"And if it is a boy?" asked Lira.

"If he is a boy, we will name him Mclanahan, after Saint Elmo's favorite uncle. He was an amazing artist and crafter of wood."

Beely, looking out over the balcony, said, "I think that's a beautiful name, Mclanahan."

Lira took a deep breath and then exhaled as she sank back into her feathery pillow. "It is so different here than where we are from. Did you know such a place even existed? This is the perfect place to celebrate the news of the new arrival."

There was a small rap on the front door. The three of them turned to see Maarab, one of the Elders of the Seyfret people, entering. She had left them alone to rest a bit in her home as she saw to other matters.

Maarab was older than Benjamin, but exactly how old she would not say. She had fine features and light brown hair that fell loosely around her angular face. Maarab came across as solemn and stern, while most other Seyfrets seemed more carefree and open.

"I'm sorry to interrupt your rest, but the men will be waiting for us."

"Maarab, before we go, may we ask you a few questions?" asked Lira.

Maarab walked out onto the small balcony and leaned against the railing, facing her guests. "Would you not rather wait until we have all assembled? Perhaps your friends would like to hear the answers."

The ladies laughed before Beely answered, "The men would have no interest in our inquiries, I assure you, Maarab."

Maarab slightly bowed her head. "Very well, ask away."

Lira walked a little closer to Maarab and framed her host's face with her hands. "How can we get this amazing glow?"

Maarab pulled back from the embrace, as she was not accustomed to such forwardness. She looked slightly perplexed as she answered, "What do you mean?"

Beely crossed her arms and placed a hand on her chin. "Are you serious? The glow all of you have here. I mean, everything here has this ethereal light, even the plants, the flowers, the people…what doesn't have some sort of glow?"

Maarab absentmindedly ran her fingers through her tousled hair. "You call it a glow?"

"What do you call it?" asked Lira.

"I think I have heard outsiders speak of such a thing, but we seldom have anyone from the outside here. I'm not sure if they called it a glow. We don't really notice such a thing."

"But you must see the difference in us, right? We don't…we don't have that…whatever it is going on about you…" Lira said this while waving her hands around and wiggling her fingers.

"I think you are lovely people. You have struggled, and it shows on your faces and hands—mostly your hands. I see that you and those with you have worked very hard." She looked at Francis, "Not so much *your* hands—but your teeth have been very busy."

Francis lost her infectious smile and promptly covered her mouth.

Beely grimaced a bit while looking at her hands. "I'm not quite sure how to take that."

"Don't you work?" asked Lira.

"Yes, of course, but we spend most of our time praying and giving praise. We memorize the great Words of the Old and New Testaments. We pass them down from memory. That's a lot of work. It takes great discipline and training to memorize and pass it on accurately."

"Where does your food come from? How do you—"

"Yes, we grow our own food, but it comes forth easily. We rely on our Lord for everything, and He has always provided."

Lira glanced at Beely with her brow furrowed and then quickly turned back to Maarab. "So, is this heaven? Are you an angel or something?"

The smile on Maarab's face was full for the first time; she even managed a chuckle. "Heavens no! The people and the creatures here are like yourselves. From what I understand, we have simply managed to keep the Word in our hearts and our minds. We have not lost our way. We are very strict in our way of living and believing. It is faith alone in our Savior that produces the fruit, and perhaps the glow, as you call it."

Beely was amazed by what the elder was sharing. "And everyone here abides by the same—"

"There have been some, so very few, that have chosen other paths. It is agreed by all that if anyone should wish to live apart from us, they may do so. The choice is always available, but when the word is so deep in the heart, one rarely departs."

Beely was silent. It was difficult for Lira to make out what Beely was thinking, but Maarab thought she might know. She could read the sorrow on Beely's face—the sorrow of time lost and so much pain that could have been avoided in realms where the Word is not cherished. She put a kindly hand on Beely's shoulder.

"Let's go meet the others. I know they are all so eager to meet you, Beely. We have waited a long time, knowing this day would come. You have done so very well to get this far."

Chapter 25

THE SEYFRET ELDERS

As the women walked along the mountainside trail to the lower valley, they heard singing coming from the courtyard. Beely thought she recognized Max's voice, but her view was obscured by the large, rose-colored crystal formations shooting out from the ground throughout the court. Lira bent down so the men would not see her coming, and she signaled for the others to do the same. While Beely readily complied, Francis was a bit too large, so she and Maarab chose to stay back, as the other girls had their bit of fun. Lira and Beely tiptoed the rest of the way down until they found a crystal large enough to hide behind. It

262

was all they could do to contain their laughter when they saw how seriously the men were taking their performances.

Even Leopold, who had positioned himself on a lampstand with his wings spread wide, looked as though he were auditioning for the Seyfret Choir.

> *Purify me from my sins, and I will be clean; wash me, and I will be whiter than snow. Oh, give me back my joy again; you have broken me—now let me rejoice.*

There was a pause in the singing, but the music played on. There were at least seven stringed instruments varying in size and sound and even more drums of varying styles. The Seyfrets were talented musicians, and their voices angelic. Benjamin and the other two male Elders, Qedem and Semol, were helping the visitors with their individual harmonies. The voices and the instruments were otherworldly.

It was particularly surprising to hear how high Propo could sing, but even more surprising was that Leopold, the smallest one in the court, had a voice lower than the bass drum keeping the rhythm. They were singing a Psalm from the Testaments of Old—one most knew well—but none of them had ever heard it sung so beautifully.

By the time the second verse came along, Maarab and Francis had joined the other two ladies, who were now sitting openly in full view of the choir and orchestra below. They were rapt by the performances of their friends and their hosts. Beely could not take her eyes off of Maximilian. It had been ages since she had heard him sing—and never had he sung so well.

"Don't keep looking at my sins. Remove the stain of my guilt. Create in me a clean heart, O God. Renew a loyal spirit within me. Do not banish me from your presence, and don't take your Holy Spirit from me."

When the song ended, the women, Maarab included, erupted in applause and cheers. Francis slapped her large tail on the ground for emphasis. They walked the rest of the way to the center of the courtyard, joining the festivities. There must have been over a hundred other Seyfrets milling about. Each one of them glowed. Beely noticed that the sky had gotten slightly darker, the stars that much brighter, and the air a bit cooler. This must be their version of evening, she thought.

She quickly ran over to her husband and embraced him tenderly, kissing him on the cheek as she whispered, "You've been holding out on me. Now that I know you sing that well, I expect a serenade on our anniversary—maybe even my birthday—and—"

"Okay, okay, that's quite enough flattery, my sweet darling. You must take into account that there were others singing with me. Anyone would sound good among voices like theirs." He motioned toward the Seyfrets.

"I am your wife. You don't think I can hear your voice amongst all the others?"

"Alright, you asked for it, sing for you, I will," he said.

Beely rolled her eyes; she knew better. She took her husband's hand, and they joined the Elders and the others under the grand canopy. Beely noticed Lira looking up in awe and asked, "What are you looking at?"

"Look at that fabric. Not even the Okrad silkworms could produce such a fine array of covering." Above them—higher than three giants standing atop one another—billowing in the slight breeze, was a soft white tapestry supported by sixteen copper pillar-lampstands. The pillars seemed too thin to stand on their own, but like most things there, they defied logic and were as strong and sturdy as any metal known in the Realms.

Even Propo noticed the delicate posts and took hold of one. When he thought no one was looking, he tried to move it, but the post defied his strength and remained unshakable.

Beely had been too mesmerized by everything beneath it to even notice the tapestry above. At the end of the emerald gemstone walkway with rocks of crystal amber towering over them, under the sixteen copper pillar lampstands and flowing white tapestry, sat the four Elders seated on natural blocks of stone. Bioluminescent lights, common most everywhere, gave the amber crystals a brighter glow than they would have emitted on their own.

The Elders waved the visitors over, and they each took a seat. Most of the other Seyfrets had slowly drifted away, back to their homes. The hosts were not as fascinated by the visitors as the visitors were with them. The Seyfrets were modest, hardworking families that kept productive and consistent routines in their daily lives, which included going to bed early.

Leopold found them to be curiously boring. "I am a creature of the night. There is no day here for night to come, and the night is like the day, and the day is as the night. It's thrown my equilibrium completely askew!" exclaimed Leopold as he watched the crowd disperse.

Saint Elmo tapped him on the shoulder. "Keep your voice down, Leopold. No one likes an ungrateful guest."

Leopold scoffed and flew closer to the front where the Elders were seated. Saint Elmo was joined by his wife. They rubbed noses before he did a double take. "What's wrong with your lips?"

Francis's huge, floppy ears turned a brighter shade of purple and stiffened—which always happened when she was embarrassed. "Don't you know anything? It's lip coloring. Lira said I looked beautiful."

Saint Elmo looked a little more closely. "Lira isn't covered in fur, nor is she a wood chipper."

"Oh, what do you know!" she exclaimed, nonchalantly wiping her lips clean with the back of her hand.

The beavers joined the others, sitting side by side on large crystal stones. The Elders were at the end of the beautiful loggia conversing quietly with one another. Propo sat in between Max and Beely. It was amazing how close Propo and Max had become. Once adversaries, they now acted like long-lost brothers. What once caused them conflict now brought them closer. Each of them loved Beely and would lay down their lives to protect her. Propo considered her as a daughter, having been so close to her father for so many seasons. Propo had watched Beely grow from a small child into the remarkable follower of Christ she had become. Propo and Max had hunted together, planned their journey together, and now, they hoped, they would see them all through to a renewed awakening. They were about to be given the miraculous painting that the Seyfrets had been hiding and protecting since time began.

Beely reached over Propo and squeezed her husband's knee. He flinched in surprise just before she whispered, "Have you seen Reverie or Thai?"

Max nodded. "They're fine. Last I saw, they were frolicking in the meadow behind the courtyard. You had beautiful gardens, but I never once saw them frolicking there."

"I didn't know empachics could frolic. I'm glad they're enjoying themselves—they've been cooped up in rucksacks for so long."

After the last of the Seyfrets had gone home, and the seven guests had quietly settled at the end of the great corridor, Benjamin stood and addressed them all. "You seven have made a great and faithful journey here—"

Maarab cleared her throat and gave a signal with her hand. Benjamin nodded in acknowledgment before continuing. "I stand corrected, the nine of you. Indeed, what would the Realms do without the enduring and special empachics?" There was a scattering of acknowledgment as everyone glanced around looking for Thai and Reverie.

"We mustn't forget the rays either," said Saint Elmo. This elicited a look of surprise from Max considering Saint Elmo's reactions to flying on them.

"Of course," added Benjamin. "It has taken many faithful followers to bring you this far." He paused, then gestured to the other Elders. "You have all met Maarab, I believe, but you have not met Qedem or Semol. Together the four of us help shepherd our people in this very special place."

Leopold moved from the lamppost to a closer spot near the front. "No one has really explained to us where here is. Where are we, exactly?"

Qedem rose and walked closer to Leopold. "That's a bit hard for us to explain. Only the salafus, along with his closest associates, are allowed to leave."

Leopold reared his head back and folded his wings around his body defensively. "This is a prison? You keep everyone captive?"

"Of course not. Anyone who wishes to leave may do so, but they may never come back," said Qedem.

Leopold pointed his wing at Qedem and exclaimed, "Even worse! If they don't obey your rules, they are banished from their homes!" Max attempted to say something to keep Leopold from escalating, but Benjamin quietly waved him off.

Benjamin remained seated and addressed the questions and accusations as if he had done so many times before. "No one here is perfect, Leopold. We live by the Word with grace; we judge actions, not the heart. Yet, this is no utopia. There are consequences for those who wish not to live according to what is moral and good."

"Utopia, you say?"

Saint Elmo whispered mockingly into Francis's ear, "He doesn't know what a utopia is."

"Do you?" she quipped back, not quite in a whisper.

"What? You think I don't?" he barked even louder, drawing looks from the Elders.

"What is it, then?" she teased him.

Beely shushed the beavers, and Leopold continued. "Well, I certainly hope our dirty feet haven't soiled your pristine and holy ground."

Qedem sat back down, giving the floor to Benjamin, who, unbothered by Leopold's bluntness, spoke in a measured tone. "Leopold, you and the others were chosen because of who you are. God has always had plans for you. You are the quenching fire for realms caught in tribulation."

He looked at each one of them: Beely, Max, the Beavers, Lira, and Propo, before continuing. "Each one of you is as a grain of salt. You are the ones that will preserve the Word and the ones that will fulfill the prophesies of these Realms."

Leopold was still not convinced, or perhaps he was just testing his hosts and showing off; either way, his obstinance was plain for everyone to see. "I know what salt represents. Have you forgotten the Word where the wife of Lot was turned into a pillar of salt? She was killed."

Leopold's last comment seemed to dishearten Benjamin. Maarab placed a hand on his shoulder before addressing Leopold. "Yes, too much salt can mean death. You crossed the salt lands to get here. It is an unnatural place where life struggles to survive."

Qedem nodded in agreement. "Young one," he looked directly at Leopold, "If you know the Word, then you know that God Himself made a covenant with salt, giving David and his descendants the Kingship of Israel forever."

Maarab added, "The Lord says that if you lose your saltiness, what are you good for but to be thrown out. The salafus came back to us, after his visits to your realms. He testified that each one of you hold the essence, the desire, and the stamina to do this work that needs to be done. Each one of you, not perfect, make no mistake, but there is a pureness, a wisdom, and a desire for preservation of all that is good."

"When did that long-nosed, diminutive winged creature ever witness my deeds?" Leopold stretched out his own wings as far as they would go. "I had never seen him before today."

All of the Elders were tickled by Leopold's feisty display. Benjamin walked closer to Leopold, who slowly retracted his wings. "Leopold, we know you very well. We even knew your parents. They were once very close to Athaliah."

Leopold immediately stiffened and looked back to see if Beely or the others had a reaction to Benjamin's revelation. He detected no negative responses but defended his parents nonetheless. "That was long before she was in cahoots with the monster."

Maarab joined Benjamin and smiled warmly. "Leopold, your parents were courageous and steadfast in their faith. They gave

269

Athaliah so much time, loyalty, and even love. They were aware of Mastad's call on her life, but their influence was not enough to change her course. Their influence on you, however, is why you are here now. You chose goodness, mercy, and love—the things your parents taught you."

"You knew my parents?" He was caught off guard and almost stumbled from his perch as he leaned in closer.

"Yes, not personally, but we knew their works, and they were good," answered Benjamin.

"Then why didn't you save them from the evil monster's experiments?" Leopold's wings trembled. "Their death was—"

"Not in vain," interrupted Maarab. "Your parents were saved long before Mastad captured them. They never feared him or the death he brought. They proclaimed their faith boldly to the very end. Mastad will pay for what he did to them, and just think, my dear, dear Leopold, you will be the catalyst for the justice that will eventually befall their murderer."

Leopold, unable to contain his emotions, dropped to the ground and sobbed. He tried his best to cover his cries with his wings, but it was useless. Everyone could sense his great pain, but even more, they sensed his relief that came with hope for justice.

Lira moved quickly to his side. Helping him up, she embraced him, holding him as he regained his composure. Leopold remained quiet for the rest of the evening, but his attention to all that was spoken was greatly heightened.

There was much back and forth between the Elders and their guests. No one doubted their insight or wisdom after Leopold's reaction. Thus far, most of the conversation about the remaining Twelve's future had been general, with few specifics. The Elders knew that when they were ready, they would ask the important questions.

Beely was the first one to bring up what had been on everyone's mind since they had arrived. "Is the painting here?"

"It has always been here, with us," answered Benjamin.

"How does it work? Are we supposed to take it from you? Are we supposed to take it someplace else?" asked Max.

Beely, not allowing a moment for the Elders to respond, pressed on: "Where did it come from? Who painted it, or was it even painted at all?"

"So, it's here, but where exactly?" asked Lira.

"How will we transport it?" asked Francis.

"It must be large," added Lira.

Saint Elmo pointed at the Elders. "Who painted it? That's the most important question on the floor, if you ask me."

"Is it a literal painting? I don't know about anyone else here, but I never thought it was an actual work of art," said Lira.

"Ah…" Qedem, who had been sitting quietly most of the evening, stood, gaining everyone's undivided attention. "Yes, it is a grand work of art." He smiled confidently.

Max raised his hands toward the Elders, eyes searching. "Have you all witnessed this work of art?"

"Yes, as have all of you," said Benjamin with raised eyebrows and a smile.

Each of the seven looked at one another, searching each other's eyes and faces, as if someone knew something that had escaped them. The beavers whispered to one another and then looked at Beely. Beely turned immediately to Max. He nodded, indicating he was as clueless as she was. Lira, with her arm still around Leopold, was simply looking up, as if lost in thought. Leopold was the only one not concerned about the questions or the answers, because he knew, deep down in his heart, that

God's will would be accomplished, regardless.

Lira hesitantly broke the silence. "I'm afraid we lost the kaleidoscope. Malora had it in his possession, and we became separated in the tunnels."

Suddenly, with Lira's comment, it seemed the tables had turned. The Seyfrets searched one another's expressions before whispering amongst themselves. No one could discern if the Elders were surprised, concerned, angry, or a little of each. The change in the Great Hall was palpable.

Lira, uncertain of the reason for their reaction, continued, "We are very concerned for Malora. He is young and inexperienced."

Benjamin remained seated, adopting a pensive pose. He rested one arm across his chest, the other elbow resting upon it, while his hand cradled his chin. "What exactly did this kaleidoscope do?"

Lira seemed surprised by the question. She was under the impression that the Seyfrets knew everything. She glanced at Propo, hoping he would be better equipped to answer. When he remained silent, she gave it her best attempt. "As I understand it, the kaleidoscope was made in order to allow us to discern if the painting was real."

Maarab seemed just as pensive as Benjamin when she asked, "How could it do that?"

Lira shrugged her shoulders, a bit embarrassed at not being able to better explain. She once again looked over at Propo for help. Although he still seemed reluctant, he finally acquiesced. "How does it work? Well…it really is sort of a miraculous instrument."

It was Qedem's turn to question. "What does that mean?"

Propo sighed, wishing for someone to intercede on his

behalf, but he was the only one that knew of the kaleidoscope's origin. "Beely's father, Mikalo, and I…mostly Mikalo, as he was the real genius behind it, built the instrument using gemstones, not too unlike these here," he motioned toward gemstones adorning a nearby lamppost. "There was one gemstone in particular that Mikalo called the keystone. He didn't tell me from where it came, just that it would allow, if used with the correct instrument, anyone to see through the painting."

There was an immediate and collective uneasiness amongst the Elders as they again whispered nervously to one another. Propo gave Max a worried glance, and in turn, Max did the same to Beely. Since they had arrived in the place that seemed to have no night or day, there was never a moment of worry or uncomfortableness. The Seyfrets had seemed unshakable. The mood had undeniably changed.

Qedem stood and paused a moment as if trying to find appropriate words, but instead, he reached inside of his vestment, retrieving a small pouch secured with a thin metal necklace around his neck. He loosened the tie around the silk-like cloth and gingerly emptied its contents into his palm.

"Did the gemstone resemble this one?" he asked, carefully holding the small, round pink stone in front of him.

Leopold, finally showing more life, flapped his wings to get a closer view of the stone but reconsidered when he saw that both Propo and Lira stood up.

Propo walked toward Qedem and more closely examined the stone in his hand. "It looks like the same stone. Maybe slightly larger, but the color is most assuredly the same, which is odd because I had never before seen anything of this color before."

Lira, who had joined Propo, nodded in agreement.

Beely noticed Maarab placing a consoling hand on

Benjamin's shoulder. His head was lowered, and he looked downtrodden. It was a look she thought not possible for a Seyfret.

She whispered to Max, "Have we done something wrong? No one ever told me of this stone—not my father, not even Propo."

Max nodded but quickly looked back to Qedem for his reaction. Qedem gave nothing away with his expression, other than his own nod to the new revelation about a pink-colored gemstone as he looked back toward Maarab.

Semol, who had remained quietly the entire evening, spoke for the very first time. "In light of this new information, we need to reconvene tomorrow. Please accept our hospitality and make yourselves at home. Your hosts will come shortly to see you to your accommodations."

The Elders, led by Qedem, walked to the very back of the hall, one after another until they were out of sight. No one pressed for clarification, as it was obvious something unexpected—and perhaps disheartening—had taken place.

After he was sure that they were alone and could not be heard by the Elders, Propo motioned for the others to gather around him. "Something is very wrong. Do you think they will reconsider giving us the painting?"

Lira shook her head. "Why would they just leave like that? What could we have possibly done or said to cause them to completely halt the proceedings?"

"Proceedings?" asked Francis.

"Yes, well, what else was this ever going to be but a proceeding to pass the torch? They have what we need—"

Leopold interrupted, "Everything is going to be just fine. What we need to do is have confidence in why we are here and in the One who sent us. The Seyfrets may be wise and the keepers of important things, but they too are servants of the same God we serve. They may glow, but they still eat, breathe, and bleed, just like we do. Give them time to sort out whatever is bothering them."

"I could not have said it better myself," added Max.

"Beautifully spoken, Leopold." Beely rubbed his back and smiled. "I for one am looking forward to a good night's sleep. Let's go find our empachics and our hosts, shall we?"

Saint Elmo gave his tail a slight snap on the crystal floor. "That sounds good to me! I wouldn't mind a few more of those starfruits before it's time to hunker down."

Francis raised her brows. "Since when do you like fruit?"

"I was hungry, and that's what was in front of me. It was fantastic!" he exclaimed.

Saint Elmo led the way, in his eagerness for more fruit, no doubt. The others followed him, quietly for the most part. They were exhausted from travel and overwhelmed by information.

The empachics were a welcomed sight as they raced toward their friends in the middle of the courtyard. There were also several Seyfrets who showed up to help them with all of their needs. They were all safe and splendidly cared for. Much-needed rest and restoration would come soon.

Chapter 26

WHAT GLOWS IN THE LIGHT

He fluttered his tiny wings, stretched out his long snout, and blew with all of his might. It was the most important wake-up call Sir Monchum had ever given. Few in the Five Realms could say they'd ever been roused by the trumpet blow of a salafus. Max, Beely, Lira, Leopold, and the beavers had all slept peacefully, but the alarming wake-up call of Sir Monchum was definitely an abrupt beginning to a day to remember.

After the empachics, who had been awake for quite some time, Lira was the first to greet Sir Monchum, followed by the beavers, Max, and Beely.

Sir Monchum could not contain his excitement. "Today is

the day. The day that you all have been waiting for, and might I say myself as well, definitely myself, and most every Seyfret here between—"

The little flower bugs, usually too quiet to be heard, emitted high-pitched, unintelligible vocalizations while repeatedly divebombing the salafus.

"I am terribly sorry to have left you all out," he said to his sweet-smelling entourage. "Of course Midie, Lots, Such, and Fuss have been eagerly awaiting this day as well." Not a second later, the tiniest flower bug sped straight down into the salafus' long snout. Sir Monchum's respiratory appendage reared up, then down, before unleashing a fearsome sneeze. Quite as expected, the littlest bug came catapulting out faster than she went in. Fortunately, her friends were there to catch her.

Sir Monchum erupted into such a fit of laughter it was quite hard to make out what he said next. "I would never forget you, Misty. I know you take this day very seriously, as we all should." He then cleared his throat and straightened his nose in an attempt to appear more dignified. "Where is our seventh guest?"

Saint Elmo pointed. "Right behind you."

Sir Monchum turned around and did not immediately see Leopold until he glanced up toward the ceiling. He was so shocked to find Leopold hanging upside down, he let out a nervous scream. It was then everyone else's turn to erupt into laughter, including Misty, Midie, Lots, Such, and Fuss.

The salafus retreated to the opposite side of the room before he spoke again. "You should have told me your bed was not adequate. Someone would have gladly rectified the situation. This isn't a cave, after all."

Leopold somersaulted to the floor, landing on his feet. "The bed was fine, no doubt, but the rafters were luxurious. I've never had the pleasure of wrapping my toes around such fine crystal beams. Never slept better."

Sir Monchum looked Leopold up and down. "Do you eat breakfast?"

"I never start the day without it."

"That's good to hear." Sir Monchum turned to face the rest of his guests. "Maarab will be hosting you for the morning fare, afterward you will meet with all of the Elders once again." He pointed his snout at Lira. "Do you remember where Maarab's home is?"

Lira nodded. "I do."

Francis chimed in. "As do I."

"Splendid, two heads are better than one," he said, before flying to the door and pointing his nose in the direction they were to go.

Lira was the first to leave, followed by Francis and Saint Elmo. When Leopold got to the door, he turned toward Sir Monchum, opened his eyes wide, let out a high-pitched screech, and seemed sincerely disappointed when his scare tactic failed miserably.

Sir Monchum waved Leopold on, using his snout once again. "I'm not scared of bats, Leopold. It could have been anybody hanging upside down and I would have screamed." The flower bugs, on the other hand, gasped and darted in all directions to find adequate hiding spots. They would not be seen for the rest of the day.

When Beely got to the door, Sir Monchum tapped her on the shoulder and whispered into her ear. She nodded and took a step back into the room. Both Max and Propo seemed confused, but it was Max who asked, "What's wrong?"

"Nothing, Sir Monchum just wanted to speak to me alone for a few moments. I'll be right along." She kissed her husband on the cheek and smiled.

"That seems a little odd, don't you think," said Max.

"I agree," added Propo. "Why the secrecy all of a sudden?"

Sir Monchum glided over to the men and reassured them. "Benjamin wishes to have a private consult with Beely. It is a highly sensitive, personal matter of a very delicate nature."

Max gave his wife a look and she nodded affirmatively. He then shrugged at Propo. They left to follow the others to Maarab's, convinced of the trustworthiness of the Seyfrets. Besides, both Max and Propo knew that Beely would relay any pertinent information back to them.

Once Sir Monchum saw that the others had turned the first corner, he led Beely out onto the pathway leading in the opposite direction. She followed him on a moss-covered trail along the hillside. The walk was not long, but this was a less inhabited side of the hill with fewer and fewer homes as they neared their destination. The only thing Beely found odd was her guide's sudden loss for words. Beely, however, relished the solitude in such a beautiful place. The flora was glowing as usual, the birds were singing sweet, languid songs, and the occasional snail looked up cheerily at the passersby.

The trail ended at a secluded dell with a hill on one side, high flowering shrubs on the other, and a shallow, steaming stream of water cascading through the center. The water pooled into a crevasse of rock. Beely was drawn to it. She sat on a rock covered in ivy and leaned over, reaching her hand out toward the mist.

"It's much hotter than it looks," said Benjamin from the other side of the crevasse.

Beely pulled her hand back. "Thanks for the warning. Just in the nick of time."

Benjamin looked at Sir Monchum, who had stayed back at the trail's end. "Did you come alone?"

"Not quite," he said.

"What do you mean?" asked Beely. "It's just me."

Sir Monchum flew lower down to the ground and stuck his ever-useful nose into a beautiful glowing bush with radiant, dark-scarlet flowers with tentacle-like blooms. He poked around until finally blowing his nose like a horn. Reverie and Thai came bouncing out of the shrubbery without so much as a squeak. Their guilt was unmistakable, despite the fur covering their faces. They moved methodically, up and down, as if two guilty spies caught in the act.

"Shame on you two. Whose idea was it to follow me?" Beely knew it was Reverie, but she didn't want to make her feel bad in front of the others. She turned to Benjamin and grimaced. "You don't mind, do you? They won't be any trouble at all, I promise."

Benjamin smiled. "Of course not, I adore empachics."

Beely called the empachics over before doing a double take. "Is it just me, or are my two cuties starting to radiate like everything else here?"

Sir Monchum flew closer to Benjamin. "I told you. In all of my travels, these creatures were the purest and most innocent of any I encountered."

"I didn't doubt you for a moment," said Benjamin.

"What does this mean?" asked Beely.

"It happens to almost anyone who comes here. Eventually those visiting long enough will reflect that which is all around them," said Benjamin.

Sir Monchum flew down to Reverie to pet her with his snout. "Never has anyone caught the glow as fast as these two, though."

Benjamin looked at Sir Monchum and gave a slight bow. "Thank you for escorting our guest, or guests as the case may be. We will join the others in the Great Hall soon."

"It was my pleasure," he said. "I must go see that the littles have come out of hiding. I doubt that bat Leopold would get the glow if he stayed here an entire lifetime!" With much flair he flew off, not by way of the trail, but up and over the wildflowers and hillside.

"Thank you for honoring my request to meet without the others, Beely. I'm afraid I have interrupted your breakfast, I hope you are not too hungry." He sat next to Beely on the large flat ivy-covered rock next to the pool of water.

"I'll be fine, thank you. How hot is it?"

"Hot enough to make tea," he answered. He leaned over and retrieved two cups from a nearby tray. "The tea is called Ognatia. It's quite good."

Beely smiled. "We have the same tea, it's Duly's favorite. I rather enjoy it as well."

Benjamin dipped her cup in the hot water. "Then you know how long to let it steep." He then filled his own cup and submerged the tea leaves. They sat in silence for a moment, as their hot water turned Ognatia blue. Reverie and Thai slowly made their way over.

"I'm sorry I did not bring any tea for them."

Beely chuckled. "That's fine, they don't drink tea. I'm sure they nibbled on berries all the way here."

"The reason I asked you here is not a pleasant one—"

Beely immediately sat up pensively with her brows furrowed

and cleared her throat nervously.

"Oh, no, it's nothing to do with you or the others, as I informed Sir Monchum. I'm afraid the subject matter is one that I thought I would never again revisit."

"You've definitely caught my attention."

"How well do you trust Propo?"

"I thought you said this had nothing to do with me or the others."

"It's complicated, I'm afraid." He paused to think. "I know you have read the Word of God. You may not have it memorized or fully realized, but you know the essentials and then some."

"I would like to think so, yes."

"The Bible, from the Earthly Realm, speaks of the connectedness of actions, repercussions, and finality. The choices made in the Old Testament flow into the New. The same is true of our actions here in these realms. What we do now, each one of us, will create everlasting waves throughout eternity. Many do not like it, especially those aligned with Mastad, but it is the Seyfret belief that we, the Five Realms of Here, are to serve the Earthly Realm. Unfortunately, we were not immune to the sin that infected them and our role has been tenuous to say the least."

"Isn't this something that you should be sharing with all of us?"

"I will, we will, but first I need to make sure you are aligned with us."

"Of course, we are. We may not have borne as much fruit as the Seyfrets, but we believe in the Christ and His ways. We are here to serve His will and His will alone. But what does this have to do with Propo? No one amongst us is more faithful. I trust my very life to him."

Benjamin sat his cup of tea on the rock and stood, looking away from Beely. "It's not just Propo. It was your father as well. The one who raised you."

"What about him?"

"Your father, along with Propo's help, it seems, has made something that will eventually lead Mastad to the painting. Mastad must never take possession of the painting. The painting itself was invisible to him, and now, as we have just learned, he will be able to not only find it, but use it."

Beely's thoughts reeled. She was slowly connecting the dots. Benjamin was talking about the kaleidoscope that her father made. "The kaleidoscope. How do you know all of this? If you Seyfrets know everything then why does this seem to be a surprise to you?"

"We are not perfect people. We have the blessings from following the ways of the Lord, but we are not infallible. We are not all-knowing. We did not know of the kaleidoscope until the revelation of the pink stone. No other people in the Five Realms of Here have those stones except for the Seyfrets. Only with that stone can an unbeliever see the painting for what it really is."

Beely swallowed hard. The color drained from her face as the realization hit her. "We never needed the kaleidoscope, but Mastad did. Mastad was behind it all along."

"I'm afraid so. Somehow, he used your father and Propo without their knowledge, if your trust in their faith is true."

"Neither of them would have knowingly helped Mastad."

Both Reverie and Thai, sensing Beely's discomfort, weaved between her legs. They vibrated and chirped as they rubbed their furry bodies against her.

"I believe you." Benjamin took Beely's hand and sat back down on the large rock, pulling her down with him. He looked deep into her eyes. "We can get beyond all of this. We will meet with the Elders and work through it."

"I don't know if I can get beyond it. My head is spinning. If this is true there are more questions than answers. How long has Mastad been manipulating things? How could we ever expect to outwit such a foe? He is so many steps ahead of us."

"There may be more questions for us, but fear not, none of this is new or unknown to our God."

Beely nodded her head and scooped up Reverie. "What if—"

"'If you need wisdom, ask our generous God, and he will give it to you. He will not rebuke you for asking. But when you ask him, be sure that your faith is in God alone. Do not waver, for a person with divided loyalty is as unsettled as a wave of the sea that is blown and tossed by the wind. But there is one more thing I need to know.'"

Beely was impressed with Benjamin's recall of Biblical verses. She was not sure, but he appeared to glow even brighter as he was speaking the words of God. She paused a moment before asking, "I have always wondered what a sea was."

Benjamin smiled. "Not too unlike our large lakes, but perhaps more like the large bodies of water that once separated our realms."

"Before they completely dried up. Now they are waves of sand."

He closed his eyes and took a deep breath before continuing. "You said yesterday that I look so much like someone you just met."

"Yes—just a coincidence, I'm sure, but the resemblance was striking. She had your eyes, an unusual combination of blue and green, very rare as you must know. Her name was Zara."

As soon as she said her name, Beely watched Benjamin's face flush, his hands falter, and his breath become erratic. She placed her hand on his forearm, subconsciously grounding him to something of substance. "Who was she to you?"

"Zara is my daughter."

Before Beely had a chance to hint at Reverie moving to the hurting man before them, Thai had already worked his way into Benjamin's lap. Benjamin distractedly stroked his fur. "It is very rare for Seyfrets to leave our home, but Zara, she chose...I suppose being the daughter of an elder wasn't easy."

"I'm so sorry, Benjamin. I've never had children. I can only imagine how difficult it must have been and still is, I'm sure."

"Where did you see her? Is she alright?"

He did not need an answer. He could see by the look in Beely's eyes that his daughter was gone. Although he had had many seasons to grieve his daughter, the impact of knowing that she had passed was heart-wrenching.

He sat Thai to the side and stuck his hands in the hot water. Beely's eyes opened wide with shock as Benjamin plunged his hands into the scalding water. When he pulled them out, they were redder than a Mindalite's head.

"Don't worry, the water is hot, but I didn't have them in long enough to cause any real damage. When I get stressed, my hands begin to itch and the only thing that brings relief is scalding hot water."

Beely stood to comfort him. She did not say anything for quite some time. Both Thai and Reverie were doing all they could to sooth him. "You know, next time try grabbing an empachic instead of turning yourself into a red-clawed Yabbie."

Benjamin rubbed his hands. "Not very Elder-like of me, was

it? You know, this spring is the one that leads to your home in Pixanese. That's why Mastad was unable to stop its flow. Of course, it's much cooler by the time it reaches you."

"If it helps to know, your daughter saved me. She gave her life to save all of us." Beely sat back down and stroked Reverie and gave Thai a gentle pat on his head. "Zara was the reason we made it out of the Salt Lands alive. She was a very kind and gentle soul. The very short time I knew her, I could tell she was very special. I know God was happy with her."

There was much more Beely could have told Benjamin, but she spared him any further pain. She would not tell him about Zara's evil mistress, Harmony, or that Harmony forced her to bleach her skin daily. The pain and suffering Zara must have endured sent a chill through Beely's spine. How could someone from Sweet Berry Hollow end up in the Salt Lands with such a sinister evil woman?

Benjamin seemed to read her thoughts before she could speak. "The pink stone was hers, no doubt. Mastad somehow influenced her and took possession of it. He was behind this." His eyes looked ahead steely, full of confidence and resolve. "But what he does not yet know is that there is an evil even greater than he, and Mastad is the one that will burn."

THE PAINTING

The Elders, along with their guests, began their walk through Sweet Berry Hollow at the Great Hall. They ascended the gently sloping mountain trails until they reached the summit of the highest peak. The walk was easy, the moss-covered ground soft, and the air still smelled fresh from the dewy cleansing; so no one was weary just yet.

The visitors were all refreshed by the gracious hospitality of the Seyfrets. Propo, in particular, had not slept well for many nights. The quiet, peaceful atmosphere—not to mention the feathered beds—was just what Propo had needed since the first meeting of the Twelve so many moons ago.

Saint Elmo made sure to walk next to Semol the entire way.

Semol, he discovered, was an expert in the agricultural refinements of the Seyfret people. "How do you think the tassel berry would do in direct sunlight?" Before Semol could answer, the beaver launched into his next question. "Do you think they would grow well next to a creek or near a lake?"

The bittersweet tassel berries had quickly become Saint Elmo's favorite indulgence, and he was already considering planting them—if and when life ever returned to normal. Francis enjoyed the tassel berries for an entirely different reason: they turned Saint Elmo's lips a bright pink, giving her much fodder for teasing.

While her husband explored new culinary delights—and with no wood to whittle—Francis had taken up a new hobby: vine twisting, taught to her by the Seyfret children. She even sported a tail sling the kids had woven, designed to keep her tail from flapping in the wind while flying on the rays.

Lira spent some time with the Seyfret children as well, memorizing Bible verses. She was embarrassed by how much more the progeny knew of the Bible than she did. There was one little boy who reminded her of her own son. They looked nothing alike, but he had the same curious spirit.

She missed her son more than she had thought possible. She had never known a heart could physically ache from missing someone. The only thing sustaining her was the thought that if the Twelve succeeded, her son might have a future. If they failed, he would have no life at all.

This would be the last night that some of those who had been searching for the painting would spend with the Seyfrets. The Elders had arranged for a farewell gathering at a place even more special than the Great Hall. Max and Beely walked hand in hand, each empachic tucked away and sleeping in their respective rucksacks.

The Wrens said nothing, but spoke volumes. Their eyes took in every detail of the special place where they found themselves—if only for a little while longer. Beely, like Saint Elmo, wished she could take some of the plants back with her to Pixanese, should they ever return. She was particularly fond of their glow.

Though doubtful they would retain their ethereal brilliance in another realm, they would still be beautiful additions to her gardens. Knowing she would more than likely never see such fauna again, her eyes busily darted from one beautiful plant to the next. Max smiled to himself, watching his wife take it all in.

As they approached the floating pedestals, Max imagined there could not be a better training ground for his rays. Learning to fly while taking commands was not instinctual for rays, and such a training place like this would be ideal. He could not help but feel pessimistic, however, as he briefly considered there may be no rays left, if Mastad got his way.

Sir Monchum brought up the rear, even behind Propo, who usually felt obligated to take that position himself. Sir Monchum only trailed the others to keep an eye on Misty, Midie, Lots, Such, and Fuss. The Elders had never seen the salafus so confounded.

The truth was, he was a bit jealous; his entourage had clearly taken a fond interest in Leopold. Either Leopold genuinely enjoyed their attention, or the bat was purposely attempting to make Sir Monchum envious. The bat flew like an aeronautical acrobat, and the flower bugs could not get enough of his antics.

Sir Monchum even heard Such and Fuss cheering as they giddily coasted behind Leopold without ever flapping their own wings. Apparently, a bat created more updraft than the tiny wings of a salafus.

When they arrived at the end of the trail, they all gathered together below a colossal pedestal. Francis noticed that the swinging bridge up to the floating pad was made from vines woven in a pattern similar to the one the children had taught her. She was also the first to comment on the color of the floating dais. "Why is this one brown? All of the others are such bright and rich colors." She did not seem bothered that no one answered her question.

Lira stared up at the floating brown mesa, thinking it resembled a large, somewhat billowy fabric, with veins spreading across its entire surface. To her, the structure appeared to be alive. The vessels undoubtedly carried nutrients, but if it was a living thing, where did the nutrients come from? It wasn't attached to anything below.

Semol, the least talkative of the Elders, looked up fondly, but when his eyes lowered, they all sensed a deep sadness. "This, which we call the Breath of the One, has been here since before even our ancestors arrived. She may not have been the first, but she is now the oldest—and she is passing."

His voice broke slightly, as if he had a personal attachment to the magnificent life effortlessly floating above him. "We think she is ill because of what is happening in the Five Realms of There, but we cannot be sure. We have not been here long enough to see any of her kindred die."

Again he paused, perhaps in an attempt to keep his emotions at bay, or simply to think of what to say next. "She has invited each of you to walk upon her frail membranes. She loves you dearly. She is connected in ways we do not understand, but she knows all of us—including all of you."

Leopold flew to the front of the gathering. "Is she connected to God or something?"

Maarab stepped toward Semol as she answered. "The Breath of the One is not God, nor does she hold any special seat before the throne. She is a creation of the One, as are we all. She is, however, ancient, beloved, and dear to her Creator—as you are, Leopold."

Leopold glanced at the others, embarrassed by his question. "Well, okay. It's just… if she doesn't communicate, how do you know we're invited to—"

"We understand your curiosity," said Qedem. "All life is precious. When a life nears its end, the time for reflection deepens. We share many memories with her. She has always been with us—greeting our children, hosting our unions, even witnessing our endings. She does not speak in ways we understand, but she has given us beauty, space, comfort, and presence."

Those standing beneath the Breath of the One looked up and suddenly saw more than just dull brown. A gentle rolling—perhaps a kind of heartbeat—pulsed through her veins. They noticed edges where small pieces had crumbled away, and a tiny hole near the base of her stem. It was undoubtedly the first of many more to come.

Semol led the way up the stem, where the vine weavers had crafted a lattice to support those ascending to the special place atop the Breath of the One. Each of them, one after the other, stepped onto her stem, which despite her deteriorating state, remained strong and firm. The stem, the Seyfrets would eventually learn, would remain until the very end.

The beavers were the last to reach the top. Francis was out of breath, as she had increasingly found herself becoming after hikes with any large incline. She huffed and puffed through the final steps, then gasped when she saw everyone else staring at a beautiful picture glowing before them.

So much light spilled forth that it overwhelmed her. She raised her arm to shield her eyes until they adjusted to the brightness. They had been in a place where the primary source of light had come from the living creatures around them and the stars above—but this light came from the sun of the Five Realms.

Benjamin watched everyone closely as they each took their first step on the floating pad. When Francis, the last of the bunch, arrived, he looked back toward the bright light. "By the looks of it, you can all see what lies before us."

"Sure," said Max. "This is where we entered when we first came here." He looked around at the smaller, more colorful floating mesas around them and saw that Searing and his beloved rays were there; however, he only counted four in total. They had arrived with seven. "Where are the other three rays?" he asked.

Qedem whispered to Semol, "He's quite fond of them, isn't he?" Semol nodded in agreement.

Maarab looked at Max. "Don't worry; they are safe. We have much to tell you, but little time for details. What we discuss now is not an edict, but suggestions—based on what we have prayed about and considered while you've been with us."

"In other words, you are all free to do as you wish, and whatever you decide, we will assist in any way we can," assured Qedem.

"Speaking of which," added Benjamin, "let us bow and pray before we proceed into this most important parting. Please make yourselves comfortable. You will find that while she is old, she is still quite accommodating."

As they each prayed silently, the Elders sat, crossing their legs as a child might. Propo was amazed at how flexible and fit the Elders were. There was no way he could sit in such a position for any length of time. Instead, he sat with his knees up, wrapping his arms around them for support.

The beavers sat in their usual positions, straight up and on their tails. Sir Monchum found this quite funny, as he could not imagine sitting on any of his appendages. Instead, he found a slightly raised bump and perched next to Lira, who was already seated comfortably with her head bowed. Beely leaned against Max, his arms wrapped around her.

After a few moments of prayer, Maarab ran her fingers gently along one of the raised veins near where she was seated. "As you know, you have all come far, but there is still farther to go. Beely has done an excellent job in choosing each of you, and none of your sacrifices have been in vain. Each act—and those of the ones whose lives were tragically taken—has contributed to what we believe will be the eventual defeat of Mastad."

Beely sighed as she thought of Cloy. He was so young—he could have perhaps stayed hidden until this was all over. Max squeezed her tightly, sensing her grief.

"We have certain knowledge, through realm prophecy, of things to come, and therefore we hope you will trust us with the things we are about to say," said Qedem.

Maarab continued, "As you all know by now, Francis is with child. And even though her kind gestate for longer than most, we feel it is important that she remain behind with us until her child is born—"

Francis interrupted, "We beavers are made of strong stock. I assure you, I am more than capable of travel and doing my part."

"Yes," said Maarab. "We are sure that you could continue. However, we ask that you take no chances, as your child will be very important in the future of the Realms."

Benjamin nodded. "Indeed, if we understand the ancient texts correctly, we believe it is you who will have a boy—and he, along with his own wife, will aid the Messengers who will come from the Earthly Realm. Their role will be crucial in the future of our realms and theirs."

Francis put her hand to her mouth in shock at the new revelation. Saint Elmo beamed with pride. "You'd better believe my boy will do right by the Realms!"

Max chuckled. "Of course, if he's anything like you, wood chipper."

"I don't know what to say," said Francis, still trying to process the information.

"I'll say it for you," said Beely. "You'll stay here with the Seyfrets. As strong as you are, we can't have you and your baby in harm's way."

"That brings us to the next, albeit similar, issue at hand," said Qedem.

"What could be similar to a future child that will aid in saving two worlds?" asked Leopold, a bit sarcastically.

Qedem smiled wryly. "Another child that will aid in saving two worlds—what else?"

Francis snorted loudly and fell back into Saint Elmo. "I'm having twins!"

Saint Elmo's grin widened even more. "Well, I do come from a long line of virile men."

"Oh please!" exclaimed Leopold.

"No, we don't believe you are having twins," said Maarab.

"Then what?" asked Lira.

Maarab did a loud trill with her tongue before calling Thai and Reverie, who each poked their sleepy heads out of the rucksacks lying beside Max and Beely. "We can't be completely sure, but we think Reverie and Thai are expecting a child of their own."

Beely shook her head. "That can't be. Reverie has been very ill for a very long time and—"

"She hasn't acted very ill lately," said Lira.

"She's right," said Propo. "Those two empachics have been gallivanting around together for quite some time. And if you haven't noticed, Reverie has been eating a lot since she's been here."

"Phew!" Francis waved her hand in front of her face a few times. "Thank you, Lord. Raising one busy beaver is enough without having to keep up with two."

Beely's brow furrowed as she protested, "What could an empachic have to do with saving the Realms?"

Max leaned back and to one side to make direct eye contact with his wife. "You of all people, doubting the prowess of an empachic! I know you better than that, Beely Wren."

"As do I," added Propo. "Beely, we know how much you adore Reverie, but if what they say is true, you must let her stay behind."

"I'll be there for you if you need a shoulder to cry on," said Lira.

Beely lowered her head in resignation as she reached into her bag to cradle Reverie, holding her tight—almost too tight. "Are you going to have a baby empa, Reverie? Could it be possible?" Of course, there was no answer, but that did not stop Reverie from making her way out of the bag and rolling around lovingly in Beely's arms. "Truth be told, I knew there was something different about her lately." Beely's lips turned downward, and she took a couple of deep breaths as she let the new information sink in. She should have been nothing but joyful about the good news, but Reverie had become such an important part of her life, and to be separated from her would be hard.

Max stood up and looked out through the door into the Five Realms. He ran his fingers through his hair and asked the only other question that had been on everyone's mind since they met the Seyfrets. "What about the painting? Where is the painting?"

"You're looking at it," said Benjamin.

Max took a step back, squinted, then looked at Beely and shook his head. He looked back at Benjamin and asked, "What? This island in the air is somehow holding the painting?"

Propo stood tall and rubbed his eyes. "It's right there, before us."

Max looked at Propo, then back at the spot where he and Searing had first flown through the cliff wall. "You mean that's the painting?" He shook his head in disbelief.

Beely—with Reverie still in her arms—joined her husband. "It's been right in front of us since we got here."

Lira rose and made her way to where the others stood. "But it's so big."

"How are we supposed to carry that with us?" Leopold asked no one in particular.

The beavers, still sitting on their tails, whispered to one another. Leopold decided to get a better look at the perplexing object and lifted off from the pedestal. Benjamin motioned to Sir Monchum to follow the curious flyer and escort him back. Misty, Midie, Lots, Such, and Fuss were not far behind.

"Maybe I'm a fool, but I really thought it was going to be a painting. You know, the kind you hang on a wall," said Beely.

Benjamin smiled. "Oh, but it does hang on a wall. You could theoretically hang it almost anywhere."

"But we flew through it, from the other side. How does it work?" asked Max.

"It only works if you have faith. You can only see it if you believe," said Qedem.

Propo thought he knew the answer, yet asked anyway. "Believe what?"

"Believe in God, of course. Only those with the gift of faith can see their path within this work of art," said Benjamin.

"Unless—" began Propo.

"Unless one has the kaleidoscope with the pink Seyfret stone."

Propo's countenance immediately sank. He sighed and shook his head. "What have I done? If we had just trusted God and not tried to circumvent His plan by making the kaleidoscope, Mastad would no longer be a threat."

Benjamin put his hand on Propo's shoulder. "We all had a part in how things have turned out. The stone came from my daughter, who left home in search of her mother. I should have never let her go, but it has never been our way to thwart the free will of any soul."

Beely stood up, still gazing at the painting. "Yet, had Zara not been where she was, I'm not sure the four of us would still be alive. She gave her life so that we could live."

Max nodded. "Not just live, but find our way here—to the painting."

"What do we do with it?" asked Lira.

Maarab smiled. "Whatever you wish. The painting belongs to the Twelve, at least for now."

Leopold, followed closely by Sir Monchum and the flowers, made a dramatic landing in the middle of everyone. With his wings wrapped around his body, he did a few spins and ended with his arms spread wide. Sir Monchum thought the display was ridiculous, but, of course, Misty, Midie, Lots, Such, and Fuss were thoroughly impressed, their tiny feet clapping enthusiastically. "If you're discussing the painting," said Leopold, "You'd better wrap it up quickly."

"Why is that, Leopold?" asked Propo.

"It's shrinking," he answered.

Benjamin smiled. "Have no worries. The painting will always be just the right size for its purpose."

"What Benjamin says is true, but if you plan on traveling through it with your rays, I would suggest you not linger," said Maarab.

Lira furrowed her brow. "What do you mean?"

"She means you should leave now," answered Qedem.

Beely held Reverie closer and looked at Max desperately. "We aren't ready. We need time to say goodbye and—"

Propo looked more steely-eyed than usual. "Our hosts are correct. We must leave now. We must also have faith that we will all meet again."

Max placed his hand on Beely's arm. "They're going to be fine. Reverie has Thai now. They have each other. Saint Elmo and Francis...well, look at them."

The beavers—rubbing noses—seemed almost oblivious to their friends' impending departure. They were focused on the future, hopeful and optimistic about its outcome. Max looked into Beely's eyes. "The Seyfrets will take good care of our friends."

Reverie, who had joined Thai, playfully weaving in and out of the legs and arms of those staring at the slowly shrinking painting, stopped in her tracks, feeling the sadness of her beloved friend, Beely. She made her way back to the one person she loved the most.

She did not jump into her lap but rather did something which she had never done before—she licked her paw and gently groomed Beely's sandal-clad foot. Beely inhaled deeply, holding in her raw emotions. She understood what the gesture meant. No words or tears were appropriate.

Beely was overwhelmed with gratitude and awe by the emotional maturity of the empachic. She then slowly knelt down and gently kissed Reverie on the top of her furry head. When she stood, looking directly at the painting, she knew it was time to go.

Max summoned the nearby rays, and one by one, Beely and Propo—who was joined by Leopold—mounted their respective rays. Max made sure Lira, who had no experience riding rays, was secure in her saddle, with reins in hand. He gave her just enough instructions for what would be a very short ride.

Finally, Max stepped onto Searing. He and Searing led the way into the painting, followed closely behind by the others until they all literally disappeared into the work of art.

Those left on the Breath of the One all looked on silently. Some prayed, others embraced, as the empachics continued playing. It suddenly struck Saint Elmo that the painting still remained. "Weren't they supposed to take the painting?"

Francis rolled her eyes. "Now how would they do that?"

Qedem looked back at the beavers. "The painting has served its purpose for now."

"The painting has another destination and more work yet to do," said Benjamin.

Chapter 28

N3580B

The portrait had led them to the middle of an open space under a deep blue sky. Max, Beely, Lira, Propo, and Leopold—along with the four broraydings, looked around curiously. Max turned slowly, completing a full circle. No matter which direction he faced, it felt as if he were looking through a prism or a kaleidoscope. Everything slowly spun around him as he remained stationary in the middle of it all. In every direction was a unique path—perhaps hundreds—rotating around them before vanishing.

The constant motion was disorienting to everyone but Leopold. Leopold was accustomed to acrobatic maneuvers, including spirals. His vestibular system was superior to that of other creatures, especially those of the wingless variety. He was, however, put off by the lack of any breeze or natural ambient sounds. At least the ground beneath his bare feet, a soft carpet of grass, felt like home. As the others grew more disoriented—some to the point of nausea—he opened his arms as wide as they would go and instructed the others to gather closely beneath his wings.

Max, kneeling on the grass next to Leopold, stared into the bat's dark flesh. He had never noticed how much Leopold's wings resembled rubbery, leather skin. He looked to his right at Beely, who was also kneeling. Her hand was covering her nose. With Leopold's wings spread so wide, his pungent odor had become overpowering. Max turned to Propo and Lira on his left. "I hope the rays will be okay."

"They are fine," said Leopold. "They're just waiting for us to make our next move."

"Which is?" asked Propo.

"Obviously we have to choose a path," said Beely.

"How? There are so many," said Lira.

Propo shook his head. "I can't even look out at them for more than a few seconds without getting dizzy."

Leopold, wings still outstretched, looked down. "I think the paths repeat—at least some of them. They come and go, but they repeat. I'm not sure there's any particular order, but in the short time we've been here, I've seen several more than once."

"Are you sure?" asked Lira.

"Yes," he answered. "I've already seen one trail twice. It led to a lone lamppost amidst a forest of trees all dressed in white. Unlike anywhere I've ever seen. Quite memorable."

Propo raised his brows. "That does sound odd. White trees, you say?"

Leopold shook his head. "As if they were covered in a white

powder."

Max was becoming increasingly agitated with each passing second. Beely was unsure if he was worried about the rays becoming disoriented or if he felt that time was of the essence. She squeezed his hand, which had been furiously tapping his thigh. He smiled knowingly and nodded.

Beely stood up and looked out at the never-ending choices circling around them. She focused on each one, following it for a few moments before shifting to the next. After a moment, Max threw up his hands and shouted, "How do we choose?"

"I think I know," Beely answered. "Look for the rainbow."

"What do you mean?" asked Max.

"I'm sure there will be a pathway with a rainbow, and that's the one we're meant to walk into," she said.

Leopold remained with outstretched arms, shielding Lira and Propo from the dizzying kaleidoscope. "What's a rainbow?"

Propo looked up. "It's a multicolored arc in the sky. I've never seen one myself, but I think it would be unmistakable once you saw it."

Lira shook her head in frustration. "A multicolored arc? What does that mean?"

"It's like a half circle with bands of red, orange, yellow, green, indigo, and violet," answered Propo.

"What does indigo look like?" asked Leopold.

Propo stood up in frustration, yet did not look out at the dizzying array of choices before them. Instead, he looked down at his feet. "Don't make it so complicated," he huffed. "A rainbow is unique, and I promise—you've seen nothing like it before. Once you do, you'll never forget it."

"What Propo says is true," remarked Beely, still analyzing the view before her. "But it's what you don't see in the rainbow that

302

makes it memorable."

Lira looked up at Beely. "I don't understand."

"The rainbow is a promise from the Creator to those in the Earthly Realm—a promise that He would never flood their world a second time," answered Beely.

Max shouted, "There it is, the rainbow!"

Everyone looked to where Max was pointing. Their heads turned in unison as the pathway with the rainbow slowly circled around them. The rainbow path lay between a trail of cobblestones and one lined with small pink flowers.

"We must go now, before it completes the full circle around us," said Beely, urgency in her voice. She immediately headed toward Joshua, who was only a few paces away. She looked back at the others and yelled, "What are you waiting for? Hurry!"

The confidence and resolve in Beely's voice spurred both Propo and Lira to move immediately. They headed toward their respective rays, but Max did not move. Leopold also remained stationary, but with his ability to fly, he could quickly make it to any pathway. Leopold, like Beely, sensed that something was wrong with Max. Something had changed in him during the short time since they'd left the Seyfrets.

Beely, now atop Joshua, breathed laboriously. She squinted toward her husband in disbelief—or perhaps confusion. Why was he not following? "Max, why aren't you moving? We don't know for sure if the path will reappear or how long it might take if it ever does. We need to leave now." She glanced back at the rainbow, which had already made it over halfway around.

Max placed his hand on his heart and then extended it toward his wife. He mouthed the words "I love you," before whistling a sharp, loud command to the rays. Even though

Joshua was bonded to Beely, he had once been bonded to Max—and it was Max who had trained him since he was a very young baby ray.

When Max whistled, he motioned toward the rainbow pathway. Joshua immediately reared up, causing Beely to stumble before steadying herself by gripping his horn. Joshua effortlessly lifted off the ground and flew confidently through the mysterious opening framed by the beautifully colored arc. The other rays followed closely behind, with Lira and her ray making it through just before the path disappeared.

"What took you so long?" said Propo. He was standing next to his ray when Lira—the last to arrive—touched down.

"What do you mean? I was right behind you," she answered. Her ray landed on the soft, sandy ground next to Propo in what appeared to be a desert landscape. Lira looked behind her, expecting Max to be close behind—but instead, she saw Beely standing on the ground, scanning the horizon.

It was refreshing to be back in a place where the world around them remained stationary. "Where is Max?"

"Evidently, he chose not to join us," he said.

"That's ridiculous. This is what we have all been striving toward for many moons."

"There does seem to be a time lag between arrivals—greater than expected—but judging by Beely's mood, he and Leopold won't be joining us anytime soon."

Lira looked back at Beely. Propo was right—her demeanor had changed. Her countenance seemed withdrawn, her face had nothing but the look of a seriously driven woman. Lira would have welcomed clarity, but she was not about to pose any questions to Beely in regard to her husband.

Her ray snorted, which Lira interpreted as a sneeze, bringing her focus back to their location. "This sandy environment must be tricky for a creature who breathes from underneath."

"It's a desert, that's obvious, but it's not too hot and it seems hospitable," said Propo.

Beely had made her way back to where the rays and their riders were waiting. She did not mention Max. She tried hard to hide her emotions and confusion. She would deal with her husband's strange actions later. For now, they had to complete what they had come to do.

"There's something up ahead. Not too far. I can't see exactly what it is, but it's reflecting the light, like a mirror."

"Speaking of light, what happened to the rainbow?" inquired Lira, repositioning her shoulder bag, which held a small portrait of her son, a woven bracelet the Seyfret children had made for her, and a light dress made from the silk of Okrad. There was plenty of room remaining for the Good News they hoped to find.

"The rainbow has disappeared," answered Propo. "I just wonder how far we are from home."

"Home? I'm not sure there is such a place anymore," said Lira.

Beely removed her rucksack, which oddly felt heavier now that Reverie was not in it. She placed it next to Joshua, sighed, and looked straight ahead. She was well aware that the others had not yet realized their homes might not even exist. It was her understanding that the painting had taken them back in time, perhaps before any of them were even born.

After they found what they had come for, she planned to break the news. She picked up her lifeless bag and dryly quipped, "We'll walk." Without looking at anyone, she added, "Like I said, it's not far. In case there is anyone around, they'll be less apt to notice the three of us on foot." Without another word, she began walking. Propo glanced at Lira before shrugging his shoulders. They trailed behind, silently.

True to her word, it was not far, but to Propo and Lira, the short journey to the shiny object felt much farther than it had looked. No one said a word. The mood was somber. Lira felt bad for Beely; she knew what betrayal felt like.

Propo, on the other hand, had known Beely long enough to trust she would bounce back soon enough. He had witnessed the ups and downs of their marriage, but somehow, she and Max always managed to find each other again. This time would be no exception.

Propo was the first to break the deadly silence. "He must have had a very good reason to stay behind."

Beely stopped in her tracks and slowly turned around to face Propo. "He didn't stay behind. He went somewhere else."

"Same difference, right?" he said.

Beely gritted her teeth and kept walking. Lira nudged Propo with her elbow. Her eyes said to stop talking. He wisely obliged.

After a few more paces, they arrived at what Beely must have seen glimmering in the sunlight—a large, odd-looking contraption. Lira had never seen anything like it and had nothing in which to draw a reference. "What is it?" asked Lira.

Beely ran her hand along the smooth metal wing of a 1950s Beechcraft Twin Bonanza aircraft. Of course, she did not know it was the wing of something that could fly, let alone something that had flown in the Earthly Realm. Beely thought it was beautifully intricate, whatever it was. The curves, the symmetry, the egg-shaped appendages with thin cylindrical oar-type inserts—she found the design fascinating.

The plane looked mostly intact, except for a broken wing

which rested a few paces to the south of the main cabin. The front end appeared to have struck something head-on. "N3580B." Propo read the letters and numbers aloud, having no clue what they stood for. "What does it mean?"

"I don't know," said Beely. "Perhaps that's its name—"

Lira suddenly let out a blood-curdling scream. Both Propo and Beely jumped at the sound, but when they looked around, Lira was nowhere to be found. Propo ran to the other side of the plane and found Lira gasping as she peered out of a small door. Beely, right behind Propo, maneuvered around him to help Lira down. "What happened?"

"Skeletons…I'm not sure how many, but bones and skulls, every one of them."

While Beely tended to Lira, Propo climbed inside of the cabin to have a look for himself. There were indeed bodily remains in the compartment. They looked humanoid to Propo, but he had never before seen a full skeleton, so it was simply an educated guess.

He bent down to walk further into the small, dark cabin with windows that had been etched by the sands of time. From his cursory inspection, there were five bodies in total. Bits of cloth hung onto a few of the bones, but for the most part they were stripped clean.

The same could be said of the interior of the cabin. It was a sterile, stripped-down version of its earlier days. There was not much else inside other than a strange configuration of mechanical devices, levers, buttons, and knobs.

Propo raised his voice loud enough to be heard on the outside of the plane. "I don't see anything in here that is of any use. I certainly don't see any books, not one. No Bible."

In order to turn around, he leaned in such a manner as to

find himself face to face with one of the deceased. He needed to get back outside for fresh air and a fresh perspective. If there was a Bible in there, he thought, they would likely need to tear the remains of the plane apart piece by piece until they found it.

Just as he was about to clear the first row of seats—there were only three rows in the small twin-engine aircraft—his foot happened upon something sticking out from under one of the seats. He looked down at a hard, box-like object. He nudged it with his foot until it fully emerged out into the middle of the aisle.

It was covered in a brown leathery type of material that had aged much better than the rest of the aircraft's occupants. He picked it up and quickly discovered that it had hinges and what must have been a handle to make carrying it easier. Like the plane he was standing in, he did not know what the otherworldly thing was. He did end up referring to it as a boxcase, which was quite similar to its Earthly name of briefcase.

He handed the boxcase to Beely and stepped down from the plane. "What is this?" asked Beely.

He took it back from her and began to shake it.

"Careful!" exclaimed Lira. "Whatever is inside could be breakable."

Propo nodded and held the case in front of him, eyeing it suspiciously. "How does it open?"

Beely felt around the top of the case as Propo held it up flat on his forearms. She scrutinized the gold hinges on the back and then the two rectangular latches resting on each side of the handle. "Maybe it's a puzzle—similar to the ones my father used to make, only larger."

"Whatever it is and whatever is inside can wait," said Lira.

"Did you find the Book?"

Propo shook his head. "No. I saw nothing that wasn't affixed to the mechanical creature. Other than the bones, obviously. We may be here a while, taking this thing apart one piece at a time."

Beely furrowed her brow and pursed her lips. "How do you suppose we take this thing apart?" She tapped on the metal fuselage and it pinged in response. "It's as solid as a rock. We don't have any tools."

Lira reached over and took the case from Propo. She gently tilted it to one side and then to the other side. "We don't have to tear anything apart. We just have to get this open. The Book is in here."

"How can you be so sure?" asked Beely.

"I always had to hide valuables from my son. His curiosity was insatiable. What would have been more valuable to those lost souls than the very Word of God?" she answered.

Propo shook his head. "Why would they hide the Bible? They were messengers—"

"The same reason we are going to hide it; so evil won't keep it from those who need it most." Beely looked the case over. Without looking up, she said, "I believe they were called missionaries. Maybe they weren't hiding it, but simply protecting it. Either way, there's no sense in going on about it. Let's get the thing open."

While Beely and Lira continued to inspect the case, Propo retrieved a piece of metal that had been torn from the plane during the crash. As he was walking back toward them, Beely looked at him and asked, "What are you going to do with that?"

"Pry the thing open, what else?" he answered matter-of-factly.

Lira held her hand up to stop him. She stood back from the case, which was now resting on the wing of the plane. She gave it one more long, serious look. She then snapped her fingers and walked confidently up to the case with both of her arms extended. She gripped the top edge of the case with all eight fingers and placed her thumbs on the gold metal latches. Beely and Propo watched intently as Lira's thumbs pushed in, up, and then to the side. Both latches magically—so it appeared to the onlookers—popped up simultaneously. They joined Lira next to the case, which was still closed. Each of them instinctively placed a hand on the smooth leathery hide and lifted the top open.

There it was. The thing that their friends had died to find. The very thing that had been lost, and now, after so much time and effort, had been found. The only hope for the future and the sole truth of the past. Wherever they were in the Realms, whenever they were in the Realms, this was the only Bible remaining. Without it, they were doomed to lose everything; with it, they had the promise of victory.

Lira and Propo both turned to look at Beely; a single tear fell from her cheek onto the black leather-bound book resting alone in the shallow case. She rushed to wipe her tear from the Holy Book as she began to sob. She could not stop herself. She was embarrassed at her show of fragility, but she did not care. The beautiful book before her, in it Words she had taken for granted, assuming they would just effortlessly find their way into her mind and heart whenever she needed them. Never again would she treat the Word of her Lord so carelessly or ungratefully.

Beely carefully lifted the Bible from the place that had held it safe for so long. She held it against her breast and inhaled the musty, smoky, woody smell of another world. For the first time she understood the sensations that Duly must have felt when he cared for the books that he loved so dearly. She could not wait to recount this experience with him.

Her two friends were gracious enough to give her a moment to compose herself. Beely thoughtfully patted her damp face with the sleeve of her cloak and after taking a few deep breaths, she placed the Bible back in its case. Until the case was closed, she never took her eyes off of the Book.

When she spoke, it was hard to tell if she was speaking to it or her two companions. "We need to find Duly as soon as possible."

Lira sighed gently. "We're the ones who need to be found. We're stuck somewhere in the past."

"We are not stuck," offered Beely as she slowly closed the briefcase. "The painting still exists. It is here, somewhere. We just need to find it once again and it will take us home."

"I've been thinking," said Propo. "I don't think we are in the past at all."

"Really?" inquired Beely.

"I'm not certain, but it would make sense. If this is from the Earthly Realm, it is more than likely from the future. I can't explain why I think this, but even though time is different here than there, it makes more sense to me that we stepped into the future, not our past."

A huge grin overtook Beely's face. She grabbed Propo by the shoulders and shook him as she laughed giddily. Her excitement was infectious, and soon the others were smiling too. "My dear Propo, you are a genius. If what you say is true, and it must be true because no one is as smart as you, I know where the painting is."

Lira was still smiling, although she was not sure why, when she asked, "How? How could you possibly know where in the future the painting would be?"

"Because I know where Max would put it!"

Chapter 29

THE RECKONING

While his wife took a path beneath a beautiful arched prism of color—like nothing they had ever seen before, a sight worthy of any painting or work of art—he and Leopold had chosen a darker path. Max saw the cave not far in the distance. He had recognized it the first time it passed before him amidst the kaleidoscope of choices. How could he ever forget it? This cave was the very place that Max had forged an alliance with Athaliah.

Max was just stepping off of Searing when Leopold, flapping his wings as he landed beside the ray, asked, "Do you mind filling me in on why we're here and not with the others?"

"I'd rather hear why you chose to follow me instead of going with them. I'm sure they could have used your help."

313

Leopold scoffed. "Deflection is not your strong suit, Maximilian. I sensed you were up to something. I could see the look in your eyes. I've seen it before in those who hold secrets."

"Perhaps you should ask God, then. It is He who presented me with a choice I never expected to have. His timing is impeccable, that's all I can say. When I saw the cave, I knew I had to avenge the death of the Woodland Shirks. It is because of me that they were all murdered."

Leopold, still looking just as confused, continued. "Am I supposed to understand what you are talking about? If so, you give me too much credit. I'm in the dark here, please explain."

Max, now standing on the rocky ground, patted Searing and sighed. "You see that cave a few paces ahead?"

"Of course."

"Not long ago, I met with Athaliah in that cave. Out of all the swirling paths around us, this was the one I recognized. The moment I saw it, I knew God was either mocking me or..." He paused. "...or giving me the chance to right a wrong. Either way, I had to follow it, or..."

"Or what?" asked Leopold.

"Or I don't know what...I just knew this was the way I was supposed to come."

"I don't think God was mocking you. Whatever you did, God will forgive you," said Leopold reassuringly.

Max shook his head. "Maybe God will, but what about Beely—and the rest of you?" Max reached up and took hold of his bow and quiver that had been secured around Searing's horn.

Leopold leaned against Searing and reached for a small bag hanging around his neck. He awkwardly took out a small, round, violet fruit. He took a bite and gestured toward the cave.

"Do you think she's in there?"

"Where did you get the bag of fruit?" asked Max as he pulled his bowstring back.

"The Seyfret children made it for me. It doesn't get in the way of my wings and it's quite aerodynamic." Leopold returned to the question of Athaliah: "Do you expect to find her here— and what if you do?"

Max began walking in the opposite direction of the cave. "I haven't a clue."

Leopold discarded the pit from the now-devoured fruit and flapped his wings. "Wait! Which is it? You don't have a clue if she is here or what to do if she is?"

"Both, I guess."

Leopold reluctantly followed Max, walking as fast as he could. He would have flown, but he did not want to get ahead of Max, since he had no idea where he was going.Max finally stopped at a large boulder. He looked back at the cave and then back at the boulder. He walked around the large rock, as if sizing it up for something specific. "This'll do just fine."

Leopold leapt to the top of the boulder and looked down at Max. "Don't you think she already knows we're here? I've heard how clever Athaliah is; she won't fall prey to such a poorly conceived ambush as this one. If she doesn't see or smell us, she will surely notice your ray."

Max chuckled, followed quickly by a scowl. "You have heard she is clever, and this is true. The genetic beast, conjured up by Mastad himself, was once a normal woman—though probably always clever. With her new heightened senses and strength came arrogance. If she doesn't know we're here now, she will soon enough."

Leopold quickly descended from the boulder and slid behind

it, out of view from the cave opening. "That's not a good thing."

Max nocked an arrow and aimed at the cave, then lowered it. He leaned his back against the rock—more than twice his height—and looked at Leopold. "Her arrogance is going to get her killed. She sees no one as a threat. It would never dawn on her to think someone would have the audacity to strike her, especially on her own turf."

Leopold waited for more. More of what, he was not sure—more explanation, more direction, more anything—but Max was in no mood to talk. Max positioned himself for a clean shot at the cave. It was far, thought Leopold, but Max was an expert marksman. He stood a good chance of hitting his target—if she showed herself.

So, they waited. And waited. Leopold finished the rest of his fruit and even had time to take a much-needed nap. When he woke, the sun was beginning to set.

"Why do you think you are responsible for the death of the Shirks?" whispered Leopold. He had waited long enough for further explanation, but since Max had not been forthcoming, he dug deeper.

For the first time since they had arrived, Max took his eyes off of the cave, but only for a moment. "I met with Athaliah at her behest. I was reluctant at first, but in the end, I thought I had nothing to lose. She was the one that told me when and where to find Mastad. When we located the Shirks, the greatest known archers in all of the Realms, it was a sure thing, or should have been. Athaliah revealed to me that Mastad was in the middle of transitioning and that he would never be as weak and vulnerable again. If we were ever going to be rid of him for once and for all, we had one shot. I knew the Shirks were the ones who could get it done. Even as good as I am, my archery skills don't hold a candle to those of the Woodlands."

"So what happened? Why didn't it work?"

"She was there," seethed Max. Leopold could see the hate in his friend's eyes as he spoke of her. "She lied to me. She took advantage of a stupid, gullible fool. When the archers arrived, they succeeded in killing all of Mastad's guards, but when they got to Mastad himself, she was there protecting him. The archers were no match against her. She had already fully transitioned. The Shirks had never faced such a creature."

Leopold looked down, saddened, as he began to comprehend the series of events. "When Mastad found out the Shirks dared to challenge him, with an attempt on his life no less, he ordered all of them—men, women, and children—to be massacred."

Max once again fixed his eyes upon the cave. He looked as though he was prepared to wait on his prey for an entire lifetime, if that's what it would have taken. "Yes, and, of course, Athaliah was the hero in the eyes of her evil lord. She thwarted his would-be assassination."

Max inhaled deeply and checked the placement of his arrow on its bowstring. He continued with his story, whispering so softly that Leopold had to lean in to hear him. "If it was not for her, Mastad surely would have been killed, and Mastad knew this. In her lust for power, she sacrificed an entire race."

An arrow flew through the air just as Max whispered his last word. It was very poetic, thought Leopold, who had turned just in time to see a black winged creature retreat into the cave opening. "Was that her? Did you get her? Did the arrow penetrate that thick coat hers?" Leopold stared toward the cave so intensely that Max had to wave a hand in front of his eyes to get his attention.

"Let's go find out," said Max with an air of confidence.

Leopold reared back. "What if you missed?"

"I don't miss."

"But what if you did?"

"I didn't."

"How can you be sure? I mean, there's no body lying on the ground."

Max smirked as he threw his bow and quiver over his shoulder. He left the security of the boulder and began walking toward the cave. Leopold silently protested with a smirk of his own. He briefly considered staying safely in the shadows, but knew he would never live it down, should one or the other of them survive.

This time he flew, joining Max who was already at the entrance. "Where's the blood?"

Max was kneeling, looking at the ground. "I don't see any blood." He stood and began walking.

"You don't seriously plan on going in there…" Leopold craned his neck in a half-hearted attempt to peer into the cave. "If that was her, she doesn't even appear to be injured. No blood! You clearly missed."

"You can stay out here if you want. I won't hold it against you." Max disappeared into the cave, leaving Leopold behind. Leopold pursed his lips and squinted his eyes before reluctantly following.

It was nearly pitch-black inside. With no bioluminescent organisms to light the way, Max moved forward as far as he could, just before the tunnel made an abrupt turn.

"What are you waiting for?" asked Leopold.

"You may be able to see in the dark, but me? Not so much."

Leopold teased, "Would you like me to hold your hand?"

Max recoiled. "Absolutely not!" He leaned against the cave wall. "If she's still here, she's already heard us."

"I could still hold your hand. If you feel uneasy?"

"What is it with you, Leo. If I didn't know any better, I'd think you were scared of her."

Leopold folded his wings tightly around his body. "Afraid of an inferior being? Never."

The cave was eerily quiet—until the moment Leopold stopped speaking. Then a faint scuffling could be heard in the distance. Max turned to look at Leopold—only to find that he had vanished.

"Leopold?"

"Not so loud," he whispered. "I'm up here."

Max looked up, scanning overhead until he finally located his fearless friend. Only a faint glimmer of his eyes was visible while the rest of his body blended in with the dark ceiling. "Why are you up there?"

"Shh. Have you no ability to speak softly? If things go badly, I will provide the element of surprise and come to your rescue."

Max nodded. "Sure you will." He peered around the corner but could not see too far. "Athaliah, is that you?"

"Who else would it be?" Athaliah stood behind Max, in the direction he and Leopold had come. Startled, Max lurched forward and gripped the side of the cave wall to steady himself.

"You seem uncomfortable, Maximilian." Athaliah moved slightly to one side, allowing more light to pass by her formidable body. She scrutinized Max, looking him up and down. Max, too, sized up his adversary, trying not to be obvious as he looked for evidence that his arrow had hit its mark.

If Athaliah was injured, she was not showing any signs. It was too dark and her body too covered, with its large, veiny, webbed wings, to detect any blood or puncture. Leopold did not move or make a sound. Yet, she need not look up to know of his presence. She could smell the fear seeping from his pores.

"Looking for this?" She held up the arrow Max had sent flying toward her heart moments earlier.

Max swallowed hard—not because he had missed the flesh of his foe, but because of his naiveté in thinking that the arrow ever stood a chance. He was no match for the Athaliah who stood before him now. The realization that she could have ended his life the moment she saw him sent chills through his body.

Although he was no longer afraid of dying, he was becoming increasingly frustrated by his incompetence. He had trusted that this evil entity would somehow do the right thing. He was ignorant enough to believe that Athaliah could change. It was this false hope that had brought an end to hundreds of innocents. He was to blame for the Woodland Shirks' deaths, not her. Evil acts according to its nature, without regard for truth or reason. It had been up to him to make the wise choice. He had failed at every turn, and his pattern of failure continued.

"Don't be so hard on yourself. It wasn't your fault." She spoke as though she were sympathizing with a small child.

"What? Do you read minds now? Is that a new ability afforded to you by the deadly experiments of your master Mastad?"

Athaliah chuckled softly. "I don't read minds, I read behavior. It doesn't take a telepath to know you came here seeking revenge."

"Something I will never get, will I?"

"That's up to you. If you think I'm the one that deserves your wrath, you've already lost," she said.

Max scoffed. "You fooled me, Athaliah. I fell right into your trap. But you shouldn't take all of the credit. I have failed at almost everything I've ever tried to do, with one exception. The only thing that I have attained victory in is not even to my credit. The only victory I have is the one that Jesus has freely given me. I have won victory in Jesus, nothing else. So, you may indeed win in this life, but you are the one that should fear the eternity that awaits you."

"Dear, man, you have it so wrong. What would I have to gain by killing those little woodland country folk?"

"I don't know. You tell me. Maybe all you really wanted was to end the life of yet another member of the Twelve. Zorian the Giant would not have fallen so easily—even with your strength—had he not been protecting those weaker than himself."

Athaliah pointed the tip of the arrow directly above her.

"Ouch!" screeched Leopold.

"If I had wanted to end any one of you, I could have done so long before now, including the giant," said Athaliah.

Leopold left his perch on the cave ceiling and joined the two below. "That's what you think! We may all die as martyrs for the betterment of the Realms, but not until you and Mastad have been defeated once and for all." Leopold was furious. He might have been afraid of his adversaries, but he would not be disrespected.

"Oh, dear, I think I poked the bat," she said wryly. "Look, you both have it wrong. I am on neither side. I hate my master, and I have little time for the likes of the Twelve."

"What exactly do you, a sick experiment gone horrifically wrong, desire?" asked Leopold.

Athaliah, ignoring Leopold's question, looked to Max. "I am

truly sorry for what happened to the woodland inhabitants."

Leopold would not be ignored. "They are called the Woodland Shirks of the High Forest. They will forever be remembered as heroes. Never refer to them as anything less."

Athaliah gave a slight bow of humility. "I stand corrected. I am sorry for the Woodland Shirks of the High Forest. But their deaths were necessary to save the Realms."

"Go on," said Max.

Leopold flapped his wings in defiance. "Go on? Go on, you say! This corrupted being has no right to defend her actions."

"Leopold, please, as hard as this may be, let her continue."

After a short pause, Athaliah pressed on. "I don't know everything about Mastad. I probably never will, but what I learned after you and I made our arrangement for the ambush, changed everything. I did not have a way or time to warn you of my newfound revelation…"

"I'm listening," said Max.

"Apparently Mastad has the ability to possess souls. Because of this, he can potentially take on any form he wishes."

Leopold hissed and threw up his wings.

"I don't understand," said Max.

"If your team had succeeded in killing Mastad's physical body, he could have possessed another—and we would never know who, or what, or where he was. As it stands now, we know exactly who and where he is."

Max exhaled loudly. "You expect me to believe this? You must know how ridiculous you sound."

"I do. But whether you believe me or not makes no difference. I was not willing to risk my evil lord becoming even more powerful. As it stands now, he is too prideful to think he could ever fall at the hands of mere figments like you. Trust me, had you succeeded in killing his current form, he would have become more guarded than ever. He would have become untouchable."

Athaliah handed Max his arrow. "The time will come. He will make a mistake and we will be there. We must bide our time."

"We?" scoffed Leopold.

"He's right," said Max. "There will never be a "we" again. This is where we part ways. If your hate of Mastad is true, then you will work as hard as we do to finish him. I hope you're sincere, because if the Twelve fail, you must succeed. Someone must save the Realms."

Athaliah made a slight bow as she moved aside so the two could pass by the narrow path toward the cave opening. Leopold skirted by her, staying as close to the wall and as far from Mastad's evil ruffian as possible. As Max followed Leopold, he paused ever so briefly to stare deep into Athaliah's cold black eyes. Her breath hit his face like a warm, stale breeze. Max desperately wanted to find any evidence that she still had a soul—that what she had told them was true.

Just as Max looked away to face the path in front of him, Athaliah spoke to him one last time. "One more thing...Beely will need the painting soon. She is in our future and without the painting, she will never make it back to this time."

Max was yet again surprised by Athaliah. There was no time to process her words; he simply needed to ask her a question, but when he turned around, she was gone. His mind was overtaken with concern. If Beely and the others were in the future and the painting was still in the past, how would they find it?

Max, now on the outside with Leopold, filled his lungs with the crisp, fresh air. "God certainly works in mysterious ways,

Leo."

Leopold stood directly in front of Max with his wings folded tight. He was not a happy bat. "She could have killed us. God gives us free will, and if you want to use yours up by doing stupid stunts, be my guest, but don't you ever include me again."

Max smiled and rubbed his hand on Leopold's furry head. "Free will? I suppose, but divine intervention is what we just witnessed."

"What are you going on about?" he asked as he tried unsuccessfully to dodge Max's hand.

"If I, or should I say we, had not followed the path that we did, the others might not ever make it back to our time. I know where to take the painting so that Beely will find it when they need it."

"Why can't you just leave it where it is with the Seyfrets?"

"It won't be long until Mastad finds it, now, but he'll never find it where we're going to take it."

Leopold shrugged. "Where?"

"Let's go, I'll show you."

Max rushed toward Searing so fast that Leopold did not have time to press him with more questions. And there were many more questions. Now that the painting was found and the Word was soon to follow, the Twelve were well on their way to defeating Mastad. The time to prepare the way for the Messengers was upon them.

The prophecy was being fulfilled and Max suddenly felt hopeful. The deaths of the Woodland Shirks, Zorian, Cloy, and Eudox would not be in vain. Max felt confident that Malora would be found and that his beloved would return with Lira and Propo.

As Max and Leopold flew back toward the Seyfrets, their hopes were high. Leopold felt Max's optimism and it was contagious. Yet, even though their hope was justified, they had no idea how much harder their battle would become.

Mastad was getting stronger and more desperate. He had spies everywhere, and few knew prophecy better than he. He would stop at nothing to kill every last one of the Twelve. He was already laying traps to thwart the Messengers when they came. The Prince of the air would destroy everything—even himself—before being defeated by inferior beings.

Afterword

Thank you for joining me on this unforgettable journey through *The Quenching Fire*.

My passion for this six-book series has been to create a compelling story with dynamic, enduring characters—an epic *Christian alternative* to the narratives often found in modern entertainment.

If this book resonated with you, I would be deeply grateful if you would consider leaving a review on Amazon and Goodreads or sharing it on social media. Your honest feedback is one of the most powerful ways to help me reach more readers and continue sharing these stories.

For those who wish to continue the adventure, the prequel, *Cruelty of Thirst*, and the entire *Messengers and Thieves* trilogy—*Where the Garden Begins*, *A Leaf of Faith*, and *Roots and Branches: The Battle for Here*—are all available now.

The final book in the *Springs of Eternal Life* series is coming in 2026.

Plays by J. Suthern Hicks

Turtle Tears:
A Play in Two Acts

Home, Hearth, and Oreos:
A One Act Play

Children's Books by J. Suthern Hicks

Charlie and Chocolate's Purrfect Prayer
Charlie and Chocolate's Furry Forgiveness

To get alerts on new releases please follow:
facebook.com/jsuthernhicks, Instagram.com/jsuthernhicks
To reach the author directly: Humbleentertainment@yahoo.com.

www.ingramcontent.com/pod-product-compliance
Lightning Source LLC
Chambersburg PA
CBHW051953240626
47153CB00005B/1739